E. M. Forster's Modernism

E. M. Forster's Modernism

David Medalie

palgrave

First published 2002 by
PALGRAVE
Houndmills, Basingstoke, Hampshire RG21 6XS and
175 Fifth Avenue, New York, N.Y. 10010
Companies and representatives throughout the world

PALGRAVE is the new global academic imprint of
St. Martin's Press LLC Scholarly and Reference Division and Palgrave
Publishers Ltd (formerly Macmillan Press Ltd).

ISBN 0–333–98782–9

This book is printed on paper suitable for recycling and made from fully
managed and sustained forest sources.

A catalogue record for this book is available from the British Library.

Library of Congress Cataloging-in-Publication Data

Medalie, David.
    E.M. Forster's modernism / by David Medalie.
        p. cm.
    Includes bibliographical references and index.
    ISBN 0–333–98782–9
        1. Forster, E. M. (Edward Morgan), 1879–1970—Criticism and
    interpretation. 2. Modernism (Literature)—Great Britain.
    I. Title: Modernism. II. Title.

PR6011.O58 Z82267 2002
823'.912—dc21   2001056133

10 9 8 7 6 5 4 3 2 1
11 10 09 08 07 06 05 04 03 02

Printed and bound in Great Britain by
Antony Rowe Ltd, Chippenham, Wiltshire

For Ann Smith, with love

Contents

Acknowledgements

I benefited greatly, when I first embarked upon this study, from the insightful advice of Jon Stallworthy, John Batchelor, Daphna Erdinast-Vulcan, Peter McDonald and Andrew Moore. I am most grateful to them all.

Subsequently, when I was revising it for publication, I had the extraordinary privilege of being able to rely upon the encouragement and critical engagement of two of my former colleagues in the Department of English at the University of the Witwatersrand: Ann Smith and Merle Williams. I cannot thank them enough for their invaluable recommendations and their generosity as colleagues and as friends.

Abbreviations: Forster's Works

A   *Alexandria: A History and a Guide* (Garden City, New York: Anchor Books, 1961).

AE   *Albergo Empedocle and Other Writings*, ed. George H. Thomson (New York: Liveright, 1971).

AH   *Abinger Harvest* (London: Edward Arnold, 1936).

AN   *Aspects of the Novel*, Abinger edition, vol.12 (London: Edward Arnold, 1974).

AS   *Arctic Summer and Other Fiction*, Abinger edition, vol. 9 (London: Edward Arnold, 1980).

CB   *Commonplace Book*, ed. Philip Gardner (Stanford, CA: Stanford University Press, 1985).

CS   *Collected Short Stories* (Harmondsworth: Penguin, 1954).

GLD   *Goldsworthy Lowes Dickinson* (London: Edward Arnold, 1934).

HD   *The Hill of Devi and Other Indian Writings*, Abinger edition, vol. 14 (London: Edward Arnold, 1983).

HE   *Howards End*, Abinger edition, vol. 4 (London: Edward Arnold, 1973).

LJ   *The Longest Journey*, Abinger edition, vol. 2 (London: Edward Arnold, 1984).

M   *Maurice* (London: Edward Arnold, 1971).

MPI   *The Manuscripts of 'A Passage to India'*, Abinger edition, vol. 6(a) (London: Edward Arnold, 1978).

MT   *Marianne Thornton: A Domestic Biography* (London: Edward Arnold, 1956).

PI   *A Passage to India*, ed. Oliver Stallybrass (Harmondsworth: Penguin, 1985).

PP   *Pharos and Pharillon* (London: Hogarth Press, 1961).

PT   *The Prince's Tale and Other Uncollected Writings*, ed. P. N. Furbank (London: Penguin, 1999).

RV   *A Room with a View*, Abinger edition, vol. 3 (London: Edward Arnold, 1977).

TC   *Two Cheers for Democracy*, Abinger edition, vol. 11 (London: Edward Arnold, 1972).

WA   *Where Angels Fear to Tread*, Abinger edition, vol. 1 (London: Edward Arnold, 1975).

1
Liberal-Humanism

> Literature loses its ardour and its inspiration. It becomes
> critical rather than invigorating: sceptical, questioning,
> sometimes with an appearance of frivolity, sometimes
> torturing itself with angers and despairs. The note today is
> that of a time of disenchantment.
>
> C. F. G. Masterman, *The Condition of England* (1911: 191)

Modernism was made of many disenchantments. There is more often
than not a lament beneath the iconoclasm and a vulnerability within
what seems to be the most implacable assertion of newness. Under
such circumstances it becomes difficult to decide which is the pile of
rubble and which the new edifice: where the elegy ends and the bold
experiment begins.

The reluctant modernism of E. M. Forster illustrates this tendency.
Beyond what it offers as a discrete set of responses to a range of early
twentieth-century anxieties, Forster's modernism also directs us towards
a broader conceptualisation and understanding of modernism itself.
In particular, it emphasises the revisionary projects that lie at the heart
of certain versions of modernism, where the rescue efforts, the recasting
of traditions, the desperate experimentalism are inseparable from the
recognition of what is no longer tenable, the elegies, and the sorrows
born of newness. The admission that new times compel new tellings is
not necessarily an exuberant one.

It is not a coincidence that Forster, who has been held up for decades
as a quintessential liberal and humanist – a reputation reinforced by
the Auden generation, who found his politics agreeably different from

1

the right-wing inclinations of many of the other male modernists – has been seen as an awkward straddler of traditions rather than as a modernist, or that it has taken so long for him to be acknowledged as the writer of one work of nascent modernism, namely *Howards End*, and of one fully fledged and seminal modernist work: *A Passage to India*. It is precisely because he has been seen as a figure of resiliently gentle liberal-humanism, one who consoled more and more as the century seemed to become less gentle and less kind to liberalism and humanism, that his status as a modernist has been under-valued.

This was particularly the case when the definitions of modernism were narrower than they are today: critics who were themselves of a liberal-humanist orientation were reluctant to include the beloved sage in a group which included fascists, calcified ideologues, misogyn-ists and obscurantists. But this perception is inaccurate because it is designed to keep Forster away from the acknowledged modernists out of a misguided political sentimentality. During the 1950s and 1960s, he was seen as one who doggedly and unfashionably clung to the lib-eral-humanist legacy and kept its values alive:

> . . . Morgan continued, during the 1950s and 1960s, to represent liberal humanism. The very name E. M. Forster symbolised the importance of personal relations, art, the inner life, the traditions of rural life, the individual; and hostility to the impersonal, the exploitative, the patriarchal, the capitalist and the imperialist. (Beauman 1993: 368)

In fact, Forster's reputation had little to do with his own liberal-humanism and what became of it: it proceeded rather from political nostalgia and the partisanship of several generations of Anglo-American liberal-humanist critics of the 1950s and 1960s.

Early twentieth-century liberalism and humanism, in relation to modernism, constitute one of the many terrains where the legacy of the past encounters the polemic of the new. It has almost become a truism to say that among the casualties of modernism is the quest for, or the belief in, a liberal society and an intact humanistic iden-tity. Certainly, it is not difficult to discern the failure of liberal ideals in the autocratic or oligarchical systems which many of the mod-

ernists favoured, while the recurrent depictions in modernist literature of spiritual and psychic fragmentation, often (but not always)
conceived of in terms of exile, withdrawal, misanthropy or despair,
would seem to point to a widespread abandonment of humanism as
a viable ideal.

In fact, the modernists – so often accused of being ahistorical or of
cultivating a deliberate historical myopia – were prescient in recognising that liberalism and humanism, particularly in their nineteenth-
century forms and ambitions, were entering a period of historical
inhospitality, as it were; and while, especially in the Edwardian period,
there were many who were hopeful that the threat could be staved off,
the modernists were articulating that uncongenial reception. But, of
course, these chroniclers were not merely observers: they not only
charted the decline, they participated tendentiously in it too. The
vigour with which T. E. Hulme, Wyndham Lewis, Ezra Pound and T. S.
Eliot, for instance, declared the deserved death of liberalism and
humanism has had the effect of obscuring the extent to which modernism was both shaped by, and implicated in, what these modernists
of a radically illiberal and anti-humanistic stance were pleased to pro-
nounce defunct. Hence, while T. E. Hulme scorned both romanticism
and humanism for 'placing Perfection in *humanity*, thus giving rise to
that bastard thing Personality, and all the bunkum that flows from it'
(Hulme 1924: 33), there were others who were not so dismissive, and
for whom the attrition of the liberal-humanist ethos was a central concern, a loss and an opportunity.

Both *Howards End* (1910) and *A Passage to India* (1924) are, in their
different ways, novels about what can and cannot be salvaged from
the interregnum that precedes what is deemed to be a terminal socio-
historical period. The Edwardian period, seen by Forster in highly partial
and selective terms, is situated as one such historical twilight in *Howards
End*; the British Raj as another in *A Passage to India*. What is significant is
that both novels offer the predicament of liberalism and humanism as a
crucial ingredient in this great drama of loss and recovery. The concern
with lost or recovered habitations, be they private, rural, symbolic or
colonial, includes an investigation of whether there can be a home for
liberalism and humanism (and for well-meaning liberal-humanists, like
the Schlegel sisters, Adela Quested and Cyril Fielding) in such dispos-
sessing environments. For creeds to have a home, they need to be granted a context in which they may be seen as efficacious. Not surprisingly,

the exploration of liberalism and humanism in these novels centres not so much on their intrinsic merit, but on their efficacy (or lack thereof) as pragmatic codes in changing and difficult contexts.

Despite the undeniable nostalgia for liberalism and humanism as they were in their heyday, the fact is that they are not presented in the novels of Forster's embryonic or fully realised modernism as transhistorical sites of value. Unlike many of his critics, Forster does not in these novels make universalist claims on behalf of liberalism and humanism. In *A Passage to India*, despite Forster's reputation as the liberal-humanist who spoke for all the century, the implication, albeit couched in wistfulness, is unflinchingly clear: liberal-humanism is no longer *tenable*; there are no longer viable contexts for its articulation. *Howards End* and *A Passage to India* are both about the legacy of loss, its shape and its possibilities.

It is in the earlier novel, however, that we find the fullest engagement with the hopes and predicaments of contemporary liberal-humanism. *Howards End* is a complex late-Edwardian response to what has been termed the New Liberalism: a strategic attempt by a number of Liberal ideologues and analysts (including L. T. Hobhouse and J. A. Hobson) to address contemporary difficulties – the Edwardian age was a time of 'severe testing and crisis for liberalism' (O'Day 1979: 2) – and to map out a series of measures to secure the future of liberalism. The New Liberalism – a term which 'had begun to flourish in the press after 1895' (Emy 1973: 68) – was 'a case study in ideological adaptation' (Freeden 1978: 3): it was a deliberate exercise in ideological revision. The 'careful political husbandry' (Eccleshall 1986: 45) advocated by theorists like Hobhouse and Hobson was both a salvage operation and an affirmation of the continued pertinence of contemporary liberalism within the changing conditions of modernity.

Broadly speaking, the New Liberalism laid far greater emphasis upon the *social* aspects of identity, whereas the older versions of the creed, reinforced by libertarian principles and *laissez-faire* economics, sought for the most part the empowerment of the individual through an 'atomistic Individualism' (Freeden 1978: 23). The aim of the New Liberalism, as it moved away from a 'creed of non-interference' (Samuel 1902: 20), was to 'convert' liberalism from 'the principle of State abstention' (28):

with the growth of experience a more matured opinion has come to recognize that Liberty (in a political sense) is not only a negative but a positive conception. Freedom cannot be predicated, in its true meaning, either of a man or of a society, merely because they are no longer under the compulsion of constraints which have the sanction of positive law. To be really free, they must be able to make the best use of faculty, opportunity, energy, life. It is in this fuller view of the true significance of Liberty that we find the governing impulse in the later developments of Liberalism in the direction of education, temperance, better dwellings, an improved social and industrial environment; everything, in short, that tends to national, communal and personal efficiency. (Asquith 1902: x)

This 'positive conception' of Liberalism would, it was hoped, provide the solution to the difficulties with which political liberalism had to contend in the early years of the twentieth century. The decade preceding the Great War, despite political successes such as the landslide Liberal victory of 1906, was a time in which liberal programmes and the nature of liberal political discourse itself seemed increasingly under pressure:

[The events of the years before the First World War] called into question the relevance of the liberal approach to problems. Liberalism was an ideology of moderation, reason and restraint. Liberals believed that differences should be resolved by rational discourse, compromise and consent. Ulster (or even English) unionists, militant suffragettes and striking trade unionists all rejected the liberal system for redressing grievances. (Bernstein 1986: 198)

Perhaps the greatest problem of all was the loss of working-class support. In response to the threat of a widespread depletion of a traditional support base, as well as a sense of social polarisation, the New Liberal theorists and strategists formulated the notion of an *organic* society:

No one element of the social life stands separate from the rest, any more than one element of the animal body stands separate from the rest. In this sense the life of society is rightly held to be organic, and all considered public policy must be conceived in its bearing on the life of society as a whole. (Hobhouse 1934: 73–4)

This new orientation, the New Liberal theorists argued, would alter the character and the fate of political liberalism: 'the elements of such an organic view . . . may inspire and direct a genuine social progress. Liberalism has passed through its Slough of Despond' (Hobhouse 1934: 226). Whereas the business of the early liberalism had seemed 'to be not so much to build up as to pull down, to remove obstacles which block human progress', the new creed would rather 'point the positive goal of endeavour or fashion the fabric of civilization' (19). This 'constructive theory of society' (48) would address the problem of ideological stagnation:

> [Liberalism's] faith in itself was waxing cold. It seemed to have done its work. It had the air of a creed that is becoming fossilized as an extinct form. (214)

The New Liberalism presented itself, not as 'fossilized' and mired in the past, but as alert to the conditions of modernity and the needs of a changing society – 'a living force in the modern world' (49).

This optimism is reflected in Forster's description of the buoyant atmosphere in which the *Independent Review* was founded. The New Liberal credentials of the *Independent Review* were unambiguous: it was 'a journal of the New Liberalism, opposed to the imperialism and protectionism of Joseph Chamberlain' (Rosenbaum 1994: 10). Forster describes it as 'not so much a Liberal review as an appeal to Liberalism from the Left to be its better self – one of those appeals which have continued until the extinction of the Liberal party' (*GLD*: 115). In 1903, when it was founded, there was the hope that a fresh Liberal spirit and agenda would provide the desired transformation:

> 'The Independent Review' . . . struck a note which was new at that time, and had a great influence on a number of individuals. . . . Those who were Liberals felt that the heavy, stocky body of their party was about to grow wings and leave the ground. (GLD: 116)

Seven years after it was founded, Forster published a novel which considers whether contemporary liberalism is indeed capable of transforming itself into a cogent force. It also deals with the knotty relationship between politics, morality and aesthetics: *Howards End*, in its own way, asks the same question which Forster posed when he was writing his biography of Goldsworthy Lowes Dickinson: 'Can you imagine decency touched with poetry?' (*GLD*: 116).

In *Howards End* Forster sets up and evaluates many of the ingredients of the New Liberal programme. The misgivings that the novel presents are the result of an inability to conceive of a place and a future for a reformist philosophy that is disabled if it cannot be construed as forward-looking: when liberalism is associated with the past rather than the future, when it is the subject of elegies rather than ambitions, it has become a spent force. The novel considers the trajectory of achievement implied by the New Liberal programmes, the tide which 'flow[s] in a steady stream towards social amelioration and democratic government' (Hobhouse 1934: 224).

The response to this is not sanguine. Contemporary liberalism, it suggests, will be overwhelmed by the conditions of modernity. The novel deprecates many of the phenomena that constitute modernity, including the increase in population, the growth of the suburbs, the attempts to democratise 'culture', the ascendancy of the plutocrats and even the proliferation of motor cars. Like many other modernist or proto-modernist works, *Howards End* presents modernity as a crisis and even as an apocalypse; something which must be opposed:

> Most of us do not experience modernity as a mode of disruption, however many disruptive historical events we may be aware of . . . modernism [is] an attempt to *interrupt* the modernity that we live and understand as a social, if not 'normal', way of life.   (Eysteinsson 1990: 6)

The entire plot of *Howards End* may be seen in terms of this notion of 'interruption', for it shows the way the world is going and then offers forms of escape or tenuous sanctuaries which stand in contradistinction to that seemingly irresistible movement. Because modernity is seen as disrupting what ought to be preserved, the novel, in response, seeks to 'interrupt' the course of modernity by refusing to sanction it, signalling it as a crisis (with potentially tragic ramifications) and, finally, veering away from it at the level of plot.

The attitudes towards various aspects of modernity which are expressed in *Howards End* have much in common with, for instance,

Masterman's analyses of England's Edwardian maladies: it immediately becomes apparent how conventional the litany of fault-finding is. Forster's novel, too, represents modern life as 'a huge apparatus of waste' (Masterman 1911: 42–3). At the same time it invests value in the countryside and in agrarian idylls, a favourite Edwardian bulwark. Throughout the novel there is a pervasive sense of modernity as a tidal force of dissolution that eats away at the islands of tradition and refuge. The ephemerality and restlessness of city life are presented as a new version of the old war between the island and the ocean:

> One had the sense of a backwater or rather of an estuary, whose waters flowed in from the invisible sea, and ebbed into a profound silence while the waves without were still beating. Though the promontory consisted of flats . . . it fulfilled its purpose, and gained for the older houses opposite a certain measure of peace. These, too, would be swept away in time, and another promontory would arise upon their site, as humanity piled itself higher and higher on the precious soil of London.   (*HE*: 5)

Here Forster manages to slip in another threat of modernity – one, incidentally, that preoccupied contemporary liberals greatly: overpopulation. In 1902, Masterman decried the rise in population, using, significantly, the same metaphor of the overwhelming flood which recurs throughout *Howards End*: 'through the gates of birth streams in the countless host' (Masterman 1980: 9). It is as if too many people jostling for too little space are pressing the very soil of England beneath the sea. The threat to English tradition is made more desperate by presenting it as a threat to the island itself. The earth has become insecure beneath one's feet: the ultimate expression of that fear is the plunge down the abyss, that favourite Edwardian nightmare.

The appeal of an island is that it can be known and measured: circumscription is a form of control. Many of the Edwardian anxieties, however, had to do with being forced by modernity into a succession of illimitable situations which provoke a feeling of powerlessness. Just as the vastness of the sea is beyond circumscription in its expanse and the depth of the void or the abyss knows no bounds, so the same lack of control is expressed in relation to social phenomena such as overpopulation, unemployment, urbanisation, the growth of the suburbs and the consequential whittling away of the countryside – all of which Forster presents in *Howards End*. Their combined effect is to threaten the very future of traditional English life, since there is a strong possibility that what is known may give way before the pressure of the unknown, which is what the apocalyptic mood of the conclusion to the novel betokens. Similarly, towards the end of *The Condition of England*, Masterman speaks of the unenviable situation of the contemporary reformer who faces 'the possible future of a society beyond measure complex, baffling and uncertain in its energies and aims' (Masterman 1911: 248).

The endorsement of rural life is a very common tactic in positioning conservative values as a phalanx of tradition and quietude – one need only think of a novel such as *Mansfield Park*. The threat comes from the city: both Forster and Masterman find urban life a modern malady and cosmopolitanism a modern curse. The dated quality of the pastoral complaint is acknowledged by the narrator of *Howards End*, who concedes also that the alliance between fashion and modernity will always strengthen the hand of the latter:

> To speak against London is no longer fashionable. The earth as an artistic cult has had its day, and the literature of the near future will probably ignore the country and seek inspiration from the town. One can understand the reaction. Of Pan and the elemental forces the public has heard a little too much – they seem Victorian, while London is Georgian – and those who care for the earth with sincerity may wait long ere the pendulum swings back to her again.
>
> (*HE*: 106)

The chronological march from Victorian to Edwardian to Georgian marks a seemingly inexorable historical progression which would seem to have little sympathy for backward glances and sanctuaries in which one may escape what Margaret describes as 'this continual flux of London . . . [which] is an epitome of us at our worst – eternal formlessness; all the qualities, good, bad and indifferent, streaming away – streaming, streaming for ever' (179). The swing of the pendulum offers the possibility of a contrary movement, one which suggests that the ruthless march towards dissolution is not inevitable. The return, however, is unlikely to occur under present conditions: in the modern world the forces of modernity will prevail and 'those who care for the earth' have no weapon other than patience. It is in this interstitial space, between present loss and recovery indefinitely deferred, that *Howards End* locates itself, and it accounts for some of its curiosities: the sense it provides of being subject to time and history and yet of having only just escaped them; the stillness, even stasis, which exists within relentless motion; the presentation of Howards End both as a doomed house and as a refuge for ever; the persistent interweaving of contemporaneity and anachronism.

In 1902 Masterman characterised the city as 'a mammoth of gigantic and unknown possibility' (Masterman 1980: 7). He warned that '[i]n the long struggle between the town and the country the former must eventually conquer; for always it has steadily advanced, never has it surrendered any of its acquisitions' (15). The city of London, treated unflatteringly by many of the male modernists – the brooding setting for Conrad's *The Secret Agent*, the 'Unreal City' of Eliot's *The Waste Land* – is established in *Howards End*, too, as the locus of overweening modernity. The 'grey struggle of the abyss' (Masterman 1911: 149) plays itself out in this vast city which seems 'satanic' (*HE*: 82), crouching beneath an 'infernal sky' (84). The city is indicted in particular for its ceaseless motion, for if nothing is at rest within it, there cannot, of necessity, be a place for the preservation of objects or traditions which accrue value precisely because they are unchanging – 'the precious distillation of the years' (146). This new 'civilization of luggage' (146) – described as a 'rever[sion]' to a 'nomadic' existence (146), thus, paradoxically, presenting modernity itself as the outcome of atavistic impulses – is producing a way of life so different that it is as if a new and foreign race is imperialistically conquering England from within: here too the novel is close to Masterman's description of London as 'a population, a nation in itself; breeding, as it seems, a special race of men' (Masterman 1911: 88). The voraciousness of the city threatens to erode the stability of the island and submerge everything. It becomes the place of restless desire, of remorseless dissatisfaction: 'London only stimulates, it cannot sustain' (147).

The 'metaphor of islands' is a trope within Edwardian literature, one which expresses a deep-seated social quandary: the 'painful need to choose between expansion and insularity' (Hunter 1982: 47). The New Liberals were, in certain respects, urging 'expansion' rather than 'insularity', including the extension of opportunities for social mobility to a wider section of the population. The preoccupation with islands, refuges and retreats has, therefore, a deeply conservative edge: it constitutes 'the substitution of small-group loyalty for the larger allegiances of racial solidarity or patriotism' (165). It is therefore far from coincidental that the country house features so prominently in much Edwardian literature: it is a retreat in both senses of the word – a place of sanctuary and of withdrawal, of dismay in the face of change. Country houses were 'microcosms, islands within the island of England' (190).

In *Howards End* the recourse to insularity is not presented in disingenuous terms. There is the understanding that it not only articulates a longing for containment and self-sufficiency, but is also an expression of exclusion. This recognition is conveyed in part through the figure of Margaret, who sees, in particular, the economic implications. Some clamber onto the safe ground of privilege and economic safety; others are not able to, and must then be thrown into an antagonistic relationship with those who 'stand upon money as upon islands' (*HE*: 58). Margaret refers frequently to straitened circumstances as a form of submergence, as seen in her advice to Helen to 'remember the submerged' (70) – an injunction which Helen later heeds when she assumes responsibility for Leonard and Jacky. Margaret refuses to be euphemistic about money, as seen when she insists upon the economic determinants of identity:

> 'I'm tired of these rich people who pretend to be poor, and think it shows a nice mind to ignore the piles of money that keep their feet above the waves. I stand each year upon six hundred pounds, and Helen upon the same, and Tibby will stand upon eight, and as fast as our pounds crumble away into the sea they are renewed. . . . And all our thoughts are the thoughts of six-hundred-pounders, and all our speeches; and because we don't want to steal umbrellas ourselves we forget that below the sea people do want to steal them, and do steal them sometimes, and that what's a joke up here is down there reality –'. (59)

For all the concern in *Howards End* with ephemerality, depletion and sad alteration, here is the frank recognition that among the most intransigent of social phenomena is the fact that those who have money tend to cling to it and that conditions of privilege tend to renew themselves. Capitalism, according to Margaret's diagnosis, is made up of exploitation and envy; it requires, too, the brutal premise that only a small section of the population will ever be able to find a place on terra firma.

Money is not the only kind of island that we find in the novel, although it is the one least romantically viewed. There are several attempts to transform insularity from an expression merely of narrowness into something which resonates with meaning – into synecdoche, 'the novel's presiding symbolic figure' (Levenson 1991: 91). There is, for instance, the panoramic vision of Chapter XIX, in which 'the imagination swells, spreads and deepens, until it becomes geographic and encircles England' (165). This 'geographic' imagination imbues England with all that lyricism and heroism may bestow:

> Does [England] belong to those who have moulded her and made her feared by other lands, or to those who have added nothing to her power, but have somehow seen her, seen the whole island at once, lying as a jewel in a silver sea, sailing as a ship of souls, with all the brave world's fleet accompanying her towards eternity?   (172)

The sea here, instead of threatening to engulf the island as elsewhere, participates in the transcendent vision of a smallness which in itself confers value – 'a jewel' – and the unity and camaraderie of the 'ship of souls'. The excerpt begins by disclaiming the kind of imperialism which has, to a large extent, made the Wilcoxes what they are. Nonetheless, it goes on to present another kind of conquest, one reserved for those who have the capacity to participate in the 'geographic' imagination. The heightened response is thus a form of possession, a notion which turns out to be prophetic, as the novel asks us, finally, to accept that Margaret and Helen deserve to possess Howards End because they have the capacity to appreciate it. The passage chimes politically with the views of the 'Little Englanders' and those within the Liberal Party – J. A. Hobson, for instance – who did not support the idea of grandiose imperial ambitions for Britain in the early twentieth century; but the romantic cargo which the 'ship of souls' bears is, in its own way, grandiose. It is Little England writ large. What is more, it establishes a pattern for the novel as a whole: the lack of expansiveness in social or political terms is offset by a symbolic sweep which combats narrowness, going beyond what can be grasped by 'the *insular* cynic and the *insular* moralist' (22; my italics).

Whether transformed by the 'geographic' imagination or not, the vexed question of land and property rights is a crucial issue in *Howards*

End. The quandary with which the novel wrestles is whether private property is to be regarded as a general right, or a special privilege reserved for a few:

> Failure to recognize that property was the basis of individual liberty in our society explains the genuine dilemma of many liberals whose loyalty has been divided between the ideal of freedom for all in a classless society and the freedom of a few exceptional beings. Like Mill, liberals have been haunted by the fear that democracy, which they have granted political freedom, would achieve real economic freedom and threaten the liberties of the individual which sprang from property. This fundamental and at times tragic dilemma has given certain liberal writers a vision of something like a doomed society.   (Spender 1937: 61–2)

For Hobson, this dilemma results from the reluctance of liberals to give up their entrenched economic advantages, a tendency which he places at the heart of the difficulties experienced by political liberalism:

> Having conceded under pressure the form of political power in the shape of elective institutions and a wide franchise to the masses, [those with vested financial interests] are struggling to prevent the masses from gaining the substance of this power and using it for the establishment of equality of economic opportunities. The collapse of the Liberal Party upon the Continent, and now in Great Britain, is only made intelligible in this way.   (Hobson 1902: 150)

In response to this, some liberals pursued schemes which would extend to more people the right to private ownership of land – always one of the most sacred of liberal tenets – or at least to establish a secure system of tenancy. The desire to free the land from the tight grasp of those who had always held onto it was a particularly strong refrain in the solutions advanced by the New Liberals:

> Through the principle of inheritance, property . . . is handed on; and the result is that while there is a small class born to the inheritance of a share in the material benefits of civilization, there is a far larger class which can say 'naked we enter, naked we leave'.
>
> (Hobhouse 1934: 186–7)

Hobhouse urges the promulgation of 'the social conception of property' (188). This includes the attempt 'to reconstitute a class of independent peasantry as the backbone of the working population' (175). The proposal to return people to the land was seen as a solution to the problems of unemployment and the vast increase in urbanisation – '[t]he English nation is becoming more and more a people of dwellers in cities. And this change is widely recognised to be full of danger to the national future' (Samuel 1902: 103). This contentious proposal divided liberals, for there were those who believed that it was not possible to 'revers[e] the trend to industrialism' and for whom 'the multiplication of owners on small quantities of land was no more than a palliative' (Emy 1973: 208). In 1907 the Small Holdings and Allotments Act was passed as 'a means of encouraging, and even compelling, county councils to satisfy local demand for small holdings' (Bernstein 1986: 106).

Howards End is, once more, full of the terms and even the language of the debate. In its support for the establishment of the small farmer and the policy of embourgeoisement as a social ambition, it is at one with the New Liberal agenda. Agricultural labourers and small farmers are elevated by being presented as potential heirs to the tradition of yeomanry:

> [In the country] men had been up since dawn. Their hours were ruled, not by a London office, but by the movements of the crops and the sun. . . . Clumsily they carry forward the torch of the sun, until such time as the nation sees fit to take it up. Half clodhopper, half board-school prig, they can still throw back to a nobler stock, and breed yeomen.   (*HE*: 320)

As the subsequent discussion will suggest, the ideas and language of the New Liberals made substantial use of eugenics – seen here in the notion of 'throw[ing] back to a nobler stock'. Those who are regarded as indicating the direction which the nation ought to follow and who 'carry forward the torch of the sun' are genetically custodians of the past; they are also 'England's hope' (320).

Howards End also echoes Masterman's lament that the English countryside is falling into the hands of the plutocrats:

> In many of the home counties . . . the bulk of the older estates have passed into the hands of the owners of the 'new wealth', the

Plutocracy which looks for its consummation in ownership of a portion of the land of England.   (Masterman 1911: 171)

This is a danger which the novel marks by allowing the Wilcoxes to retain Howards End after Ruth Wilcox's death, and which it averts by ensuring that the property goes to Margaret. The countryside around Howards End, observed admiringly by Margaret on her first visit to the house, escapes both the grasp of old, entrenched privilege (described here as 'aristocratic') and – thus far, at least – the contaminating spread of the suburbs:

> The great estates that throttle the south of Hertfordshire were less obtrusive here, and the appearance of the land was neither aristocratic nor suburban. To define it was difficult, but Margaret knew what it was not: it was not snobbish. . . . 'Left to itself,' was Margaret's opinion, 'this county would vote Liberal.'   (265)

Here some of the general ambitions of the New Liberalism do seem to be articulated sympathetically. The impulse towards more democratic tendencies seems to lie behind the description of that part of the county as being 'not snobbish'. What is problematic, however, is that we are told that what the county chiefly needs is to be 'left to itself', in which case it will, apparently, vote Liberal through instinct. The New Liberals had not the slightest wish to leave society to itself. Leonard Bast's misguided hope of 'com[ing] to Culture suddenly, much as the Revivalist hopes to come to Jesus' (48) is treated satirically by the narrator, yet there is nothing that urges the reader to consider satirically Margaret's belief that the county can just as suddenly come to liberalism. The apparent sympathy with the aims of the New Liberals is thus merely an ostensible one, for the liberal sympathies are shown as being entrenched in the wellspring of virtue which the countryside intrinsically makes possible, rather than coming from the specific set of social and political programmes envisaged by the New Liberals.

Howards End deals, at many levels, with the issue of inheritance and the question of land is continually implicated in that investigation. The different positions within the land debate are presented as a choice between the farm labourer, shepherd or yeoman on the one hand, and the two enemies of those embodiments of atavistic vigour, namely the ruthless plutocrat and the (ostensibly) innocuous clerk.

The latter, especially when he is as enfeebled as Leonard Bast, seems an unlikely opponent, but he is a threat because he represents a combination of social declension and class mobility. Many of the modernists, despite their apocalyptic anxieties and their perceptions of incipient chaos, find the greater horror of modernity to be what they regard as its pervasive banality and mediocrity. In many cases, this means the suburbs and the clerks: 'Hostility to the suburbs as ecologically destructive quickly fused with contempt for those who lived in them' (Carey 1992: 50–1). The pervasive disparagement of the clerk, whether in *The Waste Land* or elsewhere in modernist writings, may be seen in the light of the marked growth in the years between 1860 and 1910 of 'the section of the middle and lower-middle class employed in commerce, banks, insurance and real estate' (58). The reaction in part takes the form of 'the widespread intellectual cult of the peasant' (36).

In *Howards End*, the cult of the peasant is conflated with the liberal ideal of the small cultivator: the result is a nostalgic feudalism which is promoted as a progressive social programme. To return thus to the past, it is implied, is to achieve stillness and so to escape the ceaseless motion which, as we have seen, the novel repeatedly presents as one of the great curses of modernity: 'The feudal ownership of land did bring dignity, whereas the modern ownership of movables is reducing us again to a nomadic horde' (*HE*: 146).

As Leonard Bast's name suggests, he has become the 'bastard', the illegitimate child of society – a particularly unenviable fate in a novel that makes so much of heirs and the value, whether material or transcendent, of legacies. He is a bastard because he is a clerk; being a clerk effectively bars him from social ascendancy. He wears, therefore, an increasingly defeated air and has little in common, with, for instance, H. G. Wells's resourceful clerks and bourgeois heroes:

> One guessed him as the third generation, grandson to the shepherd or ploughboy whom civilization had sucked into the town; as one of the thousands who have lost the life of the body and failed to reach the life of the spirit. Hints of robustness survived in him, more than a hint of primitive good looks, and Margaret, noting the spine that might have been straight, and the chest that might have broadened, wondered whether it paid to give up the glory of the animal for a tailcoat and a couple of ideas.   (113)

The 'primitiveness' of Leonard's residual handsomeness points to its atavistic origins. Modernity has almost cost Leonard his looks – no small complaint against the modern world, for, as the beauty of the untainted (and firmly pastoral) Alex Scudder in *Maurice* and the robustness of Stephen Wonham in *The Longest Journey* suggest, the countryside and traditional life are seen as nurturing male beauty and strength. The strain placed upon traditional class identities by the ambiguous status of the upwardly-mobile clerk is recast here in terms of a failure in human potential: the humanistic slant is used to obfuscate the social commentary. In addition, instead of granting that occupations such as clerks and typists in many cases confer opportunities for social mobility upon people, it is suggested in the novel that they impede progress: Mr Wilcox gives work to clerks, but it is 'work that scarcely encouraged them to grow into other men' (179).

The description of Leonard pointedly suggests devolution: it is another instance of the common modernist perception that the present is a time of falling-off and that what this period of evolutionary disappointment breeds is mediocrity and identities that are half-formed – Leonard is 'one of the thousands who have lost the life of the body and failed to reach the life of the spirit'. In a stirring speech towards the end of the novel, Margaret speaks of the 'battle against sameness' and of the importance of finding colour 'in the daily gray' (336). She is prepared to lie to Henry Wilcox at the end and assure him that '[n]othing has been done wrong' (340): somehow wrongdoing may be indulged, if not forgiven. But the absence of colour or vividness can neither be indulged nor forgiven. Leonard Bast, despite all the romantic potential that the Schlegels recognise in him, cannot shed the greyness that cannot be condoned. A chastened Henry Wilcox may be allowed into the charmed circle at Howards End at the end of the novel, but Leonard may only be represented in the form of his child; and that child, born into a type of rustic Bloomsbury, is more the antidote to Leonard than his offspring.

Whatever the nature of the compassion elicited on behalf of Leonard, it is undoubtedly not a *pragmatic* compassion. The narrator warns us, with Tibby's unconventionality in mind, that it is 'not difficult to stand above the conventions when we leave no hostages among them' (306). By the same token, it is not difficult to feel compassion for Leonard when he can be expunged and left to participate vicariously (as a bucolic child) in the life at Howards End. The tragedy of Leonard is far easier to manage than the burdensome responsibility: the narrator's comments when he dies make it clear that his death endows the child with the opportunities which were denied to the father. In addition, it transforms the 'squalor' which characterised his life:

> To what ultimate harmony we tend [Helen] did not know, but there seemed great chance that a child would be born into the world, to take the great chances of beauty and adventure that the world offers. . . . There was nothing else to be done; the time for telegrams and anger was over, and it seemed wisest that the hands of Leonard should be folded on his breast and be filled with flowers. Here was the father; leave it at that. Let squalor be turned into tragedy, whose eyes are the stars, and whose hands hold the sunset and the dawn. (327–8)

The relief is palpable. In particular, there is the sense that, with Leonard's death, there is no longer a need to undertake practical action – '[t]here was nothing else to be done'. The child may 'take the great chances of beauty and adventure' which Leonard longed for, while in his death the romantic panoply (stars, sunset, dawn) which evaded him throughout the squalid struggles of his life is obligingly in attendance.

In addition, the fate of Leonard conveys the recognition that philanthropy may be a morally ambiguous activity, where the attempt to do good often merely entrenches the power of those who seek to confer benefits on others. Forster grew up in a tradition of philanthropy: members of his mother's family belonged to the Clapham Sect, whose predilections Forster describes in his biography of his great-aunt, Marianne Thornton, as 'affections, comfort, piety, integrity, intelligence, public activity, private benevolence' (*MT*: 20). It is the self-assurance of this – the Victorian self-assurance – which *Howards End* calls into question, as well as the assumption of continuity: between private inclination and 'public activity', between benevolent intention and desired consequence.

Leonard Bast is not only an evolutionary disappointment, he is also a *eugenic* disappointment – the language of breeding, lineage and blood is unmistakable in Forster's descriptions of him. In that respect, too, *Howards End* shows a significant engagement with the hopes and schemes of the New Liberalism, for eugenics was very much a part of

the liberals' understanding of social advancement and personal better-
ment:

> in the first great enthusiasm for eugenics liberals were prominently
> to the fore, simply because what appealed to them was the rational-
> ity of the science, the possibility that man could now control a new
> aspect of his 'environment' – his own body.   (Freeden 1978: 185)

The attraction of eugenics was that it was a form of control, a way of
minimising the power of contingency in human life. Edwardian race-
improvers, in their attempts to 'save the nation from degeneration . . .
sought to encourage the breeding of "fit" stocks and to bring the breeding of the "unfit" to a halt, once and for all' (Greenslade 1994: 47).
Eugenics was seen as possessing 'a radical and transforming potential'
(207); it was part of the preoccupation with efficiency which was 'one
of the great shibboleths of the Edwardian period' (J. Rose 1986: 117).
Many liberals, too, were attracted to the doctrine of race improvement:
Hobson, for instance, even while denying the validity of theories of
biological determinism or 'natural selection' as a justification for imperialism, nonetheless accepts as a given the need for eugenics:

> It is as essential to the progress of man as to that of any other ani-
> mal, as essential in the future as in the past, that reproduction shall
> be from the better stock and that the worst stock shall be eliminat-
> ed.   (Hobson 1902: 173)

The concern with eugenics points to a most revealing debate within
liberalism, for, even if one separates early twentieth-century eugenics
from the uses which the Nazis and others afterwards found for it – and,
in fairness, one must – it remains an indication of the extent to which
the New Liberalism still relied on programmes of extensive social
engineering determined by a few on behalf of the many. The doctrine
of social organicism had distinct Darwinian overtones, however much
Hobhouse and the New Liberals sought to nudge it away from a crude,
appetitive biological determinism and towards an idea of social evolution with a collectivist and co-operative (rather than competitive)
basis. The claim that 'biology supported ethics' (Freeden 1978: 75)
appealed to many contemporary thinkers, although by no means all:
G. E. Moore, for instance, rejected it firmly: 'Evolution has very little

indeed to say to Ethics' (G. Moore 1903: 58). The success of the incor-
poration of evolutionary thought depended upon the capacity to fashion a doctrine of social evolution which was not perceived as excessively
deterministic:

> [Hobhouse] developed his theory as part of a general philosophy of
> evolution, as did [Herbert] Spencer, but whereas Spencer saw evolu-
> tion as an automatic, mechanical and inevitable process, Hobhouse
> regarded it as a development of the power of mind, leading to a
> growth in harmony and correlation.   (Owen 1974: 9)

The harsh treatment of Leonard Bast – both in relation to the pitying
scorn with which the narrator views him and in terms of his exclusion
from the happy ending that is reserved for some – may be seen as the
failure of the New Liberal attempt to humanise eugenics and make it
something from which everyone can benefit. Eugenics is a sad fact in
Howards End, rather than an opportunity for the likes of Bast. That is
why so much is made of the unattractive possibility that always haunts
any kind of evolutionary scheme: devolution. As in Conrad's *The Secret
Agent*, where physical inferiority – in the character of the Professor, for
instance – is associated with moral decline, devolution is used as a
weapon to lambast the failings of modernity. Leonard Bast cannot
make progress – socially, economically or culturally – and the reason is
that he is an embodiment of devolution, unwittingly slipping back
even as he struggles to get ahead. The uncongenial circumstances of
his life and the forces of modernity all conspire against him:

> He knew that he was poor, and would admit it; he would have died
> sooner than confess any inferiority to the rich. This may be splen-
> did of him. But he was inferior to most rich people, there is not the
> least doubt of it. He was not as courteous as the average rich man,
> nor as intelligent, nor as healthy, nor as lovable. His mind and his
> body had been alike underfed, because he was poor, and because he
> was modern they were always craving better food. Had he lived
> some centuries ago, in the brightly coloured civilizations of the
> past, he would have had a definite status, his rank and his income
> would have corresponded. But in his day the angel of Democracy
> had arisen, enshadowing the classes with leathern wings, and pro-
> claiming, 'All men are equal – all men, that is to say, who possess

umbrellas,' and so he was obliged to assert gentility, lest he slipped into the abyss where nothing counts, and the statements of Democracy are inaudible. (43)

This passage, interestingly, offers a materialist understanding of Bast's predicament in the recognition that it is his poverty – rather than some kind of innate failing – which is accountable for his inferiority. Devolution is thus not an inevitability, for it would not have occurred had the grey Leonard still lived in the 'brightly coloured civilizations of the past'. It is modernity which has caused devolution to set in, and modernity is in this instance embodied in part in the 'Angel of Democracy', which is a devious and seductive presence, tempting Leonard to move increasingly towards the abyss. To the extent to which the New Liberals in their desire to curb the excesses of capitalism and the entrenchment of privilege sought a more democratic society, Forster may here be seen as spurning that attempt, using one liberal hope – eugenics – to respond pejoratively to another; at the same time, what is evident is his 'susceptibility to [the] clichés of contemporary degenerationism' (Greenslade 1994: 222).

In the light of the eugenics debate, it is possible to understand why, in *Howards End*, there are complaints about overpopulation and the falling birth rate at the same time: the 'dominant discourse of race-improvement' carried with it an 'attendant anxiety about the differential birth-rate' (Greenslade 1994: 208). The *wrong* people are procreating – a common complaint, seen also in Masterman's warning that 'a nation is in a serious condition if its better stocks are producing smaller families or no families at all, and its least capable are still raising an abundant progeny' (Masterman 1911: 78). In the novel procreative abundance is reserved for Charles and Dolly Wilcox, who are certainly not representative of the 'better stocks' or of the kind of people whom the novel would like to see flourishing: the younger Wilcoxes in themselves suggest a kind of devolution, being less interesting or memorable than either of their parents. The implication is that stupid and aggressive plutocrats are in danger of inheriting England: Margaret, speaking 'rather seriously', tells her siblings that 'our race is degenerating' (155).

In one significant instance, however, the novel does offer the possibility of evolutionary and eugenic recovery: the character in whom those opportunities are embodied is, of course, the child who is born to

Helen and Leonard at the end of the novel – the one who is to inherit Howards End. This child has managed to return to the country, which the unfortunate Leonard was not able to do. Circumstances have also freed him of the patriarchal and plutocratic power of Mr Wilcox, something that Leonard could not escape from either. Instead of the different strands within society being united in the form of social organicism, as the New Liberals wished, some of them have been united in the veins of one child. He is surrounded by love – itself uniquely exempt from the widespread degeneration into primal chaos: 'Love . . . knows that he will survive at the end of things, and be gathered by Fate as a jewel from the slime' (173). But if the continuation of Howards End is threatened, so too is the biological line that ends in the offspring of Helen and Leonard. He is both the culmination and the end of evolution. There is nothing to suggest that he himself will hand anything down, particularly if – as seems to be the case – he is in some way representative of the little Morgan Forster, surrounded in his childhood by his mother and a host of quasi-matriarchs. He represents a consummation that is also a cul-de-sac. The future beckons and ends in him. It is not a coincidence that it is after the birth of the child that Margaret delivers her speech in support of difference, which, however much it affirms individual difference as a general humanistic premise, is surely also a plea on behalf of that distinctive and unique difference which is homosexuality:

> All over the world men and women are worrying because they cannot develop as they are supposed to develop. . . . Don't fret yourself, Helen. Develop what you have; love your child. I do not love children. I am thankful to have none. I can play with their beauty and charm, but that is all – nothing real, not one scrap of what there ought to be. And others – others go further still, and move outside humanity altogether. (335)

The ostensibly straightforward humanistic injunction – 'Develop what you have' – is a plea on behalf of those who 'move outside humanity altogether' and who, even as they grow up amidst the richness of the unprecedented crop of hay and all the rural fruitfulness, may themselves never breed or become a link in a generational progression. Margaret asks not only that the individual should be developed, but also that he or she should be left alone, exempted if need be from the remorseless business of begetting and from the strain of functioning according to prevailing definitions of family life and identity.

The ending of the novel conspicuously refuses to supply anything resembling a conventional nuclear family: in presenting us with an illegitimate child, an unmarried mother, a dead father, an enfeebled and defeated husband and a wife who will never have children, Howards End becomes a shelter in which the broken, the defiant and the evolutionarily inert may be protected. If it is the case that 'the classic liberal paradox' consists of 'wishing to be a part, but apart' (Widdowson 1977: 19), then *Howards End* indeed opts finally to be apart and not a part. The conclusion brings not only withdrawal from the world, but also the receding of the ideal of encompassing significance. The bathos of the ending lies in the fact that the Schlegel sisters and their charmed circle are hiding *from* England in the house that was meant to *represent* England. The 'broad amplitude' (Levenson 1991: 91–2) of synecdoche fails too, so that the final note of the novel is not representation, but secession. When Howards End can no longer fulfil its metonymic or synecdochical function, the result is the loss of those contiguous relationships which metonymy and synecdoche bestow: the continuity between the private and the public, the individual life and the wider social context. This loss is expressive of an inability to make the liberal voice prevail in socially expansive terms, and thus a denial of the empowering relevance and adaptability that theorists like Hobhouse and Hobson were insisting were still within the reach of liberalism. The reader, admittedly, is invited into the charmed circle, but the hope that the geographical imagination would encircle England has been lost as the 'red rust' (337) of the suburbs draws closer: in Helen's words, 'London's creeping' (337). There are small victories, it is true, made up in part by the restoration to Margaret of the house she should have had upon Ruth Wilcox's death and the fact that the Schlegels have found a home and need no longer feel rootless. But these are set within a looming defeat: the formidable forces of modernity are advancing inexorably.

According to Masterman, those who do not find the 'riotous life' of the modern world congenial will 'seek satisfaction in quietness and common things – the untroubled horizon, the secure possession of the heart of humanity' (Masterman 1911: 184). Although the ending of Forster's novel provides a respite from the 'riotous life', the horizon *is* 'troubled' by the advance of urbanisation and the possession of

Howards End itself is far from secure. Above all, the notion of social organicism is lost amidst the bucolic pleasures: the novel not only abandons the hopes implied by the New Liberal agenda, but gives up on the polemic itself.

Patricia Stubbs and Michael Levenson both make the point that *Howards End* is, in general, inhospitable to the New Liberalism, but the conclusion that they reach is that, in consequence, it retrogressively upholds an older, archaic liberalism. Stubbs sees the novel as affirming the individualist creed of the older liberalism while awkwardly seeking to shrug off its aggressive *laissez-faire* economics:

> For although [Forster] rejected the competitive economics of liberal individualism, he continued to believe in a liberal hierarchy of values in which the rights of the individual are sacred. He gives up, if you like, the public and economic aspects of liberalism, but clings to its private morality.   (Stubbs 1979: 210)

Michael Levenson's reading is similar, suggesting, in effect, that, since Forster is necessarily a liberal of one variety or another, the unenthusiastic depiction of the New Liberalism must imply a reactionary embrace of the older creed:

> Unlike Hobhouse, Forster retains no confidence in an emerging balance between . . . personal freedom and public obligation, and faced with these alternatives, he unhesitatingly chooses private before public, friend before country, much as Margaret Schlegel makes this choice.   (Levenson 1991: 88)

The difficulty with this interpretation of Forster's position, whereby he 'appears to us now the artist of liberalism in retreat' (Stubbs 1979: 210) is, firstly, that it seems to suggest that disillusionment with one form of liberalism must necessarily imply the embrace of another; and, secondly, it does not recognise the extent to which the liberal strain in Forster's work and the modernist elements which are increasingly apparent play off against each other. In other words, it does not consider the possibility that *dialectic* – with all its accompanying tension and irresolute meanings – may be one of the choices available, and that disenchantment may function as one of its components. In *Howards End*, the perception that even the most resourceful attempts to reinvigorate liberalism are proving unsuccessful is an impasse at one level, but, on another, it becomes an opportunity for a new kind of articulation – oblique, esoteric, restless; the beginnings of Forster's modernism.

In *A Passage to India* Forster considers the possibility that liberalism will act as the remedy for the ailments of the Raj. Like *Howards End*, the novel about India that Forster abandoned in 1914 (he returned to the manuscript years later, as the discussion in Chapter 4 will indicate) also offered liberalism and its quandaries as a central focus. This is in part because imperialism was a deeply contentious and divisive issue within liberal ranks. For some, imperialism was an ideological regression, a betrayal of the progressive ambitions of the preceding century:

> The true political nature of Imperialism is best seen by confronting it with the watchwords of progress accepted in the middle of the nineteenth century by moderate men of both great parties in the State . . . – peace, economy, reform and popular self-government . . . a large section of professed Liberals believe or assert that Imperialism is consistent with the maintenance of all these virtues. . . . This contention, however, is belied by facts. The decades of Imperialism have been prolific in wars; most of these wars have been directly motivated by aggression of white races upon 'lower races', and have issued in the forcible seizure of territory.   (Hobson 1902: 132–3)

Hobhouse, too, complains that influential liberals are 'becoming Imperialists in their sleep' (Hobhouse 1934: 222) and attributes the jingoistic tendencies within British society to 'the paralysis of Liberalism', wherein 'the Imperial reaction had things all to itself' (215).

Hence, another aspect of the progressivist polemic of the New Liberalism is the anti-imperial stance of some of its foremost publicists, at odds with the pro-imperialist sympathies shown by many liberals. In a revealing comment, Hobhouse claims that '[t]he Colonial Empire as it stands is in substance the creation of the older Liberalism' (240). The New Liberalism, then, would be a corrective that would restrain this illiberal imperialistic fervour. Hobhouse even approves of the politicisation of those whom the Empire ruled, something Forster presents in Aziz's changing political attitude: 'Nothing has been more encouraging to the Liberalism of Western Europe in recent years than the signs of political awakening in the East' (Hobhouse 1934: 236). Instead of interfering in the situation – a tendency which Forster satirises so memorably – the liberal, uncharacteristically and for once, should do nothing: 'Until the white man has fully learnt to rule his own life, the best of all things that he can do with the dark man is to do nothing with him' (Hobhouse 1934: 44).

There were many liberals, however, who were entirely unwilling to leave the dark man to himself. We have seen how, in *Howards End*, England has become a possession, a legacy to be apportioned and quarrelled over, with liberals dissenting amongst themselves even as they take on the more obvious enemy represented by the plutocrats. So, too, the rule of India presented a situation of inherited power and there was little consensus amongst liberals as to what was to be done with it, which is precisely why Hobhouse devotes so much attention in his New Liberal manifesto to a review of liberal imperial policy. In a comment that says so much about the dilemma that imperialism posed for liberals, he writes that '[u]nder the reign of Imperialism the temple of Janus is never closed' (Hobhouse 1934: 94).

A Passage to India is indeed Janus-faced in its response to the Empire. It is ambivalent in its treatment of the British Raj, satirising it – in the earlier parts of the novel, in particular – as the administration of folly and showing in the Anglo-Indians an unforgivable neglect of the new contexts in which they are located; yet it also wishes to exempt from that large-scale muddle the admirable colonial administrator who is guided by distinctly liberal precepts. The fact that, for much of the novel, Forster condemns the practice of British imperialism in India rather than the idea of it – 'Forster hated imperial domineering but he had no quarrel with imperial domination' (Mahood 1977: 25) – is directly attributable to the implication of liberal precepts in the idea of a conscionable British rule in India. In fact, the alienation of Cyril Fielding within the colonial administration, was, in the early drafts of the novel, intended to convey the eclipsing of an enlightened liberal presence by a conservative, jingoistic maladministration.

It was imperial policy which, from as early as 1882 and leading up to the years of the South African War, had 'strained party unity as Liberals had sought to define what compromises were justifiable in maintaining the empire' (Bernstein 1986: 167). The strain was far greater in the years after the war in South Africa. In the battle between 'Liberal Imperialist' and 'Little Englander' (Hunter 1982: 101), the latter seemed 'in the ascendancy' after 1906 and the Liberal Imperialists had to 'take stock and strike back' (108). One of the ways in which they sought to do so in India was to institute reforms which were consistent with a liberal conception of imperial administration. The policies of 1905–14 revealed 'the bases of a liberal consensus on imperial affairs' (Bernstein 1986: 167). In appealing for a wiser and more humane form of British rule in India, as Forster did in the pre-War drafts of *A Passage to India*, he was still entertaining the possibility of a workable situation based upon liberal consensus and compromise. At that stage, Cyril Fielding's role was to suggest liberal alternatives, not, as it later became, to signify liberal impotence.

In nurturing the hope of a redemptive liberal presence in India in the years before the First World War, Forster was in respectable company: 'Intellectual liberalism gave the imperial administration a moral imperative, an ideal of service and good government to set against the anti-imperialist Gladstonian objective of early self-government' (R. Moore 1966: 41). Gandhi may have misread the nature and direction of English liberalism:

[Gandhi] calculated that a nation whose history was the growth of liberal institutions would not remain insensitive to a vigorous but restrained appeal for freedom. He . . . overlooked the fact that liberalism also nourished the imperial idea.   (R. Moore 1966: 127)

For anyone who had read *The Condition of England*, no such misapprehension would have been possible: 'No nation need be ashamed of Empire on a large scale, or apologise for the overlordship of a Continent' (Masterman 1911: 59). Indeed, it seems clear that when Forster began to write *A Passage to India*, he had no intention of apologising for the grand scale or for the overlordship: his target was pettiness, the degradation of the lofty ideal by those unworthy to be entrusted with its execution. That is why so much is made of Ronny Heaslop's attitude towards his imperial responsibilities:

How [Ronny] did rub it in that he was not in India to behave pleasantly, and derived positive satisfaction therefrom! . . . His words without his voice might have impressed [Mrs Moore], but when she

heard the self-satisfied lilt of them, when she saw the mouth moving so complacently and competently beneath the little red nose,
she felt, quite illogically, that this was not the last word on India.
One touch of regret – not the canny substitute but the true regret
from the heart – would have made him a different man, and the
British Empire a different institution.   (*PI*: 70)

Only an assumption that the British Raj was badly executed rather
than badly conceived could underlie the assertion that 'the true regret
from the heart' would have made the British Empire 'a different institution'. The excerpt points towards a superior notion of imperial governance even while it mocks imperial folly. The attitude is at one with
that brand of anti-imperialist sentiment which Forster would have
found in the *Independent Review*, a publication which was given to
denunciations of 'the philistine hypocrisy and brutality of the English
abroad' (Rosenbaum 1994: 34).

   The early parts of the novel, in undermining through satire the rule
of characters such as Heaslop and the Turtons, and seeking to entrust
India instead to those who would make it 'a different institution' along
liberal-humanist lines, are wholly in accordance with the reformist
efforts of the Liberal Imperialists. The Morley–Minto Reforms and
the Government of India Act of 1909 were welcomed by liberals as 'a
cautious, prudent step towards self-government' (Bernstein 1986:
173):

   Liberals looked with satisfaction upon the government's manage-
   ment of Indian affairs. It was one of many affirmations during the
   years of Liberal rule that liberal principles could be applied successfully to the government of the empire.   (173)

When the hope of a salvationist Liberal Imperialism began to wane,
the reassuring sense of competence went too. It is no coincidence that
the later parts of *A Passage to India*, which present the obsolescence of
liberal attempts to reform British rule, are also the sections which most
forcefully present India as resistant to the grasp of reason. It is another
way of indicating that the occidental governance of India is doomed.
Masterman, too, saw that conquest and understanding were intimately linked, but the conclusion he arrived at was quite the opposite of
what we find in *A Passage to India*:

No conquering race ever has understood the conquered: except when, understanding, its Imperial rule has begun its decline. If the English in India . . . commenced to understand India, the episode of English rule in India would be nearing its close.

(Masterman 1911: 56)

It is a curious claim: ignorance empowers, knowledge disables. For Forster, however, the inability to 'hold' India within Western cognition is precisely where the weakening and eventual dissolution of the imperial rule lie – his novel registers a recognition of a fundamental aspect of the 'colonial gaze':

To the same extent as the gaze depended on the colonizer's position in charge of a total system, it was also a potent expression of that position. To govern was to know; to see in the round, panoptically. (Boehmer 1995: 71)

That is why, even when the Indians in *A Passage to India* seem to be subservient, the landscape of India never is. Eventually some of the Indians – Dr Aziz in particular – develop the same resistance to the colonisers that the land has displayed from the start. By the same token, the ostentatiously elusive aspects of the text are a way of refusing the containment and certainty suggested by the panoptic view, of frustrating 'the spectatorial lust of Jingoism' (Hobson 1902: 227). The collective Will that is the Empire founders; civilisation, upliftment, the extension of superior technology, the Burkean notion of 'trusteeship', the idea of the 'democratic Empire' which Forster cherished initially (Das 1977: 25) – all of these lose the force of their control when they lose their self-satisfaction, for, like the major characters in the novel, they too are full of good intentions. What is even more damning than the inability of liberalism 'to offer any opposition to the enemy of its values' (Parry 1979: 132), is its inability to assert its own values; to make cogent what is creditable within itself.

In 1913 Forster was still in support of those who sought to take liberal virtues to India, as suggested by his enthusiastic response to the racial harmony which he witnessed on the trains and the symbolic importance which he conferred upon this example of amity and goodwill:

And as the Indian train goes forward, traversing an immense monotony and bearing every variety of class, race and creed within

> its sun-baked walls, it may serve as a symbol of India herself. . . . The first class – white skinned and aloof – the second and intermediate where the two races mingle – the third class many-coloured, brightly-clothed, and innumerable as the sand – the train has brought them together after so many centuries and is dragging them towards one goal.   *(PT:* 221)

Within the racial and other divisions, in other words, there is the possibility of 'connection'. However, in 1921, when Forster made a second visit to India, that colourful and energetic mix of 'class, race and creed' no longer seemed attainable to him. In the period between the wars, 'relations between East and West assumed a currency that was both widespread and anxious' (Said 1978: 248). India was decidedly not the same place that Forster had visited in the years before the war; and liberalism was not in the same condition either. It would be difficult to say where the greater change lay. In India there had been a shift in the political climate: the level of anti-British activity and polarisation had made reformist programmes virtually redundant: 'in that place and at that time the liberal virtues had been rendered powerless' (Mahood 1977: 67). The Amritsar massacre had taken place in 1919; the Treaty of Sèvres in 1920 had given rise to Muslim anger and the Khilafat agitations; Gandhi's Non-Co-operation Movement instituted its Civil Disobedience Policy in 1921; the Prince of Wales's visit in 1922 had been widely boycotted: all of these made the Montagu–Chelmsford Reforms of 1919 seem hopelessly meagre. Inadequate now were the improved manners and greater courtesy towards Indians that Forster noted in the British during his second visit. As late as 1922 he wrote that 'never in history did ill breeding contribute so much towards the dissolution of an Empire' *(PT:* 246); but, even as he wrote that, it was apparent that such humanistic accoutrements as good manners, refined behaviour and recognition of the intrinsic dignity of others would do nothing to repair the situation.

The intervening years had also brought a marked decline in the status and prospects of political liberalism. A political philosophy that prided itself upon being ever modern and thus adept at responding to contingency began increasingly to seem anachronistic. In the years between 1910 and 1914, the Liberals had also to contend with crisis after crisis. These included 'the problems of Ireland, suffragettes, industrial militancy [and] relations with the Labour party' (Cook 1976: 52).

In addition to these trying difficulties, there was the War, 'the gathering world storm' (Cook 1976: 52). When it came, it was devastating for the Liberal Party. Winston Churchill declared in 1906 that 'War is fatal to Liberalism' (in Searle 1992: 172) – a remark which, at least where the Great War is concerned, proved prophetic. The war replaced the political world which the liberals had understood with something 'brash, cheap and contemptible' (Bentley 1977: 1). Most of all, it seemed, for many, to invalidate the liberal past as well as the liberal future, undermining the belief in the adaptability of a rich tradition, those evolutionary ideas that were so reassuring to the New Liberals. Even Hobson conceded that the Great War brought a 'deplorable set-back to the rule of reason' (Hobson 1933: 31). At a certain point, self-doubt and introspection may become a disabling despair:

> By crushing the values of certainty and optimism – a complete universe encoded in the single word 'decency' – the First World War not only buried the Liberal future but rendered hopeless the past by which Liberals had chartered the course that took them there. (Bentley 1987: 152)

A Passage to India traces this general course of events, even though it never refers explicitly to the war. The 'universe' of like-minded thinking is replaced by a multiverse, the India of a 'hundred voices' (*PI*: 316) which all say different things and refuse to operate consensually. In its own way the novel, too, 'render[s] hopeless the past by which Liberals had chartered the course that took them there', and therefore, instead of imbuing their difficulties with redemptive significance, it leaves them with an unsettling sense of their own marginalisation.

One cannot consider what liberalism is and does in Forster's work without considering also the role of its traditional bedfellow, humanism. Within its greater emphasis on social concerns and its muted collectivism, the New Liberalism maintained the traditionally intimate alliance between liberalism and the customary humanistic hopes and ideals. Its language is saturated with the idea of fullness, plenitude and completion for the self, the personality and the individual, for 'the fundamental postulate of the organic view of society' is the belief that 'such a fulfilment or full development of personality is practically possible not for one man only but for all members of a community' (Collini 1979: 128). In fact, the prevalence of humanistic language suggests that the organic model is the extension of the idea of human personality as 'the motive power of social action' (Freeden 1978: 177). The conflation, even the interchangeability, of models of society and personality is suggested by Hobson's link between the rounded individual and the organic community:

> That same power of reason which brought the diverse and sometimes conflicting passions of the individual into an ordered personality, seeking its welfare as an organic and progressive whole, would perform the same service for humanity by bringing its individual members and its nations, or other groups, into finding their common good, their community, in ordered and mutually beneficial intercourse.   (Hobson 1933: 20)

It is so commonly assumed that early twentieth-century views of selfhood and personality were swayed for the most part by Freudian notions that made much of psychic inscrutability, the self divided against itself and its displacement from the Enlightenment apex of the rational mind, that it is easy to overlook the many-pronged attempts in that same period to re-establish the centrality of reason and to recover the very useful humanistic language of control, volition and self-advancement. One sees this type of language used again and again in polemic on behalf of the New Liberalism:

> Liberalism is the belief that society can safely be founded on this self-directing power of personality, that it is only on this foundation that a true community can be built, and that so established its foundations are so deep and so wide that there is no limit that we can place to the extent of the building.   (Hobhouse 1934: 123)

Where many were finding an abyss or something akin in the structures of society and in the recesses of the personality, here is an opposing view which sees society as an edifice, secured by the 'self-directing power of personality' which acts as the foundation of the building. The New Liberalism was in itself a recuperative programme: it is not surprising, therefore, that it sought recuperative possibilities within the edifice of the self:

> human personality is that within which lives and grows, which can be destroyed but cannot be made, which cannot be taken to pieces and repaired, but can be placed under conditions in which it will flourish and expand, or, if it is diseased, under conditions in which it will heal itself by its own recuperative powers.   (Hobhouse 1934: 122)

'Personality' is seen here as resilient in its adaptability and regenerative powers, but, interestingly, its capacities are also circumscribed: it can recover from disease, but not from destruction or dissolution; it 'cannot be taken to pieces and repaired'. It is significant that Hobhouse uses the word 'recuperative', for what we find in such a model of personality is an attempt to recuperate the Enlightenment self in all the power of its rationalistic rectitude, supported by a securely positivist framework. That New Liberal self, it is true, is not as fiercely individualistic in social or economic terms; it may, as Hobhouse's remarks seem to suggest, have been battered of late. But, like the liberalism which supports it, it is seen as capable of recovery.

To make a psychological model the basis for social policy amounts to more than reiterating the centrality of the individual and his or her interests within that scheme: it is also a way of setting limits to the collectivist impulse within the New Liberalism, of curbing the power of society and its vagaries, thereby minimising, for instance, the impact of the economic factors that Forster stresses in the psychological composition of Leonard Bast. That is why Hobhouse is at pains to explain that 'Personality is not built up from without but grows from within, and the function of the outer order is not to create it, but to provide for it the most suitable conditions for growth' (Hobhouse 1934: 143). The 'outer order' may nurture or fail to do so – and Forster certainly finds that it has not nurtured Bast – but, for Hobhouse, it has no greater determining factor.

Not all the New Liberals, however, felt this way: Hobson is far more willing than Hobhouse to subscribe to something resembling a materialist conception of personality and thus to accept a view of the self that is not as socially deracinated as Hobhouse's. Hobson accepts the preponderance of 'personality' as a motivating impulse within the social and political agenda, as suggested by his comment that 'no cure for poverty will be really effective unless it raises personality', but, significantly, he goes on to add that 'it is most unprofitable to identify degraded personality as the cause of poverty' (Hobson 1986: 208). Such a comment seems to offer a realignment of cause and effect, one which does not see good fortune as inevitably the consequence of merit, or ill fortune as proceeding necessarily from innate failings. However, even when Hobson seems to emphasise most strongly the materialist components of identity, the language he uses betrays once more the essentialism that underlies his compassion:

> The material conditions of poorer working-class life are hostile to the attainment of personal efficiency: they not merely stunt physical and intellectual growth, but, still more detrimental, they maim the human will, sapping the roots of character.   (Hobson 1986: 208)

The greatest debilitation, therefore, is to 'the human will' and 'the roots of character': these are the humanistic foundations from which all growth and potential proceed. If one looks past the overt message, which is about the inseparability of the inner life and the outer conditions, one sees that there is an underlying assumption that 'human will' and 'character' have a status of their own. They may be 'maimed', and are thus not inviolable; but the fact that all the other conditions of life should be in service to them reveals the hierarchical assumptions underlying Hobson's comment and betrays once more the near-sacrosanct status of humanism even within an apparently different set of priorities.

The Edwardian 'gospel' of human relations served as 'a substitute for a lost religion' (Jonathan Rose 1986: 40). This manifested itself in various ways: not only in the devotional fervour of the Bloomsbury 'personal relations' creed, but also in as socially significant an act as the drafting of the welfare legislation of 1906–11 by Masterman and others, which was 'an unprecedented affirmation of "fellowship" in national social policy' (59). This indicates the extent to which the investment of specifically humanistic potential in the individual, and in the relations between individuals, assumed vast ideological weight within the New Liberalism, its shift towards certain collectivist pro-

grammes notwithstanding. 'Fellowship' certainly does not mean socialism: Herbert Samuel, for instance, scorns the idea that '[c]omplete collectivism is now the panacea, Karl Marx the prophet and the Socialist groups
the chosen instruments' (Samuel 1902: 150), although he does warn that
liberalism must resist the spirit which 'opposes social reform out of blind
dread of socialism' (384).

Alan Bullock has sought to expose as a 'travesty' the claim 'sometimes made by both secularists and fundamentalists that secularism
represents humanism' (Bullock 1985: 160). To that end he argues that it
is capable of admitting religious belief and versions of transcendence;
it is its flexibility which ensures its survival. Yet the Edwardian period
did, in fact, extend the contours of humanism in precisely the way that
Bullock suggests, and it ought not, therefore, to have been as buffeted
as it was. Numerous scholars of Edwardian literature have emphasised
that the Edwardian age was an age of secular faith, of the attempt to
invest with a quasi-religious significance the elements of secular life as
a response to the ever-declining power of religion: the 'secular miracle'
(Ellmann 1960: 200) is a trope of Edwardian literature, a manifestation
of the vitalism of the period – what has been called 'The Cult of Life'
(Jonathan Rose 1986: 74). If there were ever a time, therefore, when
humanism was as 'protean' (Bullock 1985: 8) a phenomenon as –
according to Bullock – it is conceptually, the Edwardian period was
that time. There was romanticism to it, there was realism, there was
even secular faith. The attempt 'to incorporate *everything*, including
things that may be trying to limit it, or even totally reject it' (Robbe-
Grillet 1965: 76) has been identified as the principal characteristic of
humanism, and, indeed, that same impulse was the Edwardian obses-
sion, as Forster well knew when he made 'Only connect . . .' the
epigraph to *Howards End*.

Yet therein lay also the source of the modernists' disabling of
humanism, for when so much is made of capaciousness and malleabil-
ity, failures to include or adapt begin to damn the motivating philosophy as well as the discrete attempts. Then the humanist viewpoint that
is 'like a bridge thrown between the soul of man and that of things –
above all, a token of solidarity' (Robbe-Grillet 1965: 78) brings instead
a novel sense of the incompatibility of human volition and the
intractable world. The solidarity swiftly recedes.

Even in Forster's early work, where the humanistic strain is pervasive, there is already the perception that positivism and the primacy of

reason are constraining and provide too narrow a version of human-ism. Much of this early work is about the oppressiveness of conven-tions that cramp, confine and stifle, be they archaic moral and sexual codes or the stultifying suburbia represented by Sawston. In *Where Angels Fear to Tread* and *A Room with a View*, the contrasting expansive-ness and liberation are offered by Italy. The spirit may be trapped or it may escape: *A Room with a View* is a novel that turns on this crucial choice. Lucy manages to escape, but she is unusually lucky, for the novels and stories of this period are filled with characters for whom the perception of the 'unseen' or of romantic possibilities leaves only a wistful sense of what they have failed to seize; of what has passed them by. Lucy's happiness is guaranteed in any case by the formality of the comic mode in that novel. In no other lengthy work of Forster is the happy ending so freely permitted or so unproblematic. Mr Emerson, as befits his status as a secular sage, is granted a sermon: his message of humanistic affirmation and this-worldly contentment would be quite unthinkable in the later work:

> We know that we come from the winds, and that we shall return to them; that all life is perhaps a knot, a tangle, a blemish in the eternal smoothness. But why should this make us unhappy? Let us rather love one another, and work and rejoice. . . . Make [my boy] realize that by the side of the everlasting Why there is a Yes – a transitory Yes if you like, but a Yes.   (*RV*: 26–7)

The prevailing of the 'Yes' over the 'Why' is marked by the marriage to George and what that brings: enlarging vistas rather than claustropho-bia and viewless prospects. As Forster's novels become increasingly con-cerned with what cannot be seen or understood, no matter how much one strains to overcome the inscrutability, the elusive Why becomes much more bothersome and intrusive than it is for Mr Emerson – the contrasting bewilderment of the rationalistic Fielding in *A Passage to India* illustrates the point – and the complacent Yes becomes more and more difficult to assert in the face of increasingly intractable 'knot[s]', 'tangle[s]' and 'blemish[es]'.

There is a brief portrait of a humanistic schoolmaster in *The Longest Journey* in which the narrator's approval is offset to some extent by an unmistakably satirical note. Mr Jackson is the obverse of the stultifying Herbert Pembroke and is, therefore, in his own way, one of the emancipating spirits of the novel, along with Stewart Ansell and Stephen Wonham:

> The choice lay between Mr Pembroke and Mr Jackson, the one an organizer, the other a humanist. Mr Jackson was master of the Sixth, and – with the exception of the headmaster . . . the only first-class intellect in the school. But he could not, or rather would not, keep order. He told his form that if it chose to listen to him it would learn; if it didn't, it wouldn't. One half listened. The other half made paper frogs, and bored holes in the raised map of Italy with their penknives. When the penknives gritted he punished them with undue severity, and then forgot to make them show the punishments up. Yet out of this chaos two facts emerged. Half the boys got scholarships at the University, and some of them – including several of the paper-frog sort – remained friends with him throughout their lives. Moreover, he was rich, and had a competent wife.
>
> (*LJ*: 148)

Mr Jackson receives a mixed report card. The tendency of a humanistic creed to lack rigour and thus to deteriorate into 'chaos' is noted here: this is something that Forster develops in *Howards End* and *A Passage to India*, where the humanists are implicitly berated for leaving 'organisation' to those who, on the assumption that they are more competent to see to it, turn out to be far more likely to abuse the authority that it carries – one sees this in the Wilcoxes, the plutocratic 'organisers' in *Howards End*, and in the colonial administrators in *A Passage to India*. The portrait of Mr Jackson suggests that humanism, in not 'keeping order', is likely to be erratic in its methods and haphazard in its effects. It is also not sufficiently attentive to the idea of necessary consequence, as indicated by Mr Jackson's ordering severe punishments and then failing to ensure that they are carried out. This anticipates what is perhaps the greatest indictment of the liberal-humanists in the later novels: the fact that their good intentions, however admirable in themselves, may have meretricious consequences which they neither anticipate nor are competent to repair. The failure of good intentions is always far more damaging in Forster's work than anything that malevolence may accomplish.

Mr Jackson's successes are impressive, both in the academic achievements of some of the boys and in securing meaningful friendships. But behind these successes lie the failures – the boys who never come round to his methods, never get into university, express no sense of loyal and indebted friendship. *The Longest Journey* does not dwell on these shortcomings, nor does it take further the implications of Mr Jackson's wealth where his humanistic outlook is concerned. In the later novels the ways in which the failures of humanists compromise or even invalidate their successes are not glossed over. Similarly, the presence of wealth, privilege or power is in those works no longer an incidental detail.

In Forster's short story 'The Eternal Moment' – one of his most interesting deliberations, within a humanistic focus, upon meagreness and plenitude, loss and salvaging – we find in Miss Raby a character whom the life of the world fails at every turn. She can find solace only in the contemplation of her 'eternal moment', particularly in the face of the sad deterioration (for which she feels culpable) that she witnesses in Vorta and in Feo the concierge. The campanile itself will fall, it seems, and Miss Raby turns away from Feo and Colonel Leyland:

> In that moment of final failure, there had been vouchsafed to her a vision of herself, and she saw that she had lived worthily. She was conscious of a triumph over experience and earthly facts, a triumph magnificent, cold, hardly human; whose existence no one but herself would ever surmise. From the view-terrace she looked down on the perishing and perishable beauty of the valley, and, though she loved it no less, it seemed to be infinitely distant, like a valley in a star. At that moment, if kind voices had called her from the hotel, she would not have returned.   (*CS*: 221)

There is a neat and telling reversal: the transcendent world, often compared to a star in its remoteness, is now close to Miss Raby because of the reassuring accessibility of her 'eternal moment'. The 'perishing and perishable' world, consequently, recedes, and becomes 'infinitely distant, like a valley in a star'. What recedes with it is all the liberal-humanist language of earthly endeavour, fellowship ('kind voices') and rationalism. From this proceeds her triumph over 'experience and earthly facts', a triumph that is, significantly, described as 'hardly human'. Having felt responsible, she now feels indifferent. In the sense in which she has instigated a muddle, the consequences of which she could not have foreseen or understood, Miss Raby is the forerunner of those characters in the later work – for instance, Fielding, Adela and Mrs Moore – who wrestle with bewilderment and for whom muddle assumes existential proportions. What separates her from them is the romantic escape that is available to her. She finds another way out: when the humanistic framework fails her, the romantic possibilities come to her rescue. The characters in the later works, as we shall see, are not vouchsafed that alternative passage out of the maze.

'The Point of It', a short story which Forster completed and published in 1911, may be seen as another indication of his sense of the increasing fragility of the liberal-humanist position. In some ways, the story looks back to the fiction written before *Howards End*, since narrow rationalism – associated with a failure to respond fully to the intensity of life – is contrasted with romanticism, and found wanting as a result, which is the pattern of the earlier fiction. Harold overtaxes his heart in a recklessly heroic rowing effort (spurred on by Michael) and dies; Michael calms down considerably and becomes a humanist of the kind who 'cared for the universe, for the tiny tangle in it that we call civilization, for his fellow-men who have made the tangle and who transcended it. Love, the love of humanity, warmed him' (*CS*: 150). He believes in love, and marries Janet, who believes in truth. He is knighted and feels satisfied, towards the end of his life, with the modest accomplishments of his humanism:

> The purity of [Sir Michael's] record was not due to luck but to a purity within, and his conciliatory manner sprang from a conciliated soul. He could look back on failures and mistakes, and he had not carried out the ideals of his youth. Who has? But he had succeeded better than most men in modifying those ideals to fit the world of facts, and if love had been modified into sympathy and sympathy into compromise, let one of his contemporaries cast the first stone. (155)

The language describing his complacency is itself so much the language of balance, modulation and reasonableness that it is easy to overlook the lurking irony. The acceptance of compromise as an inevitable fact of earthly existence and the attainment of so fine a thing as a 'conciliated soul' – can these truly be deemed inadequate? But a shock lies in store for everyone. The story takes us into the afterlife, a place where secular humanists as a rule fear to tread, and we find that both Sir Michael and Janet go to Hell after they die. Sir Michael goes to the 'soft' Hell, which is reserved for 'the conciliators, the peace-makers, the humanists, and all who have trusted the warmer vision'; his wife goes to the 'hard' Hell, which is the place of punishment for 'the reformers and ascetics and all sword-like souls' (161). In Hell, Sir Michael sees that 'Love and Truth, who seem to contend for our souls like angels, hold each the seeds of our decay' (161). Like Miss Raby, he is saved, finally, from his dismally unromantic Hell by the vestiges of his romantic longings as he returns to the rowing episode of his youth.

In contrast to this, a warning is sounded in *Howards End* and taken up more fully in *A Passage to India*: the 'conciliated soul' is no longer a valid ambition; it may not even be a viable one, for the modern world does not work to conciliate and appease, although it demands compromises. The pursuit of Love and Truth *per se* is not necessarily admirable: what is more, if it is inattentive to the contexts in which it operates and neglects to consider the consequences of its actions, it is dangerous. The pursuit of moral absolutes and universal truth in a rela-tivistic world of contingent (often incompatible) truths becomes the great drama of Forster's later fiction, as it is in the work of so many of the modernists. 'The Point of It' continues the distrust of intentional-ity itself as a chauvinistic set of practices that was first seen when the Herritons rushed off to Italy in *Where Angels Fear to Tread*.

In *Howards End* we see how complex an anxiety humanism has become. As before, it is extremely useful to consider that great dis-appointment, Leonard Bast. The presentation of Bast bears directly upon the New Liberal tendency to deploy humanistic language in the attempt to reinvigorate liberalism. In the important passage in Chapter VI in which, as we have seen, his regression is considered in eugenic terms, it is made clear that Leonard will not be emancipated by conventional humanistic truisms either:

The boy, Leonard Bast, stood at the extreme verge of gentility. He was not in the abyss, but he could see it, and at times people whom he knew had dropped in, and counted no more. He knew that he was poor, and would admit it; he would have died sooner than con-fess any inferiority to the rich. This may be splendid of him. But he was inferior to most rich people, there is not the least doubt of it. (*HE*: 43)

It is significant that what brings Bast to the dangerous brink of the abyss is his quest for 'gentility', a concept which, etymologically, draws on ideas of inner nobility on the one hand, and birth or class status on the other. Through time, the latter definition has tended to eclipse the former. Thus the historical trajectory of the word suggests that the power and arbitrariness of social constructs dilute the significance of personal distinction, which is precisely what happens to Leonard Bast himself. His status as a clerk gradually whittles away everything else that he is or could be. The Schlegels, it is true, wish to look past what he is and consider instead who he is and what he could be: they wish, in other words, to consider him in purely humanistic terms. The difficulty is that no one else does, and so their efforts are futile. The gist of the excerpt quoted above is that one *cannot* separate what Bast is from who he is. There is no patronising assertion of Bast's intrinsic equality: in the recognition of the inferiority that society has bestowed upon him, there is a materialist appreciation of the ways in which 'character' is shaped that outstrips in its bluntness even Hobson's attempts to show how poverty produces a 'degraded personality'; how 'closed opportunities mean torpid minds' (Hobson 1986: 212). Leonard Bast does not have a torpid mind, but the opportunities available to him fall away, nevertheless, one by one, and he is degraded by that.

A creed, however secular, ought to be able to acquire converts; but the Schlegels acquire no converts (except Leonard, whom they harm in trying to help) to their religion of personal relations – according to Helen, 'the important thing for ever and ever, and not this outer life of telegrams and anger' (*HE*: 170). The ultimate failure of all that the Schlegels try to do for Leonard is seen in the fact that, having defiantly refused any idea of his own inferiority, he comes to accept and internalise the verdict of society in the end. This tragic submission to degradation comes when Leonard is abandoned by Helen after their love-making:

The note that she left, tender and hysterical in tone, and intended to be most kind, hurt her lover terribly. It was as if some work of art had been broken by him, some picture in the National Gallery slashed out of its frame. When he recalled her talents and her social position, he felt that the first passer-by had a right to shoot him down. He was afraid of the waitress and the porters at the railway station.   (314)

What is particularly revealing is that it is her *intended* kindness which wounds him – once more, the gap between intention and effect is stressed. Helen has given herself to Leonard sexually to affirm the equality between them: for her, it is an act of radical humanism in defiance of society and its strictures. Yet its effect is to make Leonard feel unworthy of her and deserving of the opprobrium of society. Having sought equality and self-worth through art and culture, Leonard feels that he has destroyed a priceless work of art, that the barbarism within him has made him damage something which he himself now feels ought to have been shielded from himself.

Leonard's misfortunes seem all the harsher when one considers that what is resolutely refused to him in *Howards End* is what was available to so many Edwardian heroes, whether bourgeois or fantastical: escape. Leonard is doomed because the battle raging is between the traditional past and a desecrating modernity, and he has been dispossessed by them both, for different reasons. He does not stand a chance. In fact, in addition to the kinds of devolution discussed earlier, he is even subjected to a kind of economic devolution whereby he becomes steadily poorer and more abject, a process in which the carelessness of the plutocrats and the solicitude of the liberals are both implicated. He stands, not only 'at the extreme verge of gentility' (43), but on the periphery of competing ideologies of the self. In the recognition that inner worth and intelligence come to mean nothing and achieve nothing if located in a man who is a clerk and a runt, there is an indictment of the effective power of humanism which, like alchemy, ought to be able to transform what is base into that which is desired. Yet Leonard cannot, finally, withstand even the inferiority imputed to him: his sense of self, his intrinsic worth in humanistic terms, is lacking when it is most needed.

Love and Truth, which were discovered in 'The Point of It' in Hell, 'hold[ing] each the seeds of our decay' (*CS*: 161), appear, not surprisingly, as vexed issues in *Howards End* too:

How wide the gulf between Henry as he was and Henry as Helen thought he ought to be! And [Margaret] herself – hovering as usual between the two, now accepting men as they are, now yearning with her sister for Truth. Love and Truth – their warfare seems eternal. Perhaps the whole visible world rests on it, and, if they were one, life itself, like the spirits when Prospero was reconciled to his brother, might vanish into air, into thin air.   (*HE*: 227)

That 'Love' and 'Truth' should be described as being in a state of apparently irredeemable enmity is immensely suggestive for this novel and for the uncertain status of humanism within it. Humanism rests on a fundamental compatibility between love and truth, where rationality and compassion guide each other: for them to pull in separate directions suggests misdirected compassion and muddled thinking – the very symptoms of the humanistic disappointments in the novel. The passage goes so far as to suggest that the fabric of existence, 'the whole visible world', is based on this fundamental incompatibility. This directs us once more to the importance of dialectic and meanings that, far from being absolute, are in constant and shifting relationship to one another.

In casting 'Love' and 'Truth' in the role of combatants, the traditional humanistic alliance is severed. One inevitable consequence is that they both lose their capital letters – their status as absolute values or grandiose truths. Helen is the character who most readily sees love and truth in absolute terms and will not admit compromise. The narrative voice satirises that tendency in her:

Helen loved the absolute. Leonard had been ruined absolutely, and had appeared to her as a man apart, isolated from the world. A real man, who cared for adventure and beauty, who desired to live decently and pay his way, who could have travelled more gloriously through life than the Juggernaut car that was crushing him. . . . She and the victim seemed alone in a world of unreality, and she loved him absolutely, perhaps for half an hour.   (314)

The word 'absolutely' appears twice in this passage. The absolutism and passion of Helen's creed amount to half an hour of love: here is the danger of a philosophy that will not negotiate with contingent circumstances. In Helen humanism has calcified into a kind of philanthropic tyranny that is deaf to the dialectical relationship between love and truth. It is precisely because Leonard is not 'isolated from the world' or 'a man apart' that her endeavours on his behalf do not succeed. In failing to recognise the extent to which society has enmeshed him and is curtailing his freedom, she does indeed remove him to 'a world of unreality', which is a world of love wholly devoid of truth. The passage, in so far as it stresses the social components of identity – neglected by Helen – would seem in this instance to subscribe to the New Liberal creed. However, if the diagnosis tends in that direction, the remedy, as we have seen, certainly does not follow: while ostensibly negating the perception of Leonard as 'a man apart', the novel nonetheless does nothing to insert him into society as the organic model would require.

Rather than receding, the forces of modernity – which oppress Leonard all the way through – increase in destructive potency. This is suggested by the fact that the motor car, which is associated throughout the novel with some of the worst characteristics of modernity (excessive motion, noise, fumes and the constant danger of collisions), reappears here as 'the Juggernaut car that was crushing [Leonard]'. Modernity, seen by some as a desirable destination, has become for others an agent of apocalypse: the implication is that too much motion will rush us, like Leonard, towards our ending.

The tension between essentialist and materialist understandings of the self pervades the entire novel: in fact, it becomes one of the ways in which the crisis within humanism is marked. There is no consistency in this regard: the novel gives us mixed messages and contradictory definitions, as we see, for instance, in the treatment of gender. Henry Wilcox is of the belief that there exists a 'gulf between the male soul and the female' (242), but one would not expect anything else from him. More significant are the narrator's remarks about what is intrinsic to the sexes:

Pity, if one may generalize, is at the bottom of woman. When men like us, it is for our better qualities, and however tender their liking, we dare not be unworthy of it, or they will quietly let us go. But unworthiness stimulates woman. It brings out her deeper nature, for good or for evil.   (240)

The narrative voice that mocks Helen for the absolute nature of her convictions is here shown to be capable itself of a kind of absolutism in what it attributes to men and women. The inaccuracy of this may readily be seen even in terms of the male and female characters in the novel, for few of the men respond to worthiness (or are even able to identify it), and 'pity', that supposedly essential female capacity, is absent in a number of the female characters. More interesting is the way in which such a comment deliberately compromises the authority of the narrative voice and shows – as does an ending which says some women are not made for babies, others are not made for husbands – that the essentialist identity itself is in crisis, and, with it, the humanism that has supported it for so long.

One of the cruellest ironies of the novel is that Leonard seeks to better himself through art, music and literature, which he sees as indices of the life he aspires to, as well as points of entry into it; yet, far from granting him access to that superior world, the various manifestations of highbrow culture turn out to have been his antagonists all along, thwarting his efforts, betraying him, and, finally, eliminating him, as suggested when the Schlegels' books and the ancestral sword conspire, as it were, with Charles to kill him. Culture is one of the most important ingredients of the humanistic repast; yet the highbrow version that Leonard pursues proves to be too rich for him – the morsels that come his way make him ill instead of nourishing him. The quandary which Forster outlines in his biography of Goldsworthy Lowes Dickinson is the very one that *Howards End* poses: how is culture to confer distinction, and, simultaneously, to function as an agent of democratisation?

> If [Dickinson] held aloof from ordinary people, how could he help them, and if he threw himself into their lives, should he not become like them?. . . . To abandon culture and blunt sensitiveness in the hope of breaking down barriers always seemed to him a desperate expedient.   (*GLD*: 49)

In the novel, culture becomes one of the means whereby the Schlegels 'throw themselves' into Leonard's life, not in order to become like him, but so that he should become like them. Their willingness to admit him to their world is an act of condescension disguising itself – to them, and to him – as egalitarianism. It is no coincidence that *Howards End* contains a number of references to Matthew Arnold and John Ruskin, for they both, in their different ways, represent a late-Victorian tendency to see culture in socially progressivist terms. Arnold hoped

that the cultured would seek to 'humanise [culture], to make it effi-
cient outside the clique of the cultivated and learned' (Arnold 1965:
70), thereby extending 'sweetness and light' to 'the raw and unkindled
masses of humanity' (69). However, in *Howards End*, culture is not only
profoundly inefficient, it also has the effect of entrenching 'the cultivated and learned' in the seclusion of their Bloomsbury-like coterie.
Margaret feels that culture 'had worked in her case' (*HE*: 113), but
'doubted whether it humanized the majority, so wide and so widening
is the gulf that stretches between the natural and the philosophical
man, so many the good chaps who are wrecked in trying to cross it'
(113). Instead of bringing the disparate parts of society together, culture has come to represent a cruel enticement, a type of mirage, which
bestows on people the ambition, but not the means of social mobility.
Instead of providing 'an intellectual food' (Arnold 1965: 69), it pro-
vokes a hunger which it fails to satisfy.

Arnold's tribute to Sophocles – that he could 'see life steadily and
see it whole' recurs throughout *Howards End*. It encapsulates the
entire humanistic creed: the capacity to combine discrete truth with
the capaciousness of wider understanding, to discern and include at
the same time. In the novel, however, the dictum ceases to be an
incentive and becomes the voice of the past rebuking the present, a
sanguine Victorian ambition that the Edwardian context can hear
but not heed:

> There was the girl named Helen, who had pinched [Leonard's]
> umbrella, and the German girl who had smiled at him pleasantly,
> and Herr someone, and Aunt someone, and the brother – all, all
> with their hands on the ropes. They had all passed up that narrow
> rich staircase at Wickham Place, to some ample room, whither he
> would never follow them, not if he read for ten hours a day. Oh, it
> was no good, this continual aspiration. Some are born cultured; the
> rest had better go in for whatever comes easy. To see life steadily and
> to see it whole was not for the like of him.   (*HE*: 52)

Here wealth, class, possession and culture are conflated: reading for
ten hours a day will not enable Leonard to ascend the 'narrow rich
staircase', which is too narrow and too rich for him. In a sense, however, the Sophoclean achievement eludes everyone: *Howards End* and *A
Passage to India* are novels about truths that flicker and cannot be seen

steadily, that cannot be reconciled and made whole. They deal with the failure to be inclusive and to carry out the Arnoldian injunction, with its Victorian ancestry and its liberal-humanistic cargo.

The democratisation of art was urged by Ruskin too. Chapter VI of *Howards End*, in which Leonard sits reading *The Stones of Venice* in his poky flat, is a deliberation upon the viability of Ruskin's project and upon the notion of cultural consumption – in particular, the extent to which the Victorian cultural legacy may be digested by the increasingly literate masses. Ruskin expressed great sympathy for the urban poor; in this chapter, a man who represents an attempt to escape debilitating urban poverty struggles to make Ruskin's writings compatible with his life and his social and cultural aspirations. He cannot do so. Ruskin believed that 'the universe exists as a semiotic entity that one can read if one has the key' (Landow 1993: 143) , and it is precisely as a recalcitrant *text* that Ruskin appears: Leonard reads the sage's work, but he does not have the key, the cultural *nous*, to unlock what Ruskin has to offer him. Culture is presented in *Howards End* as a syntax, a language which some speak glibly, but which confounds others:

> With an hour at lunch and a few shattered hours in the evening, how was it possible to catch up with leisured women, who had been reading steadily from childhood? [Leonard's] brain might be full of names, he might even have heard of Monet and Debussy; the trouble was that he could not string them together into a sentence, he could not make them 'tell', he could not quite forget about his stolen umbrella.   (37)

To string words into a sentence is to understand the underlying scheme, the deep structure which gives the discrete words a coherent meaning. Leonard is unable to do so because high art appears before him as a series of lofty cultural markers, not as something which has meaning in his own life. In Chapter VI, he tries to reconcile his unenviable circumstances with what *The Stones of Venice* offers him by emulating Ruskin's *sentence structure*:

> Leonard was trying to form his style on Ruskin: he understood him to be the greatest master of English Prose. He read forward steadily, occasionally making a few notes.

'Let us consider a little each of these characters in succession; and first (for of the shafts enough has been said already), what is very peculiar to this church, its luminousness.'

Was there anything to be learned from this fine sentence? Could he adapt it to the needs of daily life? Could he introduce it, with modifications, when he next wrote a letter to his brother, the lay-reader? For example –

'Let us consider a little each of these characters in succession; and first (for of the absence of ventilation enough has been said already), what is very peculiar to this flat, its obscurity.'

Something told him that the modifications would not do; and that something, had he known it, was the spirit of English Prose. 'My flat is dark as well as stuffy.' Those were the words for him. (47)

The replicated sentence is absurd because of the vast difference between Leonard's situation in his 'dark' and 'stuffy' flat, and that of Ruskin: 'The rich man is speaking to us from his gondola' (46). In addition to the recognition (implicit in so many modernist works) that words cannot be separated from their contexts, that they have no intrinsic meaning, there is also an implicit comment upon the difficulty of 'transplanting' or bestowing cultural value. The human-istic notion of elevating everyone through the civilising virtues of culture fails in this case because it is an essentially *universalist* ideal, proceeding from the assumption that everyone speaks the same lan-guage, as it were; but they do not. The appropriate sentence for Leonard is bathetic – 'My flat is dark as well as stuffy' – because the collapse of grand hopes is his destiny. His efforts are thwarted in part by 'the spirit of English Prose', which suggests that the tradition of English Letters is in itself almost ineluctably anti-populist and un-democratic; like so much else which the past has ostensibly handed down to the present, it will not readily bend itself to meet contempor-ary needs.

What is perhaps the most surprising development of all is that the chapter does not conclude, as we might have expected, with Leonard's response to Ruskin, but rather the other way around – although he has failed lamentably to 'speak' to Leonard through his elegant prose, Ruskin reacts to him nonetheless:

Ruskin had visited Torcello by this time, and was ordering his gondoliers to take him to Murano. It occurred to him, as he glided over the whispering lagoons, that the power of Nature could not be shortened by the folly, nor her beauty altogether saddened by the misery, of such as Leonard. (53)

Instead of the present contemplating the past, what we have here is the past contemplating the present. Despite the apparent impulse to democratise culture, what this astonishing paragraph suggests is that high culture actively resists such endeavours. Leonard's attempt to come to grips with Ruskin is doomed from the start, because Ruskin has already turned his back on Leonard.

Forster's failure to complete his novel *Arctic Summer* – begun in late 1911 – may also be seen in the light of his increasing difficulties in representing in fiction a viable modern humanism, even when, as in much of the earlier work, a compensating romantic alternative is made available. *Arctic Summer*, unlike *Howards End*, is not much concerned with contemporary liberalism, but is clearly an attempt to explore a central humanistic ambition, the 'sovereign ideal which humanists are bound to acknowledge', that of the 'Renaissance ideal of the "complete" or universal man' (Blackham 1976: 85). One can only speculate as to how Forster would have ended *Arctic Summer* had he completed it, but it is clear that it was to have been a novel about a resonating friendship between two men, one which has affinities with the relationships between men in *Where Angels Fear to Tread*, *The Longest Journey*, *Maurice* and *A Passage to India*, yet going beyond all of these in terms of its heavily schematic quality.

The existing fragment indicates that the progress of an increasingly intimate friendship between Clesant March and Martin Whitby was to have been invested with moral and emblematic importance. In a sense, *Arctic Summer* was also to have been a novel about connection. The evolving friendship between the two men, despite the marked differences in personality and interests, would have led to the establishment of a composite figure that was the equivalent of the Renaissance ideal: a Sir Philip Sidney, as it were, for 1911. All the humanistic ambitions of richness of self and capaciousness would have been satisfied in such a figure. In addition, the success of the men's relationship, which would nullify the individual failings of March and Whitby, would have been a pre-eminent achievement at the level of 'personal relationships'.

It was never depicted. Indeed, it is curious that such a relatively simple scheme was ever contemplated after the ambivalences and complexities of *Howards End*. What we are left with is separation and the failure to complete or unify: great Forsterian themes, yet present here only by virtue of textual incompletion. We have the skeleton of the scheme: Clesant March, the uncontemplative man who possesses physical courage and anachronistic notions of chivalry, and Martin Whitby, cultured, sensitive and contemplative, yet lacking in physical courage. However, their rapprochement remained unwritten. Forster's attempt at a grand humanistic undertaking, whereby he would provide Renaissance chivalric codes with a contemporary relevance and integrate contemplation with heroic action, did not find expression. The search for an old kind of hero in these new times was, it seems, no longer feasible for Forster. Except for *Maurice* – and that is a special case, as shall shortly be indicated – Forster could no longer write such a deliberately non-modernist novel. In *Arctic Summer* it is not the overt anachronism of March's rather quaint chivalry which is the problem: it is the covert anachronism which lies in the very attempt to modernise humanism and make it workable.

This is Forster's own articulation of the difficulties and problems he encountered in writing *Arctic Summer*:

> I had got my antithesis all right, the antithesis between the civilized man, who hopes for an Arctic Summer, and the heroic man who rides into the sea. But I had not settled what was going to happen, and that is why the novel remained a fragment.
>
> (*AS*: 162)

The situation, in other words, remained merely schematic and baldly oppositional: there was none of the *dialectic* of approach and withdrawal, of interaction and separation. Forster adds that the novel 'might have ended with the two as companions in defeat. But such an ending doesn't interest me' (*AS*: 162). The admission is most revealing. Forster was prepared to provide versions of the idea of 'companions in defeat' in the cases of Philip and Caroline in *Where Angels Fear to Tread*, Rickie and Stephen in *The Longest Journey*, the Schlegel sisters or

Margaret and Henry Wilcox in *Howards End*, Fielding and Aziz or even Fielding and Adela Quested in *A Passage to India*; why, then, was the idea so unacceptable in *Arctic Summer*? The reason must lie in the broad scope of the humanistic project in that novel. The effort to represent an unstinting plenitude in *Arctic Summer* – the very title refers us to a time when, for however brief a period, the darkness is banished – is so concerted that defeat would have been more devastating in its implications than in any of the novels where the ideological project is less ambitious.

Forster could dramatise the antithesis in *Arctic Summer*, but not the resolution. That demanded some kind of positive action to obviate Martin's unheroic flight when the fire breaks out at the cinema. Forster's inability to settle 'what was going to happen', although an ostensibly banal difficulty, is in fact a powerful comment on the failing resources of the liberal-humanist code which can no longer provide the will to act and lacks the appropriate context wherein such redemptive action would be possible.

Martin Whitby feels all the correct sympathies, but he feels none of them passionately. He gives up his Quaker background without much inner conflict, for '[t]he chasm between belief and unbelief is not very wide to those who feel religion to be an attitude of mind which may spring from either, and who have not to part with a dogma or wrestle with a sense of sin' (*AS*: 131). He is virtually a born humanist, were such a thing possible. Clesant March, on the other hand, has all the fervour and the passion – heroic action comes easily to him; but he is single-minded and rigid, and his chivalric code has become so intransigent that he causes the suicide of his brother Lance. They both lack and need what the other man possesses in abundance, for the present situation is one where heroes have become insensitive bunglers and humanists have become cowards. Had the novel been able to fulfil its own ambitions, the beleaguered status of late-Edwardian humanism might have been alleviated through access to a compensating spiritual and heroic largesse. Instead, *Arctic Summer* shows us the threadbare quality of a creed which, in desperately seeking relevance and contemporaneity, seems all the more archaic.

Along with *A Room with a View*, the novel in which Forster most conspicuously does not present 'companions in defeat', is *Maurice*. The reason for this is that they are both comedies. The reprieve that is granted to Maurice and Alec is made possible by their retreat to an idyll. There the customary comic ending of love secured and estrangement banished secures their liberation. It is not a besieged pastoralism, as in *Howards End*: here it is simply an escape. In the conclusion the comic machinery, as in Shakespeare's comedies, protects the characters from the great dangers that have afflicted them. Forster believed this to be essential:

> A happy ending was imperative. I shouldn't have bothered to write otherwise. I was determined that in fiction anyway two men should fall in love and remain in it for the ever and ever that fiction allows, and in this sense Maurice and Alec still roam the greenwood.   (*M*: 236)

Maurice and Alec, in other words, escape into the Utopia which the comic mode confers. The novel becomes a fable in order to grant them the 'ever and ever' that its homosexual polemic requires. It is a flight into a secessionist realm of existence because the world of human affairs will not permit the particular form of 'personal relations' which Maurice and Alec need in order to find happiness.

That is why *Maurice* is a modern novel, but it is not a modernist novel. It has a great deal more in common with the fables of escape and fantasy that proliferated in the Edwardian period than one might think at first. It is far closer in spirit to 'The Story of a Panic', *Peter Pan*, *The Wind in the Willows* or even *The History of Mr Polly* than to *Lord Jim* or *Howards End*. That is also why, although it deals with a specific social condition that is illiberal and inhumane, it is not, finally, an investigation of liberalism or humanism, for all it says is that a society that practises sexual intolerance cannot call itself a liberal society, and a person who suffers from that intolerance will never attain the measure of self-realisation that humanists strive for. In any case, Maurice is only required to be a humanist while he is suffering and unhappy, yet embodying that quintessential humanistic virtue, dignity:

> He hadn't a God, he hadn't a lover – the two usual incentives to virtue. But on he struggled with his back to ease, because dignity demanded it. There was no one to watch him, nor did he watch himself, but struggles like his are the supreme achievements of humanity, and surpass any legends about Heaven.   (*M*: 132)

There is no dignity in 'the greenwood', for there is no need of it. There are no struggles there with the imperfections of the world – those struggles which the humanist must necessarily take on. In that sense, *Maurice* is not a novel about the search for a habitation in the modern world for liberalism or humanism, as are *Howards End* and *Arctic Summer*. It seeks to find a refuge for the self that has been sexually oppressed, but in doing so it deracinates the self to such an extent that, in so far as they aim to be pragmatic and responsive ideologies, liberalism and humanism cannot possibly accompany it on its journey:

> [Maurice's] journey was nearly over. He was bound for his new home. . . . [He and Alec] must live outside class, without relations or money; they must work and stick to each other till death. But England belonged to them. That, besides companionship, was their reward. Her air and sky were theirs, not the timorous millions' who own stuffy little boxes, but never their own souls. (*M*: 223)

The happy fate of the two men is the obverse of what happens to Leonard Bast, for they are to live 'outside class, without relations or money', whereas it is Leonard's fate to be oppressed by the presence of the first two and the lack of the third. He is cast out by society, whereas Maurice and Alec are able to shed society at will. He remains the bastard child of England, denied his inheritance, whereas Maurice and Alec, in a grandiose acknowledgement of their heroism and sexual courage, have England handed to them: 'But England belonged to them. That, besides companionship, was their reward.' For much of the novel, it is Maurice's ordinariness, his unremarkable middle-class life, which it has been polemically strategic to stress; now, as he becomes a hero, his ordinariness is ceded along with the need to interact with society. Not surprisingly, there is then a measure of scorn for the 'timorous millions' and their 'stuffy little boxes'. The happiness of the lovers is set against their small lives in tendentious contrast, which shows how *illiberal* Forster's solution is. This is not to suggest that there is anything to be deprecated in the fate set aside for Maurice and Alec, for the homosexual polemic has its own logic: to be shunned by others is a defeat, to shun them in turn may seem like a victory. Nonetheless, the happy union of the lovers in the greenwood becomes another instance of the failure of 'connection', of the organic society and the inclusiveness which it promised.

———

In *A Passage to India*, liberalism and humanism are invariably associated with versions of failure. The struggle of these creeds for viability as shown in *Howards End* and *Arctic Summer* here gives way to an assumed or declared nostalgia. Liberal-humanists are still central figures in the novel and their concerns remain important, but the battle to fortify the philosophies they subscribe to is all but lost. This is suggested in the extraordinary passage that simultaneously salutes what Fielding and Adela represent and finds it wanting:

> A friendliness, as of dwarfs shaking hands, was in the air. Both man and woman were at the height of their powers – sensible, honest, even subtle. They spoke the same language, and held the same opinions, and the variety of age and sex did not divide them. Yet they were dissatisfied. When they agreed, 'I want to go on living a bit,' or 'I don't believe in God,' the words were followed by a curious backwash, as though the universe had displaced itself to fill up a tiny void, or as though they had seen their own gestures from an immense height – dwarfs talking, shaking hands and assuring each other that they stood on the same footing of insight. They did not think they were wrong, because as soon as honest people think they are wrong instability sets up. Not for them was an infinite goal behind the stars, and they never sought it. But wistfulness descended on them now, as on other occasions; the shadow of the shadow of a dream fell over their clear-cut interests, and objects never seen again seemed messages from another world.   (*PI*: 262)

The figure of the dwarf is revealing: when one considers the extent to which the enlargement of the individual's status and potential is central to all liberal and humanistic ambitions, the 'dwarfing' of those hopes suggests instead the meagreness of the self and the saddest admission of diminished significance. In place of the camaraderie of the 'personal relations' creed, Fielding and Adela are brought together after the trial in a poignant and shared bewilderment. On the one hand, the two represent the civilised plenitude that the post-Enlightenment world has sought for centuries to cultivate in its individual members. They are the consummate expression of a certain world view and its values as they stand on 'the same footing of insight': they are 'at the height of their powers – sensible, honest, even subtle.' They are solid and unwavering humanists, secular in their orientation and devoted to an understated appreciation of the here-and-now: they 'don't believe in God'; they 'want to go on living a bit'.

The bemusement of the two has far-reaching implications, for the Enlightenment 'is founded and flounders upon the concept of self-knowledge' (Waugh 1992: 91): here Fielding and Adela are floundering because a void has been revealed to them within what they thought they knew about themselves; within the humanistic tradition – 'the Enlightenment's grand narrative of human emancipation' (Eagleton 1986: 134) – which sustained them and brought them to 'the height of their powers'. What is more, the narrative voice that seemed for much of the novel to share their language of earnest reasonableness sudden-ly forsakes them by moving on to another type of language. It gestures towards a world which they cannot enter, impeded not – as is the case with many of the Anglo-Indians – by stupidity, ignorance or crass racism, but by the very capacity of rational discernment, the attention to 'clear-cut interests', that has made them such admirable people. The world that is denied to them, the one whose 'messages' they do not have the equipment to receive, is described in language that is deliber-ately opaque. All one can know about the 'infinite goal behind the stars' is that it cannot be reached. The 'shadow of a shadow of a dream' suggests boundless layers of inscrutability: the phrase is incantatory, subliminal, neo-Platonic, symbolist. It is also, presumably, an echo of the discussion of dreams and shadows which Hamlet engages in with Rosencrantz and Guildenstern in Act II, Scene ii, and, in particular, of Guildenstern's assertion in ll.258–9 that 'the very substance of the ambitious is merely the shadow of a dream', which conveys also the insubstantiality of aspirations and intentions. What afflicts Adela and Fielding is, in part, the chasm that has opened up between what they intended and what has come to pass, between desire and realisation. This is the moment in which, in a realistic novel or *bildungsroman*, a deserved understanding (born of the recognition of past errors) would be granted. Instead, wistfulness descends and the two are made wretched by not knowing precisely what it is they do not know.

The bathetic quality of the passage is all the stronger because of the ways in which Fielding, in particular, has been established as an estimable character prior to this. Adela's liberal-humanist orientation has been shown to be a rarefied, Bloomsbury-type chauvinism, often hopelessly inappropriate in this context; but Fielding's is unostentatious and thoughtful. What is more, he is unconventional enough to be something of an individualist:

> Neither a missionary nor a student, he was happiest in the give-and-take of a private conversation. The world, he believed, is a globe of men who are trying to reach one another and can best do so by the help of goodwill plus culture plus intelligence – a creed ill suited to Chandrapore, but he had come out too late to lose it. (*PI*: 80)

The phrase 'goodwill plus culture plus intelligence' aphoristically sums up the entire humanistic tradition that Fielding represents. Thus, although he travels light, as we are informed more than once in the novel, he is nonetheless encumbered with a great deal of ideological baggage. The importance attached to 'the give-and-take of a private conversation' shows that his political outlook is an extrapolation of the 'personal relations' ethos, the obverse of which is the adherence to caste seen in many of the Anglo-Indians. The fact that he is a rather solitary representative of a particular humanistic heritage suggests that the virtues he has to embody and uphold weigh even more heavily upon him. The schoolmaster is a loner but not a misanthrope, for that would betray the commitment to fellowship that must lie at the heart of his benign, yet principled creed. This passage pays tribute to him as the peripatetic heir to a long and great tradition.

Yet, particularly if one reads it in the light of later disillusionments, the ways in which it carries the seeds of its own failure within it are apparent. Fielding's admirable egalitarianism, which means that he is not a racist, also means that he is a universalist with his sights fixed on 'a globe of men', seeking commonality rather than difference in a context where 'the spirit of the Indian earth . . . tries to keep men in compartments' (141). But in order for this to occur, there has to be the assurance that people stand, like Fielding and Adela, 'on the same footing of insight' (262). This is the weakness within the universalist goodwill, the Achilles' heel of liberal-humanism, which, in striving for equality in all respects, often makes the fatal error of assuming its existence. The Schlegels make that error in their treatment of Leonard Bast;

it comes again in the impetuousness of Adela and the more considered humanism of Fielding. In a situation as divisive as the India which Fielding finds himself in, where religion, caste and the Empire all insist upon division, a philosophy which has 'the give-and-take of a private conversation' at its heart must face severe obstacles, as the fraught friendship between Aziz and Fielding goes on to demonstrate. The irony is that when Fielding finally achieves that apex of equality with another person, it is in the feeling of bafflement that he shares with Adela: the 'friendliness, as of dwarfs shaking hands' (262).

The gradual eclipsing of rationalist virtues in *A Passage to India* is the result, in part, of the power that the novel grants to characters whose methods of cognition would frustrate any rationalist. There are characters who may be called 'prophetic' – 'prophecy' being Forster's catch-all term for forms of inscrutability in fiction. They include Professor Godbole and Mrs Moore (particularly in her post-Marabar condition), who are the most unsatisfactory interlocutors that any rationalist could expect to meet. Reason and the conscious will give way in them to oracular and cryptic pronouncements. They are largely ineffectual at the level of directed action or endeavour. They are brusque or maddeningly unsympathetic and they do little or nothing for others. Aziz is 'puzzled by his own great gratitude' (306) to Mrs Moore:

> What did this eternal goodness of Mrs Moore amount to? To nothing, if brought to the test of thought. She had not borne witness in his favour, nor visited him in the prison, yet she had stolen to the depths of his heart, and he always adored her.   (306)

It is not in anything that can be subjected to 'the test of thought' that the value of Mrs Moore lies. Aziz is compelled to relate to her on her own, 'prophetic' terms.

In Forster's 'prophetic' characters the sheer elusiveness of identity is conveyed; what is more, there is a reconfiguration of the self – both ontologically and in its dealings with others. In representing identity, the modernists 'almost consistently reduce the role of the conscious will' (Quinones 1985: 177). *A Passage to India* presents compellingly the frustration of efforts that proceed from the conscious will and of purposive action, however philanthropic in intention. Ratiocination is thwarted and rationalistic characters are unnerved. In the end, the curiously dispassionate 'prophetic' characters have a kind of power which they cannot lose, even when, as in the case of Mrs Moore after the visit to the Caves, it seems as if they are unwilling or unable to make anything happen.

As suggested, *Arctic Summer* may be regarded as a late-Edwardian response to the problem of effective action; but in *Howards End* and, even more so, in *A Passage to India*, something more fundamental is being questioned: the notion of an essentialist self with some assurance of competence in the world: that 'assumption of a continuing self over time' (Minogue 1963: 55) which lies at the heart of both liberalism and humanism.

In a letter to Forrest Reid written in 1913, Forster, referring to his difficulties with regard to *Arctic Summer*, writes, 'I want something beyond the field of action and behaviour; the waters of the river that rises from the middle of the earth to join the Ganges and the Jumna where they join' (in Lago and Furbank 1983: 187–8). In that desire lies the final waning of the humanistic scheme that was envisaged in *Arctic Summer*, with its necessary location in 'action and behaviour'. The following year he writes to Florence Barger of a 'vague suspicion that the human relation comes second to something else', adding that 'it's not enough to go through life helping people and being helped by them' (in Lago and Furbank 1983: 209). Forster's correspondence shows that his misgivings increased in intensity in the years before he returned (in the early 1920s) to the long-abandoned manuscript of *A Passage to India*. Writing again to Florence Barger, this time in 1918, he rejects 'ideals' and 'principles', while the will fares particularly poorly:

> Living by Will is all-fashionable in these days. . . . Its drawback is that you become discontented if you fail and unpleasant if you succeed, and in either case come into conflict with the wills of others whereas is there [*sic*] no such thing as a conflict of visions, vision belonging to another cosmogony.   (In Lago and Furbank 1983: 285)

The recourse to the visionary element also has its shortcomings in *A Passage to India*, as the discussion of Forster's romanticism in Chapter 2 will suggest. What is revealing here is his perception that amongst the potential offshoots of reliance upon the will are 'discontent[ment]' arising from failure and 'unpleasant[ness]' arising from success; in *A Passage to India*, the former takes the form of Adela and Fielding's wistfulness, while the latter is seen in the intolerable chauvinism and complacency of Ronny Heaslop and the majority of the Anglo-Indians – the British Raj constituting, on a large scale, the imposition of the Will. The novel then traces how the 'unpleasantness' of that political success gives way to the 'discontentment' arising from the gradual recognition of its failure.

Humanism may be seen as teleological in terms of the trajectory of self-realisation which it assumes; it is an ideology based upon the notion of arrival. Yet, as Forster suggests in a letter to Malcolm Darling, *A Passage to India* is not about arrival at all: it is a novel of 'going away':

> I have acquired a feeling that people must go away from each other (spiritually) every now and then, and improve themselves if the relationship is to develope [*sic*] or even endure. A Passage to India describes such a going away – preparatory to the next advance, which I am not capable of describing.
>
> (In Lago and Furbank 1985: 63)

This also helps us to understand why someone who, in *Arctic Summer*, was trying to write a novel in which the coming together of two men is the central and most profound event, as it is in *The Longest Journey*, published a novel a decade later in which two men, close friends who care for each other deeply, part forever. The 'personal relations' ethos is becoming claustrophobic for Forster, as suggested by this comment in a letter to Goldsworthy Lowes Dickinson, written in 1916: 'I am losing all sense of duty towards this world of blood stained fools ... don't even bother to tell myself that creation and personal relations are arguably duties' (in Jonathan Rose 1986: 70).

This notion of 'going away' may be linked to a widespread perception of transition in the period in which *A Passage to India* was rewritten and completed. We find one expression of this in Edwin Muir's *Transition*, published in 1926: 'We live in an interregnum, between a world which has passed and one not born: not in a new order, but rather in a chaos where a new order must be preparing' (Muir 1926: 194). *A Passage to India* is located both in the 'world which has passed' and in the 'chaos' of the new. This is evident in the very uncertainty of its allegiances, as well as the fact that the only form of arrival is the perception of transition itself. What is particularly interesting in Muir's study is the way in which he links the general mood of uncertainty and transience, including his sense that '[t]he traditional, which is to say the distinctively human, conceptions of such things as love, friendship, honour, duty, are not accepted as obvious realities' (208), to an *anti-humanistic* tendency in the contemporary novel: 'the general tendency of the novel at present might be described as anti-humanistic' (216).

Muir goes on to say that 'if we are beyond good and evil we have not found the kingdom that is there. This is the stage of the tragi-comedy of modern thought which has been reached by our generation' (211). The tragi-comic note that he identifies is present in *A Passage to India* too, pervading everything and constituting an unfinished journey in itself. Simply at the level of plot, Adela's recantation averts the tragic conclusion. Yet her change of heart does not endow the novel with a comic ending since the mood of unease and failed reconciliation – despite goodwill – persists. A comedy, at least in its satisfaction of certain generic expectations, is a kind of destination; so too is a tragedy. But a tragi-comedy oscillates between the two, refusing to come to rest. In other respects, too, Muir's comment seems particularly apposite in relation to *A Passage to India*: the impoverishment of liberal-humanist values and the moral miasma that ensues do indeed approach a condition which is, in a sense, 'beyond good and evil' – even without Professor Godbole's views on that subject. Instead of the 'other kingdoms' of Forster's early fantasies and the possibilities of escaping into them – as in 'The Story of a Panic' and 'Other Kingdom' – we have here the kingdom which, as Muir suggests, has not been found; which has as its consummate characteristic the fact that it is 'not yet' and 'not there' (*PI*: 316). The novel, in common with many other modernist works, is 'balance[d] on the sensibility of transition' (Bradbury and McFarlane 1976: 49).

Forster's fiction has frequently been read retrospectively in the light of his much-quoted statements about liberalism and humanism in the 1930s and early 1940s. The result has been that the qualms, hesitations and misgivings apparent in the fiction have been insufficiently recognised, as has the fact that the essays written during this later period are explicitly polemical writings, responding to the *specific* threat of Nazism, and hence to the most illiberal set of circumstances possible – a totalitarian society. They are an expression of a particularly acute despair, suggested by Forster's comment that '[i]n 1938–9 the more despair a man can take on board without sinking the more completely he is alive' (*PT*: 295). They are not aimed at the debates within liberalism, but enunciate rather a stark opposition between a civilised code and a barbaric threat. The context is vastly different from those within which the novels were written.

In addition, what is often overlooked is the wistfulness that lies within the declamatory rhetoric, not to mention the small claims that are made on behalf of liberalism and humanism in these essays, which imply their beleaguered status. The famous essay 'What I Believe' assumes the attenuated and anachronistic condition of the very values it upholds. The 'personal relations' creed with its humanistic lineage is presented in sadly reduced, even bathetic terms:

> And one can, at all events, show one's own little light here, one's own poor little trembling flame, with the knowledge that it is not the only light that is shining in the darkness, and not the only one which the darkness does not comprehend. Personal relations are despised today. (*TC*: 66)

The wryness comes from the smallness of the flame and the little that can be done in the unambitious quest to 'keep open a few breathing-holes for the human spirit' (69).

Seen in this context, the notorious and controversial contention – 'I hate the idea of causes, and if I had to choose between betraying my country and betraying my friend, I hope I should have the guts to betray my country' (66) – takes on a different hue. It is not, after all, the provocative dismissal of patriotism or even of society itself and all its obligations that it seems to be. Instead, it is a kind of elegy for the New Liberalism and its hope of finding a marriage between the new imperative towards social responsibility and the old individualistic creed. Forster's suggestion that a choice *must* inevitably be made is much more unsettling than what he goes on to choose, since the assertion that the two kinds of loyalty are fundamentally incompatible is a renunciation of all the earlier hopes of connection. It is not the iconoclastic outburst of a traitor, or even of one excessively devoted to coteries: it is the cry of the elegist.

Within the sad tributes to the 'despised' and outmoded creed of 'personal relations', we find in these essays a number of comments that hint at the 'inhuman' consolations towards which the later novels move increasingly. For instance, in his essay on W. H. Auden's *The*

Enchafed Flood, Forster refers to 'the comfort of the non-human, the relief, when we look up at the stars, of realising that they are uninhabitable' (*TC*: 262). Similarly, the authors to whom he 'clung' for succour during the Great War were those 'who had nothing tangible to offer: Blake, William Morris, the early T. S. Eliot, J. K. Huysman, Yeats' (*AH*: 73). This may be a surprising list of writers from whom to seek comfort during a devastating war, but not perhaps for one who was shortly to return to the writing of *A Passage to India*: in his case, one can understand the appeal of esoteric thinkers and symbolists; of those who sought the oblique gaze.

Orwell's politics are praised and he is described as a 'true liberal [who] hoped to help through small things' (*TC*: 59); but the essay ends by paying tribute to Orwell's desire to do more than 'ameliorate a world which is bound to be unhappy' (59):

> We part company with a man who has been determined to see what he can of this contradictory and disquieting world and to follow its implications into the unseen – or anyhow to follow them around the corner.   (61)

In their own way, that is what Forster's later novels do: they focus upon 'this contradictory and disquieting world', but they are not restricted to it. Instead of keeping to teleological paths laid – for instance – by liberalism and humanism, they too turn the corner.

2
'Romantic Realism'

> [The Anglo-Saxon] requires a book to be serious unless it is
> comic, and when it is neither is apt to ring for the police.
>
> E. M. Forster, 'Ronald Firbank' (*AH*: 115)

As this humorous comment indicates, Forster believed that, generally
speaking, readers of English fiction in the early twentieth century were
not adventurous: he saw them as suspicious of experimentalism and
resistant, in particular, to the mixing of different genres. Yet, in his
own fiction and criticism, he tends to be receptive to generic 'hybrid-
ity', as suggested by his tribute to the work of David Garnett: 'His art is
a hybrid. It blends in a new relationship the stocks of fantasy and common sense. It is a successful experiment . . .' (*AH*: 117). He is inclined
also to approve the co-existence of different modes of writing in the
same work, noting, for instance, that, in *The Voyage Out*, '[Woolf's]
comedy does not counteract her tragedy' (*PT*: 18). What is more, he
suggests on a number of occasions that there is no hierarchy of authenticity within the competing discourses of fiction, no fictional method
that confers a more convincing reality in itself. This is evident in the
discussion of 'Fantasy' in *Aspects of the Novel*:

> Why place an angel on a different basis from a stockbroker? Once in
> the realm of the fictitious, what difference is there between an
> apparition and a mortgage? . . . The general tone of novels is so lit-
> eral that when the fantastic is introduced it produces a special
> effect; some readers are thrilled, others choked off; it demands an
> additional adjustment because of the oddness of its method or sub-
> ject-matter . . .   (*AN*: 75)

Here, in addition to marking the *theoretical* equivalence and integrity of all methods, Forster also indicates that he knows only too well that there is no *pragmatic* parity: so great has been the influence of the realistic tradition in fiction that everything tends to be measured against it; it has led to a situation where 'the general tone of novels is so literal' that every departure from the dominant mode has to contend with an inevitable resistance on the part of readers accustomed to its conventions.

Yet, as the succeeding discussion will indicate, Forster seldom gives way in his own fiction to the predilections of the unadventurous reader: in his early fiction, the realistic elements are interwoven with romantic components, constituting an example of a familiar Edwardian fictional hybrid – 'romantic realism'; in his later work, the 'romantic realism' unravels and a sense of the increasing insufficiency – even untenability – of both the realistic and romantic strands becomes a crucial aspect of his modernism.

The tendency to mix 'romance' and 'realism' is so pronounced in Edwardian fiction that one should not attribute too much iconoclasm to the 'romantic realism' of Forster's early novels and short stories:

> The Edwardian years were realistic and romantic at the same time, the tendencies being in simultaneous reaction to each other, often among the books of a single author.   (Hunter 1982: 73)

The yoking together of romanticism and realism within a single work of fiction makes 'romantic realism' a restless mode, in keeping with an age in which people lived with an 'abundance of polarities' (Hunter 1982: 73), yet sought 'connection' in various ways. One may also consider the prevalence of this generic amalgamation in the light of another contemporary preoccupation, referred to in the previous chapter: the 'secular religion' of the Edwardians, a phenomenon which is itself a hybrid. In its attempt to 'abolish the distinction between the spiritual and the mundane' (Jonathan Rose 1986: 2), this creed finds expression in a mode of writing which reinforces what the Edwardians wished to believe: that 'the transcendent is immanent in the earthly, that to go down far enough is to go up' (Ellmann 1960: 197–8).

In his 1908 study, *Modernism and Romance*, R. A. Scott-James provides one of the most vigorous defences of 'romantic realism', both as a mode of writing and as a way of retaining the spirit of romance within modern life, thus allowing 'a greater spiritual force . . . to break through the crust of sceptical common sense' (Scott-James 1908: 29). As suggested by his tribute to Robert Louis Stevenson, Scott-James admires the work of writers who 'bring out the marvellous and the unexpected from the midst of the familiar' (218), and who have sought to 'invest common things with a new meaning'(219). What he urges is the compatibility of realism and romance (as he construes them), although the force of his polemic works to bring realism within the reach of romance:

> ['Romance'] is not used in opposition to realism. On the contrary, the realism of some of the great Russian and French novelists brings with it that profound sense of the significance and mystery of life which satisfies the deeper romantic instinct.   (11)

Scott-James's conceptualisation of 'realism' does not, therefore, exclude a preoccupation with what Forster calls 'the unseen'; it seeks a kind of transcendence which nevertheless does not imply a renunciation of this-earthly, human obligations: 'To be lifted beyond the appalling sense of our own weakness, yet to remain human, is to experience that romance which lures [sic] to quests and adventures, to hopes and bolder actions' (4). It is a flexible, capacious realism, as far from naturalism as possible:

> [The 'realism' of Galsworthy] is not the unsparing, often sordid realism of Zola or Gorki. It is realistic only in that it takes its cue from the ordinary, unalterable course of real life . . .   (259)

It is revealing that Scott-James describes the work of the naturalists as 'unsparing', for Edwardian realism, in contrast, is marked by a 'benign' quality, as well as a tendency to 'spare' both the characters and the readers:

> Although realism continued to hold a central place in British fiction, there was a marked change in its tone at the turn of the century. . . . The combination of gentle humour, precise social observation, and a realism kept firmly in check, was both popular and influential. To the reading-public it announced that realism was no longer threatening,

and to many novelists of the time it provided a similarly welcome breathing-space.   (Keating 1989: 318–19)

In keeping with this, Keating detects a 'related relaxation of mood' in the work of various writers, including 'the early novels of E. M. Forster' (319).

This 'welcome breathing-space' proceeds, in part, from the prevalence of 'romantic realism' during the period, as well as from what this mode conveys. The interweaving of realism and romanticism means that neither of them remains unchanged: what they have in common is accentuated, while the differences between them grow smaller. They accommodate themselves to one another – where the one mode seems to close opportunities off, the other makes them available. It is a fictional mode which confirms that ' "escape" is the prominent aspect of to-day's art . . . a deliberate turning away from the realities of the present, which only a few accept as substance for artistic interpretation' (Masterman 1911: 193). Not only do characters escape (usually to agrarian idylls) at the level of plot, but these 'parables of escape' (Hunter 1982: 79) offer also a mode of writing, 'romantic realism', which communicates a 'reversal of the lines of causality, the presence of an escape hatch through which the fictional being may in some way evade the apparently ineluctable limitations of his existence' (Becker 1980: 102). The romanticism is of a kind that makes what one may call an accessible transcendentalism possible, and the version of realism is far removed from any naturalistic attempt to represent deterministically the contexts that may pertain in people's lives. The widespread vitalism of the period – the Edwardian 'Cult of Life' or, as Masterman calls it, 'Life Worship' – was also well served by a fictional cocktail of this sort, for '[Life Worship] rebels always against the mechanic pacing to and fro; the set grey life; the apathetic end' (Masterman 1911: 208).

English realism *per se* has generally tended to provide 'escape hatches' – webs of causality with large loopholes in them – and the Edwardian period brought an intensification of an existing trend, rather than an entirely new emphasis. English realism may even be seen as a continuation of the tradition of the romance, 'which insists on the power of the hero to overcome the limits of his constricting social context' (G. Levine 1974: 252). One of the 'paradoxes of the history of realistic fiction' is that, in the frequent avoidance of 'resolutions in death, missed opportunities, and absence of meaning', realistic fiction becomes 'an essentially comic form' (252). Despite the emphasis on environment and social context in realistic works, there is an indulgence which tends to *protect* individuals from their environment as much as locate them within it; the social context is a constant, but not implacable, backdrop.

It is the 'escape hatches' in this tradition of realism, and its general tendency to view contingency as something to be shaped and altered, that account for the affinities between it and nineteenth-century liberalism and humanism: the realistic novel 'has much more in common with liberal humanism than it has with either Christian or pagan world views' (Lodge 1977: 50). There is a 'fundamental assent' (Stern 1973: 45) to the realist method with its empirical and positivist biases; liberal-humanism, too, as we have seen, is a form of fundamental assent, and, like realism, it proposes possibilities of transformation or escape from unenviable circumstances.

Needless to say, a preoccupation with escape implies that there is something to escape *from*. This implies that all the different kinds of escape in Edwardian literature – whether into agrarian idylls, realms of fantasy or mythology, or even into good fortune and happier circumstances – proceed from a lurking fear that opportunities may be receding and that uncongenial circumstances may prevail. Forster was only too aware of this: *Howards End*, in particular, deals extensively with the mythology of escape, even while it demythologises it and explores its etiology. A few years earlier, he had emphasised the anxieties underlying the predilection for light-hearted escapism: in 'Pessimism in Literature', he claims that the 'general tendency [of modern literature] is pessimistic, and that optimism is the exception' (*AE*: 130). The pessimism of the contemporary artist 'results, not from wrongheadedness, not from spiritual blindness, but from an honest attempt to interpret the spirit of the age' (140). Particularly revealing in relation to the escapist elements in Edwardian literature and the benignity of its realism is Forster's claim that 'the modern mind' is able to discern pessimism and morbidity in what other ages may have regarded as light-hearted relief: 'It has detected the discomfort and misery that lie so frequently beneath the smiling surface of things' (142). There is even a desperate quality to the popular comedies:

> Perhaps we do not often realize how very far this pessimism extends in modern work – especially in what we term comedy. The

> sentimental comedy of J. M. Barrie, the tit-for-tat comedy of Ellen
> Thorneycroft Fowler, the cynical comedy of Pinero – all pay their
> ultimate homage to something that is certainly not a laugh. We
> are so keenly – if you like, so morbidly – alive to sorrow and
> suffering, that human action seems impossible without them . . .
> (140–1)

Seen from this perspective, the lighter side of 'romantic realism' – the
comedy, the romance, the fortunate escapes – is also a manifestation of
'something that is certainly not a laugh'; of an undercurrent of trepida-
tion and unease in Edwardian life.

Not surprisingly, the Edwardian period brought a widespread antipathy towards naturalism, which 'took shallow root in England'
(Eagleton 1970: 12); it had its supporters – in particular, George Moore,
George Gissing and Sarah Grand – but even they were only 'half-
persuaded by Zola's determinism' (Trotter 1993: 121). The naturalist
endeavour to 'extend mimetic realism to its furthermost logical limits'
and, thereby, to cast the artist 'into the role of a photo-phonographic
recorder of reality' (Furst and Skrine 1971: 70) was regarded by many
Edwardian writers as too inflexible, too grim, insufficiently *accommo-
dating*.

H. G. Wells expressed disdain for the ' "colourless" theory of fiction',
whereby the personality of the author is suppressed, resulting in a
novel's extending 'the purview of the police-court reporter to the
details of everyday life' (Wells 1980: 142). Authorial interpolation and
the absence of 'objectivity' are thus inevitable:

> men must needs be partisans, and whatever their resolves may be,
> the idealizing touch, the partiality, the inevitable taint of justifica-
> tion, will mar their handiwork.   (148)

In contrast to this, one sometimes finds Arnold Bennett presenting
the ambitions of realism in terms of an 'uncontaminated' verisimilitude:

> To take the common grey things which people know and despise,
> and without tampering to disclose their epic significance, their
> essential grandeur, that is realism as distinguished from idealism
> and romanticism.   (In Simons 1936: 81)

However, contemporary realism consisted, for the most part, of a great deal of tampering, not a little idealism and romanticism, and a widespread reluctance to leave the 'common grey things' as they were: the realists tended 'to write about [reality] as they believed it ought to be' (Stubbs, 1979: 55). Their works confer possibility; they are liberating rather than restrictive.

Modernism, in contrast, begins 'with the search for a literature which is no longer possible' (Barthes 1967: 44). The reaction against realism is central to that search. However, if one looks past the ostensible targets of attacks upon the realists by writers such as Virginia Woolf, what emerges is that it is not so much what they *ignore* that is so unsatisfying to the modernists, as what they *permit*. The realists tend to find ways of limiting the power of contingency, while the modernists are faced with an 'awareness of contingency as a disaster in the world of time' (Bradbury and McFarlane 1976: 26). This is not to suggest that modernism does not have 'escape hatches' of its own: nonetheless, there is a perception that the modernist writer must contend with restriction as well as possibility. Following on from this, there is the recognition that restriction itself confers new kinds of possibility. Most of the early modernists 'thought of themselves as realist in one or another sense' (Butler 1994: 273): their project was revisionary, their quest to rescue realism from the realists.

In Forster's tribute to Chekhov, published in 1919, he identifies a kind of 'romantic realism' in Chekhov's work, and acknowledges the plenitude that is achieved when the ostensibly contradictory impulses are successfully yoked together:

> We have travelled through the world of his creation, and enjoyed its imaginative fullness, nothing has happened that might not happen in the world of daily life, but the particular sequence of events is not to be experienced this side of poetry. Tchehov [*sic*] (if one cares to label him) is both realist and poet. With one hand he collects facts, with the other he arranges them and sets them flowing. (*PT*: 29)

Forster's earlier works, too, show very clearly how much is made possible when one is 'both realist and poet'. Failures at the romantic level have recourse to realistic alternatives, and, more commonly, failures at the level of the realist mode find romantic consolations. The realist elements are so closely interwoven with the romantic components that disentangling the two is almost impossible, as Masterman recognises in his unsigned review, published in 1908, of *A Room with a View*. His description of the 'fusion' Forster achieves in that novel provides, incidentally, one of the best definitions of 'romantic realism' itself:

> Mr. Forster can describe with sure touch the queer satisfactions and still queerer repugnances which make up the strange region of modern things. Had this element been there alone, the book would have been merely an excellent satirical judgement of manners and conventions. Had the other element stood alone – the revelation of the hidden life – it would have been mystical, intangible, illusory. By the fusion of the one with the other, he is able to present work humorous and arresting, with a curious element in it of compelling strength and emotion.   (In Gardner 1973: 115)

The degree to which the realist focus upon 'manners and conventions' and the romantic preoccupation with 'the revelation of the hidden life' are intertwined in Forster's writings sets him apart from some of his Edwardian contemporaries. In Wells's *The History of Mr Polly* (1910), for instance, the entire episode at the Potwell Inn is couched in romantic and pastoral terms, thus granting Mr Polly the freedom, the comic heroism, and even the good digestion that are his once he has 'broken through the paper walls of everyday circumstance, those unsubstantial walls that hold so many of us securely prisoned from the cradle to the grave' (Wells 1953: 193). But the novel is able to function only in terms of diametrically opposed contrasts, the one represented by Mr Polly's life in Fishbourne, and the other by the Potwell Inn; there is no sense that the rejuvenation Mr Polly finds at the Potwell Inn can ever permeate the dreariness of Fishbourne. There is no illumination of the quotidian, and Mr Polly does not so much transcend his life as flee from it.

In Forster's early work, however, the romantic elements have precisely the function of irradiating the mundane – although the narrowest kinds of suburban existence (usually represented by the fictitious suburb of Sawston) are excluded from that possibility. This transformation is frequently achieved by means of the 'eternal moments' which feature so prominently in his works of this period. The idea of the 'eternal moment' represents 'one of Forster's most obvious debts to nineteenth-century Romanticism' (Colmer 1975: 37). It is a moment that is, paradoxically, located within time and yet able to transcend the flux of time; consequently, it is left behind and yet never left behind. The 'eternal moment' has always to do with preservation. In his essay 'The Beauty of Life', published in 1911, Forster indicates that the panoply of High Romantic longings – 'the comprehensive ecstasies' – may have been curtailed dramatically in the modern world, but this makes the retention of beauty, aesthetic and spiritual, all the more important:

> Here then is what one may call the irreducible minimum, the inalienable dowry of humanity: Beauty in scraps. It may seem a little thing after the comprehensive ecstasies of Whitman, but it is certain; it is for all men in all times, and we couldn't avoid it even if we wanted to. The beauty of the fine day amid dingy weather; the beauty of the unselfish action amid selfishness; the beauty of friendship amidst indifference: we cannot go through life without experiencing these things, they are as certain as the air in the lungs.
>
> (*AE*: 171–2)

The 'eternal moment' expresses the romantic desire for 'beauty' which Forster universalises and presents as transhistorical; it is also a symptom of his sense that modernity tends to scale down grand nineteenth-century aspirations – 'the modern mind . . . can never recall joy on a large scale – the joy of the gods' (143) – and induce fragmentation: 'Beauty in scraps'. The above excerpt also makes it clear that the 'eternal moment' depends as much upon the quotidian as upon the transcendent – it requires 'dingy weather', 'selfishness' and 'indifference' as a counterpoint to what it both expresses and preserves. It is interesting to note that Masterman, too, speaks of an 'eternal moment', and suggests that its effect is the preservation of something precious, especially through exemption from the otherwise remorseless movement of time: 'an Eternal "moment" [is] something that is good in itself apart from remembrance of what has been or anticipation of what shall be.' (Masterman 1911: 212). Scott-James, too, discerns in the paradoxicality of those ' "moments" of vision which seem to promise "some instant fulfilment of life" ' (Scott-James 1908: 7) an attempt to escape the exigencies of time:

All artists have desired that that moment of perception should be eternal; all have found it fleeting. But though the mood itself is fleeting, that which is experienced lies outside time, and so is eternal.   (7)

In *A Room with a View*, which, of all Forster's novels, most obviously maintains a formal comic structure, the 'eternal moments' perform their act of rescue very successfully. It is significant that there are romantic elements of one sort or another in both Florence and Windy Corner – they are not the irreconcilable contrasts presented to Mr Polly. It is not only the Emersons' appearance in England which brings about Lucy Honeychurch's salvation: it is clear that the 'eternal moments' she experiences in Florence – such as the incident in the Piazza Signoria and George's kiss amongst the violets at Fiesole – remain with her, and they rescue her from the 'medievalism' of Cecil Vyse and the life he offers, and return her to the anti-ascetic plenitude of her 'renaissance' with George. Mr Emerson's words help her to a realisation of the lasting influence of these 'eternal moments', and to what she has been suppressing within herself; they do not in themselves effect the change. The realist trajectory tends to move towards marriage, closure and resolution, the 'Comic Muse' (*RV*: 117) also impels Lucy towards that resolution, and the novel's romantic elements work further to save her from 'the vast armies of the benighted . . . [who] have yielded to the only enemy that matters – the enemy within' (174). With all these forces hastening Lucy on towards her happiness, it is not surprising that there seems so little choice in her eventual selection of George rather than Cecil – she merely wakes up to truth.

If there seems to be less tension between the realist and romantic elements in *A Room with a View* than in *The Longest Journey*, for instance, it is because they are less evenly arrayed in the former novel. *A Room with a View* is largely a romance, and the 'escape hatch' provided by the 'eternal moments' is readily attained.

This is true also of most of Forster's early short stories, which resemble closely what Wells calls 'scientific romances':

the living interest lies in their non-fantastic elements and not in the invention itself. They are appeals for human sympathy quite as much as any 'sympathetic' novel, and the fantastic element, the strange property or the strange world, is used only to throw up and intensify our natural reactions of wonder, fear or perplexity.

(Wells 1980: 241)

Like *A Room with a View*, these stories present relatively uncomplicated escapes and make 'appeals for human sympathy' through starkly drawn polarities. Years later, when Forster rejects fantasy in favour of 'prophecy' in *Aspects of the Novel*, it is partly because fantasy is found to be too 'easy': its gods are 'rather small gods', and, despite its attention to the supernatural, its focus is on 'all that is medieval this side of the grave' (*AN*: 76). If one considers these short stories (most of which rely on fantastical elements) in the light of that distinction, it is clear that they do not involve a fundamental reshaping of experience.

This is evident in the way in which they frequently equate transcendence with flight, and in their presentation of virtually every version of quotidian reality as irredeemably objectionable. Some escapes are successful, such as Eustace's in 'The Story of a Panic' and Evelyn Beaumont's in 'Other Kingdom'; others are not – 'The Road from Colonus', for instance, where Mr Lucas misses his opportunity and returns to his mundane life with all the concomitant pettiness and shrinking of the spirit. Ethel, his daughter, is 'aghast at the narrowness of [his] escape' (*CS*: 108) from disaster, but what is more remarkable is the narrowness of the choices available to him: death in Greece while he is overcome by his 'eternal moment', or an existence that is so devoid of meaning that it is worse than death.

In one of Forster's short stories, 'The Eternal Moment' – significantly not a fantasy – there is no easy escape, and no dilution of the tensions inherent in the 'romantic realism' mode. Miss Raby's 'eternal moment' of so many years ago, when Feo proclaimed his love for her on the mountain, returns to her with its romantic significance intact even when she is confronted with the horror of what has happened to Vorta, to Feo, and, by implication, to herself. Amidst the sullied world which she, in effect, has created through the success of her novel, she sees that, unlike the new tower which will fall, her 'eternal moment' will survive: 'she realized . . . that the incident upon the mountain had been one of the great moments of her life – perhaps the greatest, certainly the most enduring' (*CS*: 216). But her victory is only partial: it cannot be disentangled from defeat, for the tainted reality prevails simultaneously, and Colonel Leyland is part of it. The story ends with a mean little pact between Feo and Colonel Leyland; the sordidness closes in again. It is entirely appropriate that the final note of the story should be bathetic: in itself, bathos here suggests the incompatibility of the impulses that 'romantic realism' seeks to reconcile and integrate. It reinforces the chasm which exists between 'the eternal remembrance of the vision which had made life seem endurable and good' (217) and the debasement which ensues when it becomes the subject of a grubby transaction between people who are expedient.

A similar note is struck in *Where Angels Fear to Tread*. Philip Herriton is appalled by the incongruous jumble of romance and bathetic ordinariness in Monteriano:

> A dentist at Monteriano! A dentist in fairyland! False teeth and laughing-gas and the tilting chair at a place which knew the Etruscan League, and the Pax Romana, and Alaric himself, and the Countess Matilda, and the Middle Ages, all fighting and holiness, and the Renaissance, all fighting and beauty! . . . he feared that Romance might die.   (*WA*, 19–20)

But the narrator does not support this view and immediately warns us that 'Romance only dies with life. No pair of pincers will ever pull it out of us' (20). The use of 'romantic realism' as a fictional mode in itself suggests that romance is not expunged by the mundane aspects of life; but it is not left untrammelled by it either:

> [Forster's Italian novels are] completely and properly indecisive as to the relation between personal commitment to action in life and the transformative, reality-bearing power of the 'unseen', exemplifying shiftingly as they do that the worldly will and the contemplative imagination each touch on something like 'reality' yet also run counter to one another.   (Graham 1988: 14)

This is true, in particular, of *Where Angels Fear to Tread*, which explores – as does 'The Eternal Moment' – this 'indecisiveness', including the chafing that ensues when the romantic and unromantic aspects of life, instead of being conciliated, grow further apart. In contrast to *A Room with a View*, the comic resolution is conspicuously avoided, and the conclusion brings a strong sense of expectations unfulfilled. In particular, there is an avoidance of the use of marriage as an ending: Philip

Herriton and Caroline Abbott do not marry – Philip believes, at the end, that he loves Caroline, but Caroline loves Gino, and is able to offer Philip only her friendship and gratitude. The repudiation of marriage as a conclusion is a way of marking a departure from both the comic and the realist modes, both of which use it extensively as ending and resolution. In 'Pessimism in Literature', Forster declares that the 'social feeling of the period' will no longer accept this 'Victorian' tendency:

> We of today know that whatever marriage is, it is not an end. We know that it is rather a beginning, and that the lovers enter upon life's real problems when those wedding bells are silent. Our better education, and the better education of women has taught us this. The early Victorian woman was regarded as a bundle of goods. She passed from the possession of her father to that of her husband. Marriage was a final event for her. . . . And so the early Victorian novelist might reasonably end his book with a marriage. The social feeling of the period approved him.   (*AE*: 135)

Not conforming to the traditional marriage plot has, therefore, sociological and narrative implications:

> Marriage had been essential to the novel, both as a subject and as a structuring principle, from its inception: marriage served as a paradigm of social integration and stability within the narrative, while the desire for marriage provided narrative impetus and the achievement of marriage offered a means of narrative resolution. To question that paradigm entailed (at least implicitly) a questioning of the narrative conventions and forms that novelists used to depict romance and marriage.   (Miller 1994: 44–5)

The movement towards marriage is, arguably, the most common trajectory in fiction. At the very least, what it requires is *activity*. It is, therefore, significant that activity in *Where Angels Fear to Tread* tends to be satirised – especially in the expedition to retrieve the baby. The title itself ('fools rush in . . . ') suggests that ill-considered activity will meet with catastrophe, as, indeed, it does. The presence of Santa Deodata, the patron saint of Monteriano, who, '[i]n her death, as in her life . . . did not accomplish much' (*WA*: 119), and who gained her sainthood through inactivity, hovers over the events: 'sweetness and barbarity mingle strangely in her story' (79), as they do in the novel as a whole. An inactive saint is already a bathetic notion, and the description of her extraordinary restraint makes the bathos even more pronounced:

> So holy was she that all her life she lay upon her back in the house of her mother, refusing to eat, refusing to play, refusing to work. The devil, envious of such sanctity, tempted her in various ways. He dangled grapes above her, he showed her fascinating toys, he pushed soft pillows beneath her aching head. When all proved vain he tripped up the mother and flung her downstairs before her very eyes. But so holy was the saint that she never picked her mother up, but lay upon her back through all, and thus assured her throne in Paradise. She was only fifteen when she died, which shows how much is within the reach of any schoolgirl.   (79)

The novel, in refusing to sanction certain kinds of activity, may be regarded as following the ironic and bathetic example of Santa Deodata. There is not only a retreat from marriage and the path to marriage through courtship, but also from the fictional paths, the narrative conventions, which that movement traditionally relies upon.

In addition to conforming more closely to the marriage plot, *A Room with a View* also adheres more closely to the conventions of comedy. Forster admired George Meredith, and it is significant that Meredith, in his influential 'An Essay on Comedy and the Uses of the Comic Spirit' (1877), while conceding that 'Life, we know too well, is not a comedy, but something strangely mixed' (Meredith 1979: 242), nevertheless insists that, for the 'Comic Spirit' to prevail, an emphasis on only one of the ingredients in the mixture must come into play:

> You must . . . believe that our state of society is founded in common sense, otherwise you will not be struck by the contrasts the Comic Spirit perceives, or have it to look to for your consolation. You will, in fact, be standing in that peculiar oblique beam of light, yourself illuminated to the general eye as the very object of chase and doomed quarry of the thing obscure to you. But to feel its presence, and to see it, is your assurance that many sane and solid minds are with you in what you are experiencing . . .   (447)

In other words, the Comic Spirit – like the conventions of realism – requires consensus, a belief in a community of 'many sane and solid minds', if it is to be successful. That is the 'consolation' which underlies the intricacies of comedy – 'the masterly muddles and the semi-quarrels and the shifting of positions which are essential to comedy' (*PT*: 145). But when the individual cannot be consoled and begins to feel estranged from the 'general eye', or suffers from feelings of self-consciousness, vividly suggested by Meredith's description of one caught in a 'peculiar oblique beam of light', then the Comic Spirit must falter. This is indeed the case in Forster's work: there is a gradual movement away from the conditions of assent in which the Comic Spirit is most at ease, as in *A Room with a View*, until we reach *Howards End* and *A Passage to India*, in which elements of comedy remain, but where consensus dissipates and the 'peculiar oblique beam of light' becomes itself an object of investigation.

The departure from the customary trajectory of the realistic or romantic novel is even more strongly in evidence in *The Longest Journey* than in *Where Angels Fear to Tread*, for the former deals much more fully with the oppressiveness of conventions. It subverts so many of the realist conventions that it would not be going too far to describe it as an anti-realist realist novel. Although it does not make use of the technical innovations generally associated with modernism, *The Longest Journey* presents us with an agnostic or decadent realism, a creed in crisis, so distrustful of its own conventions and what they imply that it is not surprising that we find Forster turning away from realism (to some extent) and towards the deployment of modernist strategies in his next novel, *Howards End*. (Although *A Room with a View* was published after *The Longest Journey*, the first drafts of the former were written earlier.)

Mrs Failing – a falsely sibylline figure – declares that 'conventions . . . are majestic in their way, and will claim us in the end' (*LJ*: 276), but Rickie, at the end of the novel, has the implicit support of the narrator when he repudiates her assertion: 'He stood behind things at last, and knew that conventions are not majestic, and that they will not claim us in the end' (278). One of the conventions which the novel emphatically refuses to endorse is marriage, both as a sociological phenomenon and as a fictional convention. The marriage plot, which was undermined in *Where Angels Fear to Tread*, is presented here as a form of entrapment which brings only unhappiness. Although there are many romantic elements in *The Longest Journey*, a concerted attempt is made to locate them wholly in Cambridge, the English (specifically Wiltshire) countryside, and in relationships between men, and thus to dissociate them from conventional heterosexual courtship and marriage:

> There are men and women – we know it from history – who have been born into the world for each other, and for no one else, who have accomplished the longest journey locked in each other's arms. But romantic love is also the code of modern morals, and, for this reason, popular. Eternal union, eternal ownership – these are tempting baits for the average man.   (272)

There are several echoes here of Shelley's 'Epipsychidion', including the phrases 'the longest journey' and 'the code of modern morals'. Shelley's poem is invoked in the novel because it rejects the 'idealism of Romantic passion' (Rosenbaum 1994: 242), including the creed of single attachment and unalterable devotion in love – the 'doctrine . . . that each one should select / Out of the world a mistress or a friend, / And all the rest . . . commend / To cold oblivion' (126). (The lines that follow on from those quoted by Forster reinforce this: 'True love in this differs from gold and clay, / That to divide is not to take away'.) The invocation of 'Epipsychidion' also provides a compelling irony: the High Romantic poem itself treats ideas about romantic love with suspicion, while what ought to be a more wary and sceptical age seems to have taken this kind of love over unthinkingly, investing it with its own forms of 'ownership'. The narrator asserts that '[t]here are moments for all of us when we seem obliged to speak in a new unprofitable tongue' (206); the discourse of romantic love, by contrast, has become the old, profitable tongue, debased by its own popularity. It served, in a qualified sense, for Lucy Honeychurch, but it will not do for Rickie Elliot and Stephen Wonham.

One of the main reasons why *The Longest Journey* treats its own realist conventions with such suspicion is that heterosexual love, channelled into courtship and marriage, is a staple of realistic fiction, and Forster's novel is a thinly-veiled protest against the oppressiveness of heterosexist pressures and expectations. It is true that Rickie does not universalise the failure of his marriage: 'I'm not so silly as to think that all marriages turn out like mine. My character is to blame for our catastrophe, not marriage' (275). None the less, there are no successful marriages in the novel, and, although Stephen does marry at the end, his wife remains a shadowy figure and we are told that 'love for one person was never to be the greatest thing he knew' (242). What Rickie calls his 'character' is something more than his personality or disposition: it is the covert homosexuality which he represents and yet cannot claim for himself, and which he has betrayed in his marriage to Agnes. Ansell, in his letter to Rickie, says 'You are not a person who ought to marry at all' (81), and the novel warns us (as blatantly as it can) that 'those who stray outside their nature invite disaster' (198). In Rickie's relationship with Stephen, homosexual desire is rendered 'acceptable' by the revelation that they are brothers, and can come to love one another as brothers; but, in comments such as the following, the subversiveness of the relationship flickers and declares itself as openly as it dares:

> 'Come with me as a man,' said Stephen. . . . 'Not as a brother; who cares what people did years back? We're alive together, and the rest is cant . . . ' (257)

Seen in this light, the misogynistic elements in *The Longest Journey* are easier to understand, although this does not make them less unpalatable. Ansell, from whom Rickie, in marrying Agnes, is estranged, is deeply misogynistic. He sees 'feminine' behaviour solely in terms of reprehensible wiliness and as a series of strategies designed to entrap men, and cries 'Damn those women. . . . Their diplomacy was ladylike. Their lies were ladylike. They've caught Elliot in a most ladylike way' (79). Nor is there anything in the novel as a whole that seriously challenges this, although there is a modicum of sympathy for Agnes. All the important female characters – Rickie's mother, Agnes, Mrs Failing – practise deception and suppress or distort the truth in one way or another; all play a part in separating Rickie from the men whose love and companionship are essential to his happiness. In *The Longest Journey*, the resentment of marriage becomes a resentment of women. The misogyny that this implies is not common in Forster's writings; whenever it does appear, it has always the same etiology: an inability to exempt women from the social pressures and strictures that frustrate the expression of male homosexual desire.

The forces arrayed against the special kind of 'friendship' that is homosexual love are shown to be daunting – in particular, the procreative impulse is presented in this novel as so powerful that those who do not participate in it are relegated to an afterthought in the long history of the world:

> Nature has no use for us; she has cut her stuff differently. Dutiful sons, loving husbands, responsible fathers – these are what she wants, and if we are friends it must be in our spare time. Abram and Sarai were sorrowful, yet their seed became as sand of the sea, and distracts the politics of Europe at this moment. But a few verses of poetry is all that survives of David and Jonathan.   (64)

Rickie wishes that 'there was a society, a kind of friendship office, where the marriage of true minds could be registered' (64), but the social exclusion of this type of 'friendship' is as uncompromising as, according to the above excerpt, Nature is towards those who do not conform to the pattern in which she has 'cut her stuff'. The reference to David and Jonathan and the echo of Shakespeare's sonnets in 'the marriage of true minds' suggest that a tradition, even a discourse, of loving male friendship does exist, but it has been suppressed to such an extent that it has been all but drowned out by the clamour of more dominant discourses. To some extent, the novel participates in the naturalisation of heterosexuality in that it seems to accept a necessary continuity between the procreative impulse in nature and the social institutions that entrench heterosexual desire and marriage: this is suggested not only by the comment that '[d]utiful sons, loving husbands, responsible fathers' are what '[Nature] wants', but also by the fact that Stephen, who is at one with nature, becomes both a husband and a father at the end, despite little enthusiasm prior to that for either role. Yet there is also a protest lodged against what Nature prefers or is deemed to prefer: Ansell, in an argument with Tilliard, who suggests that allegiance to a wife must take precedence over loyalty to friends, because 'it is ordained by nature', cries out '[t]he point is, not what's ordained by nature or any other fool, but what's right' (80). Hence, although natural beauty is as much admired in *The Longest Journey* as in any Edwardian idyll, Nature is also a fearful presence, shown by the extraordinary ruthlessness with which it is imbued. Rickie, for instance, is afflicted by heredity in the form of a lame foot, and, when he dares to override his own earlier caution – 'He says he can't ever marry, owing to his foot. It wouldn't be fair to posterity' (50) – eugenics and Darwinian notions of the starkest kind seem to conspire in punishing him for seeking to procreate: his infant daughter is similarly deformed and her death is seen as a merciful release.

Like Vita Sackville-West's *Challenge* (which was written in 1918–19), *The Longest Journey* is a homosexual novel forced to masquerade as a heterosexual one; its strained realism is the result of that. Sackville-West's novel is a traditional romance, except for the subversiveness lying at its heart – so, too, is *Maurice*, which, in dealing overtly with homosexuality, was silenced by its own explicitness and remained unpublished for decades – but *The Longest Journey* is 'pessimistic' (in Forster's terms) and an abrasively realistic novel, full of cruel disappointment, poor choices, understanding that comes too late, disability and death; it does not conform to the 'benignity' of much Edwardian realism, and does not generously offer escape. There is in it a great deal, including the plot 'that manipulates death so arbitrarily, the . . . sometimes overt and sometimes quite subtle symbolism . . . [that] can be read as resistance to conventions of Victorian and Edwardian fiction' (Rosenbaum 1994: 250). It shares with many modernist novels the sense that contingency cannot readily be held at bay by the comic or realist mode: 'There is much good luck in the world, but it is luck. We are none of us safe. We are children, playing or quarrelling on the line' (110). It reflects also the capriciousness, the 'extraordinarily unreliable' (117) quality of life in general – in Stephen's words, 'One nips or is nipped . . . and never knows beforehand' (117). Realist novels make much of the lessons of experience, but, in the capricious world of *The Longest Journey*, experience has only a circumscribed value. The sadder-but-wiser tone which marks the ending of much realistic fiction, and which has a redemptive quality because it suggests that misfortune may be instructive, does not prevail here. Not all experiences are shown to be valuable or worth undergoing – Rickie's marriage and his life with the Pembrokes are examples of regrettable experiences which he ought to have spared himself. The difficulty, as the narrator acknowledges, is to know when to stop drinking from 'the teacup . . . of experience' (61), for, 'it is not easy, after accepting six cups of tea, to throw the seventh in the face of the hostess' (61). Stephen possesses instinctive knowledge, despite limited worldly experience, while Ansell, who does not participate in many of the conventional experiences of life, does not require them in order to be prescient.

The concern with different kinds of knowledge bears also upon the complex philosophical stratum of the novel. *The Longest Journey* has been read as a repudiation of philosophical idealism, including the Berkeleyan dictum '*esse est percipi*', and as an endorsement of the philosophical realism of G. E. Moore; indeed, the argument with which it begins – whether the cow is there or not when there is no one to see her (a debate similar to the one about the kitchen table in Woolf's *To the Lighthouse*) makes explicit from the start the overriding question of what constitutes 'reality' in ontological terms. The novel goes on to imbue the question with an ethical dimension – 'Bloomsbury's and Forster's Moorist inoculation was both epistemological and ethical' (Rosenbaum 1994: 231) – so that, for instance, when Rickie leaves Agnes and his marriage, he says he is happy at last: 'Because, as we used to say at Cambridge, the cow is there. The world is real again' (277). There is therefore an equation between the false idealism of marriage and the falseness of philosophical idealism. Seen in this light, there is a connection between Moore's philosophy and the ideas expressed in 'Epipsychidion':

> The monogamous ideal of modern morals results in the practice of an Idealism that denies the independent human reality of all but the loved or jealous one. Like cows when unperceived, all but the friend or foe are commended to the 'cold oblivion' of non-existence. The longest journey is thus a trip into subjective unreality.
>
> (Rosenbaum 1994: 241)

This would seem to promote 'objective reality' rather than 'subjective unreality', and to entrench philosophical realism and, by implication, fictional realism, despite the attempt to repudiate the marriage plot and its heterosexist orientation. But it is clearly not as simple as this. Part of the problem lies with Ansell: although he is the most vociferous critic of the two kinds of idealism referred to by Rosenbaum, he is himself not immune to Idealism – he 'fails to get his fellowship because he has read too much Hegel, and is in other ways tainted with Idealism' (Bernard Harrison 1991: 99). His mandalas are 'symbols of his incipient Idealism' (Rosenbaum 1994: 236), and it is significant that, when Rickie is regaining the romantic inclinations from which he had allowed himself to become estranged, it is in terms of these mandalas that the recovery is framed:

In the midst of lessons he would grow dreamy, as one who spies a new symbol for the universe, a fresh circle within the square. Within the square shall be a circle, within the circle another square, until the visual eye is baffled. Here is meaning of a kind.   (183)

Rickie's renewed pursuit of the kind of vision that requires more than the 'visual eye', as suggested by his awakened romantic sensibility, involves, therefore, a *reinstatement* of philosophical idealism, of 'imagined creations beyond the external world's perceived actualities' (Rosenbaum 1994: 235). This is what he returns to when he can look beyond the stultifyingly unromantic world of Sawston and 'the heart of all things' (144) is no longer obscured from his sight. This leads to the deeply romantic 'eternal moment' when he and Stephen play with the lighted paper in the tunnel, and the arch is transformed and becomes 'a fairy tunnel, dropping diamonds' (273), the burning paper a 'mystic rose' (282).

Yet here, too, the novel does not follow the pattern it had seemed to construe. Rickie and Stephen quarrel over the decidedly quotidian issue of Stephen's drinking, and Rickie is overtaken with despair, feeling that he has '[g]one bankrupt . . . for the second time. Pretended again that people were real' (281). He saves Stephen's life '[w]early' (282), and his last words are 'You have been right' (282), whispered, not to Stephen or Ansell, but to Mrs Failing, who has never counselled him wisely or really cared for him. This does more than refuse the consolation of understanding gained through hardship which realist novels tend to offer; Rickie's regression into despondency also calls into doubt the authenticity of the 'reality' bestowed by two trajectories, two kinds of meaning: realism and idealism. What was once intimately and vitally related – in ancient Greek society, the ideal 'was originally related to the real' (Dickinson 1904: 228) and the 'impulse to reconcile divergent elements' (229) was central to the Greek way of life – has drifted apart in the modern world. Although Forster does not discard 'romantic realism' (he uses it in both *Arctic Summer* and *Maurice*, for instance, and there are elements of it in *Howards End* and even in *A Passage to India*), *The Longest Journey* marks the beginning of the recognition that, in works which address the more stringent conditions of modern life, 'romantic realism' (or equivalent attempts to fuse 'divergent elements') can no longer serve as an escape from 'the implacable defiance of present things' (Masterman 1911: 193).

After *The Longest Journey*, a new element in Forster's writing begins to become prominent, moving it beyond what 'romantic realism', even in its most agnostic form, can signify. In *Howards End*, and *A Passage to India*, Forster makes use of symbolist ideas and techniques. This is an extremely significant progression in terms of his growing modernist tendencies: much modernist literature may be seen 'as a second phase of *symbolisme*' (Michael Bell 1980: 29), and it had a renewed impact in the years before the First World War, and even in the 1920s.

One of the earliest expositions of the symbolist creed, Arthur Symons's *The Symbolist Movement in Literature* (1899), already indicates the extent to which symbolism marks a departure from the premises underlying the enterprise of realism. Realism sponsors 'the myth of its own authenticity' (Furst, 1995: 77), but symbolism, by contrast, selfconsciously attests to its own artificiality – it is 'a form of expression, at the best but approximate, essentially but arbitrary' (Symons 1899: 3–4). This includes the recognition that language itself is made up of arbitrary imputations of meaning:

> What are words themselves but symbols, almost as arbitrary as the letters which compose them, mere sounds of the voice to which we have agreed to give certain significations, as we have agreed to translate these sounds by those combinations of letters? (3)

Forster's essay 'Anonymity: An Enquiry' (1925) offers a romantic theory of inspiration – the artist 'dips a bucket' (*TC*: 83) into the 'lower personality' (82) – but in fact provides an account of artistic creation that is essentially symbolist. In it he argues for a more 'impersonal' kind of literature – a notion that has both symbolist and modernist implications. All literature, he claims, 'tends towards a condition of anonymity' (81); 'great literature' reminds us 'that it was not the speaker who was in the beginning but the Word' (83). The combination of impersonality and the primacy of the Word means that an autotelic, entirely self-referential text – poetry, for Forster, has this capacity – may be envisaged: 'We have entered a universe that only answers to its own laws . . . internally coheres, and has a new standard of truth. . . . A poem points to nothing but itself' (81). An autotelic text is, of course, an impossibility; but the search for one speaks of a desire to move away from conventional modes of signification. Symbolist techniques do, in any case, accentuate the self-referring elements of a work:

Narrative is often suppressed or implied rather than made explicit; the connections and transitions between parts of the writing are often omitted; the sign function of words is diminished so that lines of reference to the real world are either blurred, made ambiguous or paradoxical, or reduced to a minimum. For these reasons, a symbolist writing, with its 'clues and indirections' tends to be more self-referring than other kinds of writing.   (Bigelow 1976: 124–5)

The emphasis on causality and consequence, so central to realism, is thus replaced by a stress upon that which is inscrutable. The symbolist creed reaches after the most elusive of visions – 'invitations to journeys into the ineffable' (Stern 1973: 184). It is 'a making rather than a matching; a "dis-figuring" of the things the world contains rather than a retracing of them' (157), and, because it asserts the primacy of the private and the esoteric over the communal, because 'shared knowledge gives way to intimation', symbolism violates that 'balance between public and private meanings' (84) which is so crucial to realism. If realism asserts 'an ideal intelligibility of things' (Barthes 1967: 75), then what symbolism offers by contrast is the inviolability of the dream – as suggested by the epigram that Lukács quotes from Heraclitus: 'Those who awake have a world in common, but every sleeper has a world of his own' (Lukács 1981: 20). Alternatively, it provides access to a state that lies between waking and dreaming, where 'the visible world is no longer a reality . . . the unseen world no longer a dream' (Symons 1899: 6).

Symbolism deliberately problematises the relationship between language and meaning through its insistence upon multiple referents, and the irreducibility of the symbol to a single meaning. The closer language comes to divesting itself of reference, the more it approaches the condition of music. In what may be regarded as its non-referential 'purity', music is the ultimate aspiration of symbolist writing: it represents 'the ideal form of "disinterested" expressivity' (Nicholls 1995: 48–9). It is significant that Forster describes 'prophecy' – which is his broad term for symbolist elements and techniques of various kinds – as 'song' (AN: 86). 'Prophecy' is 'a tone of voice', but not one in which the 'prophetic' novelist, whose 'theme is the universe' is going to ' "say" anything about the universe' (86). From this perspective, 'a poet's message is far greater than anything that he manages to say' (PT: 53) and, in this tendency, the 'prophetic' novelist becomes more like a poet. Forster is fully aware of the difficulties of combining symbolist techniques with other fictional modes:

> the strangeness of song arising in the halls of fiction is bound to give us a shock. How will song combine with the furniture of common sense? we shall ask ourselves, and shall have to answer 'Not too well': the singer does not always have room for his gestures, the tables and chairs get broken, and the novel through which bardic influence has passed often has a wrecked air, like a drawing-room after an earthquake or a children's party.   (*AN*: 86)

A mixture of modes and tones of this kind is the result of a situation where what one may call the residue of realism – by no means a spent force – is present along with fictional ingredients which work to destabilise it and wreck the 'furniture of common sense':

> the contemporary desire in poetry for a symbolist wholeness comes to preside in one whole strain of the modern novel as well; the world beyond the contingent detail and haphazard reality acquires that luminosity which, for instance, Virginia Woolf sought in fiction. One result is a progressive fading of that realism which has long been associated with the novel; language ceases to be what we see through, and becomes what we see. The novel hangs on the border between the mimetic and the autotelic species of literature . . .
> (Fletcher and Bradbury 1976: 401)

This is precisely what occurs once Forster begins to use symbolist elements in his writings: a form of double vision ensues, the expression of a dual commitment that comes of being 'on the border between the mimetic and the autotelic'.

Howards End is the novel where this is most in evidence, for, on the one hand, it reaches towards new techniques in a way that the earlier works do not, while, on the other, it retains a greater allegiance to realism and romanticism than does *A Passage to India*. Forster 'had been reading poetry the year he began [*Howards End*] . . . and works like Baudelaire's "Correspondances" are in the novel's background' (Rosenbaum 1994: 451); this is borne out by the fact that, in a letter to Syed Ross Masood written in 1909, Forster, in giving advice on 'how to

scan French poetry' (in Lago and Furbank 1983: 101), chooses lines
from Verlaine's 'Chanson d'Automne' and Baudelaire's *Les fleurs du
mal* to illustrate the point he is making.

In part, the symbolist elements of the novel are related to the anxiety
that the aggressive spirit of modernity will destroy everything of
value that the past wishes to confer as a legacy upon the present.
Forster sees the incantatory aspects of symbolism as having to do with
the preservation of the past and the resurrection of the dead:

> Most of us see the past as a swamp. Events do not flow past us; they
> neither go down into the mighty ocean nor are they lost in the
> sand; no, their behaviour is otherwise; the moment they move out
> of our physical reach they begin to sway and interlock, and they
> remain quite near. It is no wonder that amateurs all through the
> ages have indulged in incantations, and have hunted for the Word,
> the Gesture, the Sensation which should evoke their unburied
> dead, and bring back the richness and sweetness which had scarcely
> ceased to breathe.   (*PT*: 323)

In this respect, the use of symbolism constitutes a kind of 'connection'
between the past and the present, an elaborate attempt to retain the
plenitude of the past and its ghosts, the 'unburied dead' who, like Mrs
Wilcox, do not cease to influence the present once they are dead.

In another sense, however, the use of symbolism in *Howards End* is at
odds with the notion of 'connection', for symbolism of necessity makes
certain kinds of 'connection' impossible: Forster, 'who as a moralist
esteems "connection", as a narrator and a symbolist deliberately follows
words into the places where no connection is possible, and where the
grammar of relationships and perceptions fails' (Graham 1988: 155). In
the manner of its telling, the novel therefore conveys the same falling-
short of the Arnoldian injunction that it implies in the area of socio-
political ambitions: there can be no wholeness or steadiness of vision
when one is required to look in so many different directions at once,
when opacity and flickering truths become part of what one ought to see,
and when, through the movement into symbolism, representation and
meaning are inflected by the intimation of 'a hidden (but, obviously,
occult and non-consensual) universe of analogy' (Butler 1994: 7).

These problems of vision and insight are captured when Margaret, in
an epiphany, sees through to the essence of London: 'The mask fell off

the city, and she saw it for what it really is – a caricature of infinity' (*HE*: 277). Immediately after this, however, she enters St Paul's, only to find that the unwavering vision has not prevailed – like the lighthouse in Woolf's *To the Lighthouse*, the cathedral is comprised of diverse symbolic associations that are present at the same time, and that do not cancel one another out, but are also not reconciled to one another:

> [St Paul's] dome stands out of the welter so bravely, as if preaching the gospel of form. But, within, St Paul's is as its surroundings – echoes and whispers, inaudible songs, invisible mosaics, wet footmarks crossing and recrossing the floor. *Si monumentum requiris, circumspice*: it points us back to London.   (278)

The cathedral thus both represents London and opposes it; it stands as an embodiment of the city and as a countermanding presence. It is formally declarative and confident – 'preaching the gospel of form' – but, within, it contains much that is subdued, even furtive. In heeding the injunction to look around ('*circumspice*'), Margaret – like the reader – does not find a monolith seen steadily and whole, but a nexus of divergent meanings.

A more conspicuous example of this is the wych-elm tree, which is a powerful symbolic force precisely because its many meanings cannot be subsumed within any one meaning. The wych-elm tree accrues significance gradually and achieves its fullest import when Margaret finally sees it:

> It was neither warrior, nor lover, nor god; in none of these roles do the English excel. It was a comrade, bending over the house, strength and adventure in its roots, but in its utmost fingers tenderness, and the girth, that a dozen men could not have spanned, became in the end evanescent, till pale bud clusters seemed to float in the air. It was a comrade. House and tree transcended any simile of sex . . . to compare either to man, to woman, always dwarfed the vision. Yet they kept within limits of the human. Their message was not of eternity, but of hope on this side of the grave. As she stood in the one, gazing at the other, truer relationships had gleamed. (203)

Several romantic expectations are refuted in the description of the tree, including the traditional heroic identities implied by 'warrior', 'lover' and 'god'. Despite the progression from solid, earth-bound physicality to 'evanescent' spiritual delicacy that it embodies, it does not exceed the 'limits of the human' and does not, therefore, urge a passage to a transcendent realm. Everything suggests the inefficacy of conventional categories, including those derived from traditional romance, metaphysics and gender divisions. Even though the tree is extremely old and associated with ancient mythology – suggested by the talismanic pigs' teeth embedded in the bark – the description of it points the way to a new and oblique language.

There is in *Howards End* the fear of what symbolism may lead to, something which is explored more fully in *A Passage to India*. The anxiety that the silence towards which symbolism frequently moves may simply be nothingness is expressed in the image of the abyss, which, in this case, takes on a significance beyond its usual status as a favourite Edwardian nightmare. It is not only Leonard Bast who is threatened by it, although he is most starkly affected; Margaret, too, draws back intuitively from the furthest limits of 'the unseen':

> All vistas close in the unseen – no one doubts it – but Helen closed them rather too quickly for her taste. At every turn of speech one was confronted with reality and the absolute. Perhaps Margaret grew too old for metaphysics, perhaps Henry was weaning her from them, but she felt that there was something a little unbalanced in the mind that so readily shreds the visible.
>
> (*HE*: 192)

One of the ways in which the extremeness of Helen's position is marked is through the exposure of her tendency to form 'an *idée fixe*' (275) and her corresponding lack of pragmatism, the blunders she makes, and her inability to read situations correctly – for instance, when she drags the Basts to Evie's wedding, or when she allows Leonard to seem 'not a man, but a cause' (309). Her failure to respond appropriately to the discrete contexts that pertain and her oversight of contingent truths in her eagerness to pursue absolute truths show us that Helen has not learned the lessons of realistic fiction, in which the importance of negotiating with the imperfect and changing conditions of life is stressed continually. This is certainly not true of Margaret, however, and the novel which endorses so much of what she says retains a substantial allegiance to the tradition which best serves her pragmatism.

Within the larger question of inheritance which the novel poses, there is the matter of spiritual continuity:

> Is it credible that the possessions of the spirit can be bequeathed at all? Has the soul offspring? A wych-elm tree, a vine, a wisp of hay with dew on it – can passion for such things be transmitted where there is no bond of blood?   (96)

Margaret is the spiritual 'heir' to Mrs Wilcox only in so far as she shares her love for, and appreciation of, Howards End, but she never becomes a 'prophetic' character like Mrs Wilcox or Miss Avery, characters wholly in accord with the symbolist elements of the novel; her eventual possession of Howards End, rather than answering the questions posed here, makes the issue even more problematic. There is also the romantic legacy that has been passed on to her and her siblings from their father: he, too, has sought to 'bequeath' the 'possessions of the spirit'. The father's beliefs represent an Idealist tradition which affirms the supremacy of the spirit and assumes the lesser status of the materialist sphere of existence:

> He was not the aggressive German, so dear to the English journalist, nor the domestic German, so dear to the English wit. If one classed him at all it would be as the countryman of Hegel and Kant, as the idealist, inclined to be dreamy, whose Imperialism was the Imperialism of the air.   (26)

But this is not the kind of spirituality which Margaret inherits when she takes possession of Howards End. This 'Imperialism of the air' is at odds with a legacy which is emphatically English, strongly rooted to the earth, to a specific place, and to keeping 'within limits of the human' (203). The implication is that some of the erstwhile traditions of the spirit, including those with a High Romantic derivation, will no longer suffice. Just as modernity has brought profound material changes in people's lives – for instance, new modes of transport, the growth of the suburbs and increased urbanisation – so, too, it has brought a need for a different kind of spirituality, a new configuration in reply to what Helen communicates so urgently: 'the vague yet convincing plea that the Invisible lodges against the Visible' (236).

At the same time, the novel draws attention to the consequences of abandoning, even partially, the spiritual traditions of the past. The displacing of romanticism from its pre-eminent position is associated with disquiet and foreboding. The goblins that Helen hears in the music of Beethoven's Fifth Symphony represent the potential for mean-spiritedness and spiritual paucity in a world without romanticism:

> They were not aggressive creatures; it was that that made them so terrible to Helen. They merely observed in passing that there was no such thing as splendour or heroism in the world. . . . Panic and emptiness! Panic and emptiness! The goblins were right. (30–1)

The goblins, like the Marabar Caves, do not represent malevolence or evil. Instead, what makes them terrifying is the utter denial of value which they communicate, the insidious acceptance of a situation in which 'there [is] no such thing as splendour or heroism'. Forster warns in 'The Beauty of Life' that 'Modern civilization does not lead us away from Romance, but it does try to lead us past it, and we have to keep awake' (*AE*: 175); the goblins represent the possibility of a world which has not been sufficiently alert and which has permitted a hollow banality to prevail, expunging 'that zest and sparkle and inner glow of accepted adventure which alone would seem to give human life significance' (Masterman 1911: 70–1). The goblins are 'scattered' by Beethoven, but not banished – 'They could return' (32).

The ending of the novel invites us to consider not only the implications of the continuation of Margaret and Henry's marriage, but also the uneasy 'marriage' between Margaret's rationalist orientation, her family's romantic heritage – which, for Leonard, makes her one of the 'denizens of Romance' (120) – and the Schlegels' habitation of a symbolist house. This accounts in part for the discordant notes which the final chapters bring and the impression of compromises which go either too far or not far enough. The ending emphasises that the concern with inheritance – familial, social, political, financial and spiritual – pertains also to the question of *fictional* inheritances: the novel has 'inherited' certain literary modes, including realism and romanticism, some of which may have begun to seem inappropriate. Having everyone living together, despite their being so different, is not as simple a solution as it seems. At the level of plot, Leonard is dead and Henry enfeebled; similarly, there is not necessarily a place for every fictional 'inheritance', or, if a place is found, it may involve a diminution of status. The 'capaciousness of the great Victorians' (Levenson 1991: 86) can no longer be asserted unequivocally; nor can the realist mode favoured by the Victorians and Edwardians.

Margaret says that 'very early in the morning in the garden I feel that [Howards End] is the future as well as the past' (337); the attempt to rescue the house from the threat of anachronism has its fictional counterpart too. The implication is that what the past 'bequeaths', however estimable, will lose its value if it is received unquestioningly and kept unaltered. The respite which the relatively tranquil ending of the novel suggests is a lull, not an escape: as in Beethoven's symphony, it represents merely the temporary 'scattering' of the goblins. In this instance, too, they could return.

In his discussion of *Howards End*, Michael Levenson has suggested, with justification, that '[l]iberalism and symbolism, both unwieldy terms, become more unwieldy when brought together' (Levenson 1991: 78), adding that they seem to belong to 'such different orders of description and such different strains of modernity' (78). But this incongruity is part of what *Howards End* is about. In the realist novel, there is generally a confident assumption that the fictional methods will be efficacious in representing a shared social reality; in this case, however, the 'unwieldiness' which Levenson discerns marks the inability to assume commonality in the social context (suggested by the crisis in liberal-humanism) or in fictional terms (suggested by the use of symbolism, with its esoteric meanings). The incompatibility of paradigms is thus another version of the inability to see things steadily and to see them whole. Whereas realism seeks to conciliate the warring parties in 'the border warfare . . . between things as they are and as they ought to be' (*HE*: 228), the awkwardness arising from Forster's seeing 'with one liberal and one symbolist eye' (Levenson 1991: 78) marks, in characteristically modernist fashion, the increasing enmity between the two sides.

A Passage to India is not without its romantic elements: it contains, for instance, one of the most significant 'eternal moments' in all of Forster's writings – the meeting between Aziz and Mrs Moore in the mosque. But that meeting occurs in the first section of the novel, when the possibilities of 'connection' at the romantic and liberal-humanist levels have not yet been negated by the Marabar. The 'eternal moment' in the mosque belongs to this time of hope and goodwill, and it endures as such moments do – it perpetuates Aziz's adoration of Mrs Moore, and is revived when Aziz meets Ralph Moore in Mau. Yet it survives without the contexts that gave it meaning: by the time Aziz meets Ralph, Mrs Moore has moved on to disillusionment, apathy and death; friendships in general have come to little or nothing; and, although the memory of the encounter makes Aziz warm to Mrs Moore's son, at the same time the repetition of the words 'Then you are an Oriental' (*PI*: 306) disconcerts him, for he realises that the cycle cannot be renewed without the renewal also of the suffering which he has sought to escape by leaving Chandrapore. The romanticism has been sullied by the fact that it is another Western 'visitor' that has come to India with good intentions, unaware of the implications of its foreignness, and Aziz cannot think of it in unambiguously positive terms.

It is at the Marabar that romanticism receives a series of devastating blows. On the way to the Caves, Adela and Mrs Moore witness a false dawn that anticipates the fate of romanticism:

> As she spoke, the sky to the left turned angry orange. Colour throbbed and mounted behind a pattern of trees, grew in intensity, was yet brighter, incredibly brighter, strained from without against the globe of the air. They awaited the miracle. But at the supreme moment, when night should have died and day lived, nothing occurred. It was as if virtue had failed in the celestial fount. The hues in the east decayed, the hills seemed dimmer though in fact better lit, and a profound disappointment entered with the morning breeze. Why, when the chamber was prepared, did the bridegroom not enter with trumpets and shawms, as humanity expects? The sun rose without splendour. He was presently observed trailing yellowish behind the trees, or against insipid sky, and touching the bodies already at work in the fields.   (149–50)

The anticlimax occasioned by the false dawn is the result of the disappointment of romantic expectations – the sun rises, but it does so without 'splendour' (the very quality which the goblins denigrated in *Howards End*), and the imperviousness of the Indian landscape to romantic formulations is intimated. An important point about the circumscribed and culturally specific nature of symbols is also being made: in the hot Indian climate, the sun is not a 'miraculous' and longed-for presence as it may be in parts of the world that are further from the equator. The expected climax is built up linguistically and imagistically – particularly in the syntactical crescendo of 'grew in intensity, was yet brighter, incredibly brighter'. Phrases such as 'supreme moment', and 'celestial fount', as well as the reference to 'bridegroom' and 'chamber', serve to render romantic fulfilment in terms of sexual consummation, a deeply ironical association in view of what occurs at the Marabar.

Significantly, the description of the false dawn witnessed by Adela and Mrs Moore is followed almost immediately by a discussion of sunrises in which mention is made of Grasmere:

> 'Ah, that must be the false dawn – isn't it caused by dust in the upper layers of the atmosphere that couldn't fall down during the night? . . . Well, I must admit that England has it as regards sunrises. Do you remember Grasmere?'
>
> 'Ah, dearest Grasmere!' Its little lakes and mountains were beloved by them all. Romantic yet manageable, it sprang from a kindlier planet. Here an untidy plain stretched to the knees of the Marabar. (150)

The reference to Grasmere is telling, considering the importance of the Lake District for several of the English High Romantics. Here it is striking in its incongruity, and the fact that it is associated with nostalgia and wistfulness suggests, bathetically, the enervation of the romantic creed in this foreign environment. Grasmere is described as being '[r]omantic yet manageable', and the inference is that romantic conceptions (and preconceptions) are themselves ways of 'managing' what seems to be unmanageable; here, however, they will not serve.

Mrs Moore is, in her mild way, a romantic as well as a Christian and a humanist – she relies on intuition and first impressions, relishes mysteries, and dislikes regimentation and bureaucracy. Her romanticism suffers as greatly as do her other beliefs in the Marabar Caves; in fact, it never recovers. In the Caves she finds that 'Devils are of the North, and poems can be written about them, but no one could romanticize the Marabar, because it robbed infinity and eternity of their vastness, the only quality that accommodates them to mankind' (161). This anticipates the recognition that '[t]he abyss also may be petty, the serpent of eternity made of maggots' (213), which suggests that the quest for transcendence may not only have entered a decadent phase, but may even have grown rotten at the core – an unenviable fate from which spirituality is usually exempt. A further implication is that, despite any assumption of amorality, or at least of transcending mundane versions of morality, romanticism is still bound up with categories of good and evil, both of which may be granted the status of a revelation, and transported to the realm of the visionary by virtue of being distanced from the 'pettiness' of their quotidian origins. It is the 'escape hatch' once more, and the Marabar Caves will not grant it. Instead there is the fear that the quest for transcendence may lead only to 'Panic and emptiness!' (*HE*: 31)

The 'intermittent' (*AN*: 93) or 'spasmodic' (94) realism which Forster detects in the works of 'prophetic' novelists such as Dostoyevsky and Melville is present in *A Passage to India*. What are we to make, for instance, of the opening paragraph of Chapter XIV?

> Most of life is so dull that there is nothing to be said about it, and the books and talk that would describe it as interesting are obliged to exaggerate, in the hope of justifying their own existence. Inside its cocoon of work or social obligation, the human spirit slumbers for the most part, registering the distinction between pleasure and pain, but not nearly as alert as we pretend. There are periods in the most thrilling day during which nothing happens, and though we continue to exclaim 'I do enjoy myself' or 'I am horrified' we are insincere. 'As far as I feel anything, it is enjoyment, horror' – it's no more than that really, and a perfectly adjusted organism would be silent. (*PI*: 145)

Here is the interpolating voice of realist fiction, confident and confiding, and – of significance in a novel where so much is silence and inscrutability – claiming the privileges of such a voice in order to assert the predominance of mundane life, the sheer 'dullness' of existence. There is the assumption of commonality and shared perspectives ('we'), as well as the attribution to itself of a vantage point of superior insight. Yet the experiences at the Marabar Caves undermine all of this – the confidence, the insight, the ostensible omniscience, even the assumption that banality is unremarkable and unthreatening. The insouciance of the realist position would seem to be amongst the other 'casualties' of the Marabar.

The opening paragraph of the 'Temple' section, which is also the first description of the Gokul Ashtami festival, begins thus:

> Some hundreds of miles westward of the Marabar Hills, and two years later in time, Professor Narayan Godbole stands in the presence of God. God is not born yet – that will occur at midnight – but He has also been born centuries ago, nor can He ever be born, because He is the Lord of the Universe, who transcends human processes. He is, was not, is not, was. He and Professor Godbole stood at opposite ends of the same strip of carpet.   (281)

Almost all conceivable violations of the realist method are present in this short extract. The initial identification of time and place is immediately undercut by the fact that Professor Godbole stands 'in the presence of God', which must, necessarily, move him beyond both time and place. The ostensibly contradictory assertions ('God is not born yet . . . but He has also been born centuries ago, nor can He ever be born') cast doubt upon the reliability of the narrative voice, or, at the very least, its suitability as a guide to what is clearly removed from its characteristically rationalist stance. The confusion of tenses has the same effect of contradiction, and when we finally come to the preterite, which is the traditional tense of realist prose, it is to be told that '[God] and Professor Godbole stood at opposite ends of the same strip of carpet.'

Realism is 'an ambitious exercise in bringing the novel to terms or at least to a truce with the essential artificiality of art' (Furst 1995: 10); it is a mode which relies upon 'a canny concealment of any cracks', whereby 'fictional referents are presented as prolongations of referents known outside the fictions' (110). A passage such as the one which introduces the 'Temple' section is signalling to us that, in order to appreciate the philosophy and religion of Professor Godbole, the realist contract must be abandoned, the truce that it rests upon forsaken, the cracks that it conceals exposed. It seems as if every realist premise must now be declared invalid, the narrative voice exposed as an interloper at an event which is beyond its ambit.

On the basis of this, one would expect to be guided through the 'Temple' section by a different kind of narrator, one that has moved even further away from its realist ancestry than the voice that recounted the events at the Marabar. Yet this is not what we find. Even if the narrative voice is not able to enter fully into the esoteric mysteries of the Hindu festival, it is clear that it does not give up the right to evaluate it; it does not, in other words, cede its *authority*. We see this, for instance, when the ecstasy occasioned by the celebration of the birth of Shri Krishna is described not long afterwards:

> the human spirit had tried by a desperate contortion to ravish the unknown, flinging down science and history in the struggle, yes, beauty herself. Did it succeed? Books written afterwards say 'Yes'. But how, if there is such an event, can it be remembered afterwards? How can it be expressed in anything but itself? Not only from the unbeliever are mysteries hid, but the adept himself cannot retain them. He may think, if he chooses, that he has been with God, but, as soon as he thinks it, it becomes history, and falls under the rules of time.   (285)

Here is the narrator stepping back from the mystical experience, subjecting it to the scrutiny of a sceptical and rationalist viewpoint. Miracles, it is suggested, are beyond the scope of narrative; only the approach to the miracle and the inevitable retreat from it can be rendered. The experience itself is closed to fiction, to writers and to readers. But a description of it may well be rendered and, in view of the close relationship which realism has with 'history' and the 'rules of time', it may serve to convey what can be conveyed, and leave the rest unsaid. The authoritativeness of the narrative voice in this excerpt would not be out of place in a realist novel. What it communicates is the extraordinary resilience of realism: confounded by the Marabar, excluded – or so it seemed – from the Gokul Ashtami festival, it nonetheless returns, towards the end of Forster's least realist novel, to evaluate what it cannot comprehend.

In the last paragraph of the novel, however, we are told that the union between Aziz and Fielding can take place only in a 'No, not yet' and 'No, not there' (316) realm of existence which requires the suspension of the social, political and phenomenal conditions of their present existence. Only in a symbolist world can they clasp one another, and that is a world which Aziz and Fielding, *qua* Aziz and Fielding, cannot inhabit. Nor can 'science', 'history' and the 'rules of time' prevail in such circumstances. Instead of the closure towards which realist fiction conventionally moves, these final sentences are, so to speak, a 'dis-closure': they do not disclose what they cannot know in the sense of revealing what is hidden; but they disclose the limits of knowledge, of certainty, and of confidence.

3
The Debate about Form

> form is as important to-day, when the human race is trying to ride the whirlwind, as it ever was in those less agitating days of the past, when the earth seemed solid and the stars fixed, and the discoveries of science were made slowly, slowly.
>
> E. M. Forster, 'Art for Arts Sake' (*TC*: 92)

A preoccupation with form is not in itself characteristically modernist. What is distinctly modernist, however, is the attempt to impose shape and form and, at the same time, to undermine them even as they are being employed – the idea of form as *order* being thus offset by the notion of form as *stricture*. Kenneth Graham has written of James, Conrad and Forster that, for all three writers, 'forms of art . . . are always under pressure, always a compromise at best, an unending open negotiation between the mind's shaping and the world's recalci-trance' (Graham 1988: 156). The use of form in modernist works fre-quently implies an assertion as well as a retraction; to posit, in this regard, is also to deny, or – to use terms particularly significant in Forster's case – to include is also to exclude.

The formal experiments of the modernists were not only diverse in nature, but also frequently disparate in their implications. Christopher Butler, in rejecting the argument that the modernists' 'experimental-ism of technique' implies that they 'were devoted to the production of an art primarily concerned with its own procedures' (Butler 1994: 14), offers an alternative way of interpreting their technical innovations:

> What makes a work of art Modernist is not just the loyalty of its maker to the aesthetic of an evolutionary or disruptive tradition . . .

but its participation in the migration of innovatory techniques *and* their associated ideas. In this period, concepts like 'intuition' and 'expression', or 'subjectivity' and 'inner division', or 'harmony' and 'rhythm', are parts of a changing framework of ideas which inspired stylistic change in Modernist work in all the arts.   (16)

Forster's work (which, as we shall see, includes a particular interest in 'harmony' and 'rhythm') illustrates this very clearly, for, as has been suggested, change and 'disruption' are never ends or explanations in themselves for him, but are to be seen in the context of 'their associated ideas'; there is no definitive exchange of allegiances.

Forster is an 'ambivalent formalist' (Rosenbaum 1982: 60). This ambivalence emerges in a number of the essays, as well as in *Aspects of the Novel*, his most important theoretical work, and one of the most popular and enduring critical studies ever written. Yet, for all that it has been regarded for so long as an accessible and informative guide to novel-writing and novel-reading, *Aspects of the Novel* is in fact a whimsical, quirky, even eccentric work – 'an anti-critical work of criticism' (Rosenbaum 1982: 68) – which frequently subverts itself and disclaims its own objectives. If read as a general introduction to the art of the novel, it does not take one very far – or, at least, it leads one down some idiosyncratic paths. Where it is extremely useful, however, is as a guide to Forster's own fiction and, more generally, as an example of modernist theory, bringing to light, in particular, through its 'mixture of formalistic and non- or even anti-formalistic ideas' (Rosenbaum 1982: 63), the ambivalent attitude to form which we find in many of the modernists. From that perspective, its hesitancies, tendentious pronouncements, tentative assertions and reluctant concessions are easier to understand.

Forster defines the central preoccupation of *Aspects of the Novel* in the following terms:

> The idea running through these lectures is by now plain enough: that there are in the novel two forces: human beings and a bundle of various things not human beings, and that it is the novelist's business to adjust these two forces and conciliate their claims.   (*AN*: 73)

At the end, it becomes clear that the novel that contains all the 'aspects' discussed probably does not exist: a situation of perfect 'adjustment' and 'conciliation' is not possible. Putting it another way: there is nothing 'rhythmic' and 'prophetic' (in Forster's terms) that does no injustice to 'people', to the representation of character in fiction. The novel Forster regards as coming closest to this theoretical harmony between the subject matter of novelists and their methods is *War and Peace*, but it remains, for him, 'an untidy book' (116).

In the absence of this desired 'conciliation', the critic is required to consider the novel in terms of its different 'aspects', and to take up and lay down 'a different set of tools' (101). In other words, criticism becomes, necessarily, an eclectic activity. Forster accepts that this is unavoidable, but finds it lamentable none the less:

> The human mind is not a dignified organ, and I do not see how we can exercise it sincerely except through eclecticism. And the only advice I would offer my fellow eclectics is: 'Do not be proud of your inconsistency. It is a pity, it is a pity that we should be equipped like this. It is a pity that Man cannot be at the same time impressive and truthful.'   (101)

The claim that it is not possible to be 'impressive and truthful' simultaneously is deeply significant, both for Forster's own writing and for modernism itself. What it suggests is that something has crept between the modes of expression and what they purport to convey; that iconic truth is no longer tenable; that discourse itself has become infected with cynicism and compromise, with 'this double aspect of the modern – that the thing observed is changed, and the observer also is changed in his manner of perceiving' (Spender 1963: 133). The eclecticism Forster offers ruefully as the only available choice is an admission that the realist assumption of potential compatibility between the word and the world is no longer possible; it conveys the crucial modernist recognition that 'what previous generations had taken for *the world* was only *the world seen through the spectacles of habit*' (Josipovici 1971: xiii–iv). There is thus a close connection between epistemological scepticism and the search for new forms – something which is borne out by Forster's later fiction and criticism.

Aspects of the Novel is, in part, an elaboration upon the dispute about form in fiction that had engaged Henry James and H. G. Wells more than a decade before Forster delivered the Clark Lectures at Trinity College, Cambridge in 1927. (They were published as *Aspects of the*

Novel later that year.) It is also a response to Percy Lubbock's defence of James's methods in *The Craft of Fiction*, published in 1921. However, despite Forster's disparagement of James and Lubbock, and his apparent support of Wells in the dispute, it is important to note that what is being treated dismissively in *Aspects of the Novel* is the dispute itself. It features far less prominently than one might have expected, and the implication is that the famous quarrel has produced an oversimplification of the issues involved. The criticisms of James seem so similar to those made by Wells that it is easy to overlook the fact that Forster is criticising James for *excessive*, constraining formalism, and not for his interest in formalism *per se*, and that much of *Aspects of the Novel* is a defence – however sceptical and reluctant – of form in fiction.

Wells and James had argued about the respective merits of 'discursiveness' as opposed to 'selection', with Wells maintaining 'the novel I hold to be a discursive thing; it is not a single interest, but a woven tapestry of interests' (Wells 1980: 195), and James dismissing the realist quest for discursiveness as 'saturation' (James 1948: 184). For the latter, '[t]he function of form was to make capital of that selection, of the very difference between art and life, and thus, paradoxically, to suggest sufficiency and "truth" ' (Jones 1985: 156); Wells, however, believed that this would lead to an impoverishment of the unmanageable plenitude of life itself. Forster's criticisms of James's methods, however much they echo Wells's, need to be seen in the context of Chapter 8 of *Aspects of the Novel*, and the distinction that he makes there between 'pattern' and 'rhythm': what he offers is not a contrast between form and the absence thereof; instead, he distinguishes between *formalistic alternatives*, between different ways of applying form to fiction.

Although some of Forster's criticisms of James's work may be seen as an extension of Wells's polemical remarks – including the assertion that '[m]aimed creatures can alone breathe in Henry James's pages – maimed yet specialized' (110) – there is no corresponding defence of Wells's general hostility towards technical innovation. As far back as 1913, Forster had written that 'the influence of Galsworthy Wells &ct . . . is certainly bad for me' (in Lago and Furbank 1983: 200); in *Aspects of the Novel* there is little that endorses unequivocally the methods or philosophical assumptions of realism, and much that assumes the need to move beyond it. Yet most early responses to *Aspects of the Novel* saw Forster as supporting Wells and the realists unambiguously:

Edwin Muir, for instance, while recognising that 'the pattern of no novel, however formless, can ever be so formless as life as we see it; for even *Ulysses* is less confusing than Dublin' (Muir 1928: 11), does not see that *Aspects of the Novel* works with exactly the same premise, for he places Forster firmly in the 'Life' camp: 'Mr Forster argues that the novel must give us life because life does' (10). However, there is no sense in which the 'discursiveness' Wells stresses as a novelistic ambition is regarded as viable: selection and curtailment are accepted as the *sine qua non* of fictional methods, and it is for his '*drastic* curtailment, both of the numbers of human beings and of their attributes ... in the interests of pattern' (*AN* 110; my emphasis) that James is criticised.

It is not sufficient, therefore, to see *Aspects of the Novel* as merely a continuation of the debate about 'life' as opposed to 'art', for, to a significant extent, Forster refuses the terms of that dispute. He does not offer a way of capturing 'life' in the novel in any crudely referential sense. Even in the representation of character ('people'), where Forster is least inclined to renounce the methods of realism, the correspondence between fictional representation and experiential reality is seen as arbitrary, as the revealing comparison between 'Homo Sapiens' and 'Homo Fictus' indicates:

> Homo Fictus is more elusive than his cousin. . . . He is generally born off, he is capable of dying on, he wants little food or sleep, he is tirelessly occupied with human relationships. And – most important – we can know more about him than we can know about any of our fellow creatures, because his creator and narrator are one. Were we equipped for hyperbole, we might exclaim at this point: 'If God could tell the story of the universe, the universe would become fictitious.' For this is the principle involved.   (38–9)

This is very far indeed from being a defence of realism and its claims that it can appropriate or approximate 'life'. In fact, as Forster suggests, only the omniscience of God could provide the ultimate realist narration, in which case the universe and the telling of it would become as one. Lesser forms of omniscience attempt to pass 'Homo Fictus' off as 'Homo Sapiens', and to elide the difference between the two.

Seen in this light, the distinction Forster draws between 'flat' and 'round' characters is less straightforward than it seems. This is perhaps the most famous of all the critical tools which is offered in *Aspects of the Novel*; it has been used for decades as a measure of assessing and responding to characters in fiction. The tendency has been to regard 'flat' characters as representing a unidimensionality which is absent in 'life', and 'round' characters as embodying the multidimensionality which we find in 'life', and thus as one of the great achievements of realist fiction. Yet, if one looks closely at the way in which Forster uses these terms, it becomes clear that he does not regard 'flat' *or* 'round' characters as capable of embodying the kind of psychological verisimilitude associated with realist representations of character. A character in a book is regarded as being 'real' under the following conditions:

> the novelist knows everything about it. He may not choose to tell us all he knows – many of the facts, even of the kind we call obvious, may be hidden. But he will give us the feeling that though the character has not been explained it is explicable, and we get from this a reality of a kind we can never get in daily life.   (44)

Being 'real' in fiction, therefore, means something different from being 'real' in 'daily life'. The distinction between 'flat' and 'round' is so well known and so convenient, that it is generally not recognised for what it is: a radical admission of the impossibility of representing mimetically in fiction the ultimately elusive nature of 'character'.

The difference between a 'flat' and a 'round' character also does not lie in the common distinction between caricature and character:

> The test of a round character is whether it is capable of surprising in a convincing way. If it never surprises, it is flat. If it does not convince, it is flat pretending to be round. It has the incalculability of life about it – *life within the pages of a book*.   (54; my emphasis)

'Flat' characters are caricatures of unidimensionality, which is why Forster regards them as most effective when they have a comic function; 'round' characters are caricatures of multidimensionality, signifying in their limitations the inevitable frustration of novelists in their attempts to do justice to the fullness and capriciousness of human personality. In a deliberate inversion of the notion that the novelist (especially the realist) has unlimited control over his or her creations,

Forster suggests that the characters in a novel are 'full of the spirit of mutiny':

> [They] are . . . often engaged in treason against the main scheme of the book. They 'run away', they 'get out of hand' . . . if they are given complete freedom they kick the book to pieces, and if they are kept too sternly in check they revenge themselves by dying, and destroy it by intestinal decay.   (46)

The novelist is '(qua plot-maker) continually negotiating with himself qua character-monger as to the best effect to be produced' (67); compromise, not omnipotence, is the note of modern fiction.

The ambivalence regarding form in *Aspects of the Novel* is introduced at the start with the description of the novel as a 'spongy tract' which is 'bounded by two chains of mountains neither of which rises very abruptly – the opposing ranges of Poetry and History – and bounded on the third side by a sea – a sea that we shall encounter when we come to *Moby Dick*' (3). 'Poetry' and 'History' in this context signify art without referents and referents without art respectively, and the 'sea' of *Moby Dick*, is, of course, 'prophecy'. 'History' also refers, presumably, to writing that is not free of the exigencies of time, and this leads to one of the most startling features of *Aspects of the Novel* – its notorious anti-historicism:

> Time, all the way through, is to be our enemy. We are to visualize the English novelists not as floating down that stream which bears all its sons away unless they are careful, but as seated together in a room, a circular room, a sort of British Museum reading-room – all writing their novels simultaneously.   (5)

In this vein, we are told that the lectures will seek to 'exorcise that demon of chronology' (8). The insistence in *Aspects of the Novel* upon synchrony rather than diachrony is its most extreme formalist premise. Yet Forster is not alone amongst the literary critics of the 1920s in proposing it: in Muir's study, for instance, we find a deprecation of the widespread contemporary preoccupation with 'period detail':

> The bondage of the novel to period has degraded it. But it also insensibly falsified for a time the standards of criticism, and they still show

its influence. Exactitude of contemporary detail became more important than exactitude of imagination.   (Muir 1928: 118–19)

A comparison between these two objections to historicity reveals,
however, how little they have in common. Muir's is merely the result
of a general aversion to the tradition of formal realism:

> The period novel . . . does not try to show us human truth valid for
> all time; it is content with a society at a particular stage of transition,
> and characters which are only true in so far as they are representa-
> tive of that society. It makes everything particular, relative and his-
> torical. It does not see life with the universalising imagination, but
> with the busy, informing eye . . .   (117–18)

Forster, as we have seen, never moves so far from realism that he abandons his allegiance to what is 'particular, relative and historical', or forsakes 'the busy, informing eye' of the realist. The difference in tone is
an indication that the polemical objectives are entirely different.
There is no trace of irony in Muir's comments, whereas Forster's
description of a room resembling the British Museum reading-room,
in which all the English novelists are writing their novels at the same
time, is tongue-in-cheek.

The playful expunging of history at the beginning of the lectures
turns out to be a deceptive ruse: before the end, it is back again, but
the requirement that depictions of historical situations be interwoven
with artistic and formal considerations has been established. It becomes
clear that it is the tendency to present time and history in deterministic
terms in the work of the naturalists and some of the realists that is the
target of the anti-historicism of *Aspects of the Novel*. This is what underlies the pejorative treatment of Bennett and Hardy: according to Forster,
there is too much time in *The Old Wives' Tale*, too much 'fate' (external
circumstances triumphant) in the novels of Hardy. Those who take
Forster's reading-room too seriously – finding in it, for instance, a stance
akin to the ahistoricism of New Criticism – have overlooked the fact
that, at the very end of the lectures, there is an important retraction of
the initial position regarding time and history:

> as I look back at my own scraps of knowledge, and into my own
> heart, I see these two movements of the human mind: the great

tedious onrush known as history, and a shy crab-like sideways movement. Both movements have been neglected in these lectures: history because it only carries people on, it is just a train full of passengers; and the crab-like movement because it is too slow and cautious to be visible over our tiny period of two hundred years. So we laid it down as an axiom when we started that human nature is unchangeable, and that it produces in rapid succession prose fictions, which fictions, when they contain 50,000 words or more, are called novels. If we had the power or licence to take a wider view, and survey all human and pre-human activity, we might not conclude like this; the crab-like movement, the shiftings of the passengers, might be visible, and the phrase 'the development of the novel' might cease to be a pseudo-scholarly tag or a technical triviality, and become important, because it implied the development of humanity.   (*AN*: 118–19)

Here the arbitrariness of the anti-historicist position is being admitted. History and time have been neglected, not because they are unimportant, but because they are too important to be treated simplistically, either by novelists or critics. Diachrony is being suspended because it has too often been abused. The hyperbolically synchronic British Museum reading-room is a scenario which violates the 'great tedious onrush known as history' in order to provoke an awareness of how easy it is to do so; similarly, the assertion that 'human nature is unchangeable' draws attention to its converse, to changing perceptions of personality and of the self, as suggested in the comment that 'if the novelist sees himself differently he will see his characters differently, and a new system of lighting will result' (*AN*: 118).

What this indicates is that *Aspects of the Novel* is not only unusual for being that rare thing, an amusing work of literary criticism; it is also a sly text, full of contradictions – as one might suspect, considering that it is written by an influential critic who is, nonetheless, deeply suspicious of the practice of criticism itself.

Percy Lubbock's *The Craft of Fiction* proposes a formalism so extreme that it is not surprising that it was not well received by Forster. Lubbock's contention that '[f]orm, design, composition are to be sought in a novel, as in any other work of art; a novel is the better for possessing them' (Lubbock 1947: 9) is not in itself at odds with Forster's views. However, Lubbock emphasises the formal properties of fiction to such an extent that all other considerations are deemed to be of secondary importance – 'There is nothing more that can usefully be said about a novel until we have fastened upon the question of its making and explored it to some purpose' (272). Towards the beginning of his study, he describes the method of analysis to which he will be subjecting '[a] few familiar novels':

> And I shall consider them . . . with no idea of criticizing all their aspects, or even more than one. How they are made is the only question I shall ask; and though indeed that is a question which incidentally raises a good many others – questions of the intention of the novelist, his choice of a subject, the manner of his imagination, and so forth – these I shall follow no further than I can help.   (12)

It is possible that the title Forster gave to his lectures was, in itself, a response to the limitations upon the work of the critic which Lubbock imposes when he says that he has 'no idea of criticizing all [the chosen novels'] aspects'. Forster's title suggests a desire to broaden the field and methods of investigation where Lubbock seems content to accept narrowness: 'I have chosen the title *Aspects* because it is unscientific and vague, because it leaves us the maximum of freedom' (*AN*: 16). This does not mean that there is no principle of selection operating in Forster's study; the difference is that, unlike Lubbock, Forster expresses in various ways the notion that there is no curtailment, no narrowing of the range of investigation (in other words, no *exclusion*), however inevitable, that does not come at a cost, a recognition which he also explores in fiction – in *Howards End* and, especially, in *A Passage to India*. Where Lubbock makes no apologies for the eclecticism or tendentiousness of his critical method, Forster, as have seen, urges his 'fellow eclectics' to lament their eclecticism; to accept as the most appropriate critical tone the 'drooping regretful voice' of the person who says 'Yes – oh dear yes – the novel tells a story' (17). Forster's critical style is ironic and self-satirising where Lubbock's is declamatory – a difference which says a great deal about their attitudes towards the practice of criticism itself. While Lubbock does not hide the fact that what he seeks amounts almost to a taxonomy of the 'laws of art'

(Lubbock 1947: 10) as applied to the novel, Forster offers what he disingenuously calls a 'ramshackly survey' (*AN*: 54).

The orientation of *The Craft of Fiction* is in many respects strongly anti-realist, as we see in the following putative description of the method of composition of a writer to whose work Forster also devotes attention – Tolstoy. After surveying 'the free and formless expanse of the world of life', Lubbock's Tolstoy goes to work:

> His hand is plunged into the scene, he lifts out of it great fragments, right and left, ragged masses of life torn from their setting; he selects. And upon these trophies he sets to work with the full force of his imagination; he detects their significance, he disengages and throws aside whatever is accidental and meaningless; he re-makes them in conditions that are never known in life . . . he liberates and completes.   (Lubbock 1947: 18)

The loaded word 'selects' takes us back to the dispute between Wells and James and identifies Tolstoy with the latter writer. In an act of extraordinary critical ventriloquism, Lubbock here transforms Tolstoy into Henry James – or, rather, his version of James. Disputing his characterisation of Tolstoy (or, for that matter, Forster's reductive representation of James's methods) is less important than recognising what it says about the relationship between 'life' and 'art' which is being construed. What Lubbock offers unhesitatingly is the triumph of form. He is making available to the modern novelist a version of the High Aestheticism of the 1890s. Within the idea that form can confer freedom and 'completion' lies the implication that what is truly liberating is the power of art to remake the world on its own terms.

What is problematic for Forster (and for many of the other modernists) is not so much the desirability of this, but rather the confident belief that it is possible. Central to modernist fiction are the very difficulties that Lubbock dismisses: the imperative to engage with fragmented and inchoate reality, even if the realist method no longer serves; the knotty and profoundly complex relationship between what is to be represented and the modes of representation; and, in the face of the intractability of the world, the powerlessness (as well as the power) of the word.

This comes across clearly in Forster's essay 'Art for Art's Sake', in which, while he asserts the 'pertinacity' (*TC*: 92) of art and its capacity to bestow order and shape, he modifies significantly the Aestheticist creed which the title of the essay recalls. For Forster, 'Art for Art's Sake' means making art important while recognising (not ignoring) the opposing tendencies of a recalcitrant world:

> Many things, beside art, matter. It is merely one of the things that matter, and high though the claims are that I make for it, I want to keep them in proportion. . . . Man lives, and ought to live, in a complex world, full of conflicting claims, and if we simplified them down into the aesthetic he would be sterilised. Art for art's sake does not mean that only art matters . . .   (87)

The difference between Lubbock's and Forster's perspectives emerges very clearly here: Lubbock values form because, as he sees it, it is able to renounce the 'complex world, full of conflicting claims'; Forster values it because it can be made to serve and represent that very complexity.

Lubbock does not regard form merely as one 'aspect' of the novel, but rather the overarching compositional principle which subsumes all else:

> with the book in this condition of a defined shape, firm of outline, its form shows for what it is indeed – not an attribute, one of many and possibly not the most important, but the book itself, as the form of a statue is the statue itself.   (Lubbock 1947: 24)

For Forster, the form is not 'the book itself'; for him, the formal properties are important, but they are some, not all, of the 'aspects' of the novel. In particular, the 'prophetic' element escapes Lubbock's quest to consider the novel as 'matter to be wrought into a single form' (16). Where Lubbock's comparison of the form of the book to a statue suggests that it is a static entity which is there merely to be apprehended and seen for what it is, Forster's musical analogies, as we shall see, emphasise rather the notion of process.

Another area of disagreement between the two critics concerns the question of point of view in fiction. For Lubbock, the virtue of this aspect of fiction lies not so much in the opportunities it presents for exploring the nature of perception and subjectivity, but in the way in which it can be used to accentuate the formal wholeness of a novel.

A shift in point of view is deemed reprehensible when it detracts from the impression of aesthetic unity, as in his reading of *Vanity Fair*, where he discerns 'an inconclusive look, something that draws the eye away from the book itself' (115). His sense of how point of view ought to operate becomes a yardstick against which novels are measured: *Madame Bovary* is found wanting because '[t]here is nothing more disconcerting in a novel than to *see* the writer changing his part in this way – throwing off the character into which he has been projecting himself and taking a new stand outside and away from the story' (87); *The Awkward Age*, on the other hand, is applauded as 'one novel in which method becomes as consistent and homogenous as it ever may in fiction' (194). Point of view becomes another method of communicating the idea that 'in fiction there can be no appeal to any authority outside the book itself' (62).

In contrast, Forster is open to the possibilities of experimenting with point of view. In a letter to Goldsworthy Lowes Dickinson, written in 1922, Forster describes the difficulties he is experiencing in his writing at the time:

> I am bored not only by my creative impotence, but by the tiresomeness and conventionalities of fiction-form: e.g. the convention that one must view the action through the mind of one of the characters; and say of the others 'perhaps they thought', or at all events adopt their view-point for a moment only. If you can pretend you can get inside one character, why not pretend it about all the characters? I see why. The illusion of life may vanish, and the creator degenerate into the showman. Yet some change of the sort must be made[.] The studied ignorance of novelists grows wearisome. They must drop it.   (In Lago and Furbank 1985: 26)

Forster's objections to rigid conceptions regarding point of view, such as Lubbock's, may be seen as part of a dissatisfaction with realist authorial control, which manifests itself alternatively as omniscience or as 'studied ignorance', which is, of course, another kind of omniscience. It is significant that, in his discussion of point of view in *Aspects of the Novel*, Forster singles out for praise nineteenth- and twentieth-century novels (Dickens's *Bleak House*, Tolstoy's *War and Peace*, Gide's *Les Faux-Monnayeurs*) in which the writer 'bounces' the reader into accepting 'the shiftings of the viewpoint' (*AN*: 55):

[In *War and Peace*] we are bounced up and down Russia – omniscient, semi-omniscient, dramatized here or there as the moment
dictates – and at the end we have accepted it all. Mr Lubbock does
not, it is true: great as he finds the book, he would find it greater if
it had a viewpoint; he feels Tolstoy has not pulled his full weight.
I feel that the rules of the game of writing are not like this. A novelist can shift his viewpoint if it comes off, and it came off with
Dickens and Tolstoy. Indeed this power to expand and contract
perception (of which the shifting viewpoint is a symptom), this
right to intermittent knowledge – I find it one of the great advantages of the novel-form, and it has a parallel in our perception of
life. (56)

Forster's endorsement of flexibility in the matter of point of view is
characteristically modernist in a number of ways: first, in its acceptance
that the subject matter must dictate the method of telling, rather than
having a conventional form of narration imposed upon it; second, in
its suggestion that breaking away from the existing rules of fiction may
lead the novelist towards a more authentic or greater realism – an
instance of 'the forms of modernism discover[ing] that in realism that
realism did not know about itself' (Jackson 1994: 165); and, third, in
the important recognition that experiments in point of view may
reflect mimetically a preoccupation with the workings of consciousness and perception, as well as the 'intermittent knowledge' which so
many modernist writers seek to render.

It is important, also, to situate *Aspects of the Novel* in relation to
Bloomsbury aesthetics and, in particular, the ideas of the art theorists
who were part of the coterie – Roger Fry and Clive Bell. Many of their
ideas can be traced back to G. E. Moore, who established an important
connection between aesthetics and morality: since '[Moore] believes
good taste to be very important to morals, and since the appreciation
of beauty is the most essential constituent of the good that he
describes, a theory of aesthetics is necessary to complete his ethics'
(Johnstone 1954: 46). Moore's definition of 'the Good' establishes
precisely the conjunction of aesthetics and ethics to which Johnstone
refers:

> By far the most valuable things, which we know or can imagine, are
> certain states of consciousness, which may be roughly described as
> the pleasures of human intercourse and the enjoyment of beautiful
> objects.   (G. Moore 1903: 188)

The claims made by Moore on behalf of these 'valuable things' could
not be greater: he sees them as forming 'the rational ultimate end of
human action and the sole criterion of social progress' (189). He is preoccupied with judgements of 'intrinsic value', the advantage of which
lies in the fact that 'they are always true' (166). Forster, as the discussion of liberal-humanism in his work has indicated, interrogates
increasingly the notion that 'the pleasures of human intercourse'
have an intrinsic value; similarly, his later fiction and criticism suggest that aesthetic considerations, too, need to be considered in relation to the contexts which pertain, and which may or may not confer
value upon them. Moore's criterion for assessing intrinsic value is that
things must be good even when they exist 'in absolute isolation'
(187); Forster's concern with 'connection' includes the implication
that nothing exists 'in absolute isolation'. His work (like Virginia
Woolf's) problematises what Moore offers as desirable in absolute
terms; what is more, it presents as a quandary the relationship
between right conduct and aesthetic value which Moore proposes as a
necessary harmony.

Forster recognises that the search for 'pure form' brings an erasing of
'human interests and emotions' (Carey 1992: 80). To admire the formal and compositional aspects of a work of art to the extent that he
does, and yet to draw back from espousing wholeheartedly the consolations it makes available, is another way of avoiding the 'escape
hatches' of art (akin to the movement away from 'romantic realism' in
his later work): an admission that there is too much that is impervious
to private patterns of meaning and resolution for art to be 'pure'.
Instead we find in his later fiction an example of an important characteristic of modernist narrative, the 'equivocal negotiation and testing-
out that for its dynamism depends . . . on the pressure between shaping
and obstacle' (Graham 1988: 204).

In this regard, Forster's views differ markedly from those of Fry and
Bell. In his biography of Goldsworthy Lowes Dickinson, he refers to
Dickinson's reservations about Fry's ideas and those put forward in
The New English Art Club:

[Dickinson] was conceded form, but he was conceded it rather too insistently, and was asked to sacrifice on its rigid altar the one thing for which he did care: subject matter. (*GLD*: 69)

Dickinson 'contradicted the sterile formalism which separated art and life, form and content' (Advani 1984: 107), and, in this regard, Forster's sympathies are entirely with Dickinson. The warning that form can be a 'rigid altar', requiring sacrifices that are too great, is what sets Forster apart from Fry and Bell, who embraced unreservedly the doctrine of 'form':

Form is the talisman. By form the vague, uneasy, and unearthly emotions are transmuted into something definite, logical, and above the earth. (Bell 1947: 283)

'Thou shalt create form' is, according to Bell, the 'first commandment of art' (44). Hence, for all their ostensible iconoclasm, seen in particular in their support for Post-Impressionist art, the theories of Bell and Fry also reveal a conservative High Aestheticist belief in the Religion of Art. This is evident also in their quest for artistic 'purity':

All art depends upon cutting off the practical responses to sensations of ordinary life, thereby setting free a pure and as it were disembodied functioning of the spirit; but in so far as the artist relies on the associated ideas of the objects which he represents, his work is not completely free and pure, since romantic associations imply at least an imagined practical activity. The disadvantage of such an art of associated ideas is that its effect really depends on what we bring with us: it adds no entirely new factor to our experience. (Fry 1920: 242)

Fry and Bell 'celebrate the decline of art's traditional illustrative or iconic function' (Harrison 1994: 59); the 'purity' they seek thus extends also to a rejection of art that 'aim[s] at representation' or pursues 'fidelity to appearance' (Fry 1920: 11) – in other words, realistic art. In this, as in most other matters, Bell's position is more extreme than Fry's:

The representative element in a work of art may or may not be harmful; always it is irrelevant. For, to appreciate a work of art we need bring with us nothing from life, no knowledge of its ideas and affairs, no familiarity with its emotions. Art transports us from the world of man's activity to a world of aesthetic exaltation.

(Bell 1947: 25)

Hence, '[e]very sacrifice made to representation is something stolen from art' (44). Not surprisingly, Bell's objections to representational art include a distaste for realism and naturalism in fiction, suggested by his declaration that 'with all their gifts, neither Zola, nor Edmond de Goncourt, nor Mr Arnold Bennett ever produced a work of art' (Bell 1922: 47).

Fry suggests that the successful artist is one who has 'ben[t] to our emotional understanding by means of his passionate conviction some intractable material which is alien to the spirit' (Fry 1920: 302). But for Forster, especially in *A Passage to India*, as well as for many of the other modernist writers, there is much 'intractable material which is alien to the spirit' and which remains thus, despite all efforts to transform it.

In addition, modernist fiction tends to present moral complexity – it is seldom amoral, and Forster's work, in particular, is never so. Fry's ideas about form lead him, as one may have predicted, to view the 'correct' artistic response as essentially amoral – an attitude which also links him to the High Aestheticism of the 1890s:

Art . . . is an expression and a stimulus of [the] imaginative life, which is separated from actual life by the absence of responsive action. Now this responsive action implies in actual life moral responsibility. In art we have no such moral responsibility – it presents a life freed from the binding necessities of our actual existence. (Fry 1920: 20–1)

In Bell's comments on this subject, the voice of G. E. Moore may be heard:

Art is above morals. . . . Once we have judged a thing a work of art, we have judged it ethically of the first importance and put it beyond the reach of the moralist.   (Bell 1947: 20)

The result is that art is removed to a rarefied sphere where it is invested with universal significance: considering an object 'as an end in itself' makes us aware of 'its essential reality, of the God in everything, of the universal in the particular, of the all-pervading rhythm', as opposed to 'its accidental and conditioned importance' (69). In contrast, Forster's refusal to see a work of art solely 'as an end in itself' brings a preoccupation with the very qualities which Bell seeks to expunge – the particular in the universal, the fitful and episodic (rather than the 'all-pervading') rhythm, the contingent and the 'accidental'.

In *Principia Ethica*, Moore devotes a great deal of attention to the idea of organic wholes or unities, something which was also taken up by the Bloomsbury art theorists. For Moore, the term 'organic' implies that 'a whole has an intrinsic value different in amount from the sum of the values of its parts' (Moore 1903: 36). Fry's comments about the quest for unity suggest that, for him, it has to do with the desire to ensure that the work of art is autotelic:

> unity of some kind is necessary for our restful contemplation of the work of art as a whole, since if it lacks unity we cannot contemplate it in its entirety, but we shall pass outside it to other things necessary to contemplate its unity.   (Fry 1920: 31)

Fry claims that 'art has . . . turned its vision inwards' (14), and his concern with order and unity reflects the belief that 'the rhythms of life and of art . . . are distinct' (10). In Forster's later work, by contrast, there is a refusal to submit to the idea that art should turn 'its vision inwards', or that the reader should be placed in a state of 'restful contemplation'; instead there is a compulsion to make the form of the novel convey the recognition that the 'rhythms of life and art' are *not* distinct, but, instead, are interwoven in complex and often unpredictable ways.

Forster also differs from Bell and Fry in that he does not conceive of a direct relationship between the formal aspects of a work of art and the response of the reader, auditor or spectator. This is the subject of his essays 'Not Listening to Music' and 'Not Looking at Pictures', and it is explored in the intricate speculations about the reception and appreciation of art in Chapter V of *Howards End*. The Bloomsbury art theorists' notions of 'significant form' and 'aesthetic emotion' do, however, posit an intrinsic connection between what the work of art is and how it may be received:

lines and colours combined in a particular way, certain forms and relations of forms, stir our aesthetic emotions. These relations and combinations of lines and colours, these aesthetically moving forms, I call 'Significant Form'.   (Bell 1947: 8)

In 'Not Looking at Pictures', Forster treats ironically his own undisciplined and unmethodical response to paintings:

in galleries so many of us go off at once into a laugh or a sigh or an amorous day-dream. In vain does the picture recall us. 'What have your obsessions got to do with me?' it complains. 'I am neither a theatre of varieties nor a spring-mattress, but paint. Look at my paint.' Back we go . . . and resume the looking business. But something is sure to intervene . . . and to draw us away.

(*TC*: 127)

The description of his amateurish response to the paintings, the flippant tone notwithstanding, violates several of the premises underlying the idea of 'significant form' and 'aesthetic emotion': in particular, the idea that the formal composition of the painting will elicit the 'correct' response and that it will remove the spectator from mundane preoccupations. Instead, the act of interpretation, as presented by Forster, is fluid, subjective, unpredictable, and inseparable from a sense of the vagaries of everyday life.

———

Benjamin Britten describes Forster as 'our most musical novelist' (Britten 1969: 81); it is not possible to consider his contribution to the debate about form in fiction without considering also his interest in music. Forster accepts – as does Roger Fry – the Paterian notion of music as the 'purest' of the arts: it is 'the deepest of the arts and deep beneath the arts' (*TC*: 105). However, in his responses to music, and even more in his use of musical analogies and structures as applied to fiction, there is evident once more an ambivalent attitude to form, which is related to an important dualism in Forster's work:

The problem of whether art can redeem life by transcending it is crucial to modernism. . . . Forster's view is, like that of most modernism, dualistic: art may reach beyond the world of men and things – the world of 'story' – but it can never leave that world behind, and must seek meanings and connections in it.

(Bradbury 1969: 129)

Although Forster shares the Bloomsbury predilection for the inter-mingling of ideas and techniques drawn from different art forms, his choice of music rather than painting or sculpture as the most suitable analogy for the ways in which fiction may be constructed and read suggests, in itself, a distrust of the extreme formalism of the Bloomsbury art theorists: unlike a painting or a sculpture, a novel or a piece of music cannot be considered as a contained entity; the arrangement of harmonious interrelationships becomes far more difficult to determine where these interrelating elements are not simultaneously apprehensible. Responding to music or to a work of fiction of necessity involves taking account of the movement over time, of process. Forster was not alone amongst contemporary literary critics in considering such issues – we find Muir, too, comparing the different art forms in seeking to isolate the distinguishing characteristics of the novel:

> The annihilation of time in the statue and of space in music has in reality the effect of making both absolute. The plastic artist, concentrated on his spatial image and on that alone, attains a state which we justifiably call timeless; the processes of time have stopped for him, or have become irrelevant.   (Muir 1928: 90)

This leads Muir, like Forster, to a view of fiction as the least 'absolute' or 'pure' of all the arts:

> Both [plastic art and music] are more unmixed than the art of imaginative literature, and very much more so than the novel, which is the most complex and formless of all its divisions.   (89)

Forster's analysis of music is, however, much more intricate than Muir's. The symbolists and the Bloomsbury art theorists regard music as the most autonomous of all the arts because, from their perspective, its 'purity' is not compromised by extensive reference to phenomena beyond itself – musical form is 'pure art with a tremendous significance of its own and no relation whatever to the significance of life' (Bell 1947: 31). This is a view which Forster sometimes echoes, as in his assertion that 'music which is untrammelled and untainted by reference is obviously the best sort of music to listen to; we get nearer the centre of reality' (*TC*: 124); at other times, it is the extent to which music can express the conflicting impulses towards completeness and incompleteness which he values, for music, 'more than the other arts, postulates a double existence. It exists in time, and also exists outside time, instantaneously' (*TC*: 116). In any case, the 'purity' of music must necessarily elude even the most 'musical' of novelists, for language can never be 'untrammelled and untainted by reference' – the 'pure expressiveness of music' may only be conveyed through 'linguistic equivocation' (Aronson 1980: 22).

The ambivalence of Forster's attitude to music lies in his 'waver[ing] between two reasons for [the] exalted status of music':

> Sometimes he held the view that it was the form or the order of the art, as indeed believed Roger Fry. At other times he also seemed to want to attribute music's power to something that reminded him of something else, or even to something ineffable, almost mystical in it. The formal and the impressionistic impulses seem to be at war in Forster.   (Hutcheon 1982: 85)

Forster treats these apparently contradictory impulses in himself ironically in 'Not Listening to Music', where he writes that he hears 'two sorts' of music: 'They melt into each other all the time, and are not easy to christen, but I will call one of them "music that reminds me of something", and the other "music itself"' (*TC*: 122). The first response – which he calls 'wool-gathering' (124) – involves responding to the music imagistically; thereby 'transform[ing] even music into a representational art form' (Hutcheon 1982: 89). What is not clear in 'Not Listening to Music' is whether the 'wool-gathering' is solely a response on the part of the listener, or whether it is called for by the properties of the music itself. It seems to be a combination of the two, for Wagner is described as writing music in which the phrases 'ordain' certain meanings, while Forster goes on to say 'I accepted his leitmotiv system much too reverently and forced it on to other composers whom it did not suit, such as Beethoven and Franck' (123).

The mention of Beethoven immediately calls to mind the description of the concert in Chapter V of *Howards End*, which is, among other things, a deliberation upon the question of structure and referentiality in art, reflecting in part, as we have seen, upon the composition of the novel itself. The chapter also refers implicitly back to *Principia Ethica* and to the debate about ways of responding to a work of art – it is interesting to note that Moore, too, is concerned with this very symphony and how one ought to appreciate it:

> What value should we attribute to the proper emotion excited by hearing Beethoven's Fifth Symphony, if that emotion were entirely unaccompanied by any consciousness, either of the notes, or of the melodic and harmonic relations between them?   (Moore 1903: 192)

The Schlegel sisters embody the two approaches identified in 'Not Listening to Music': Helen is an incorrigible 'wool-gatherer'; Margaret, 'who can only see the music' (*HE*: 29), represents what Forster calls listening to 'music itself'. Helen's response is a type of imaginative synaesthesia and is presented with gentle irony; yet, significantly, it is described at length, whereas we are told no more at this stage of Margaret's response, for, it seems, there can be no satisfactory linguistic depiction of her ability to see only the music. Neither attitude is endorsed unequivocally by Forster – one could say, to apply the terms used in *Aspects of the Novel*, that Helen is being 'impressive' and Margaret is being 'truthful'. Margaret's response to the music implies the belief that the work of art can exist without referents, and it is not surprising, therefore, that she can contribute nothing at this stage to our understanding of the structure of the novel. If the 'intermingling' of the arts as practised by Bloomsbury – the idea that the arts can be 'enriched by taking in one another's washing' (*TC*: 123) – is being parodied in Helen's response, the insistent formalism of the Bloomsbury art theorists is being parodied in Margaret's, and even more in Tibby's, for Tibby is 'profoundly versed in counterpoint, and holds the full score open on his knee' (*HE*: 29); '[he] implored the company generally to look out for the transitional passage on the drum' (30). Margaret criticises Helen's response shortly afterwards, in conversation with Leonard Bast:

> 'What *is* the good of the arts if they're interchangeable? What *is* the good of the ear if it tells you the same as the eye? Helen's one aim is to translate tunes into the language of painting, and pictures into the language of music. . . . Now, this very symphony that we've just

been having – she won't let it alone. She labels it with meanings from start to finish; turns it into literature. I wonder if the day will ever return when music will be treated as music.'   (36)

Here Margaret mocks Helen's tendency to transform music into 'the language of painting'; later, in conversation with the guests at the luncheon party given in Mrs Wilcox's honour, she satirises the obverse of this – her sister's conversion of a visual spectacle (a view of the Oder) into 'the language of music':

'The course of the Oder is to be like music. It's obliged to remind her of a symphonic poem. The part by the landing-stage is in B minor, if I remember rightly, but lower down things get extremely mixed. There is a slodgy theme in several keys at once, meaning mud-banks, and another for the navigable canal, and the exit into the Baltic is in C sharp major, pianissimo.'   (72)

Margaret's response is the rational one, but that is also its limitation. As she moves closer to an appreciation of the 'unseen', concretised by her occupation of Howards End, there is increasingly the suggestion that there are connections that can only be achieved by moving beyond rationality, whether her own liberal-humanist version of it, or the unimaginative responses of Mr Wilcox, which assume the status of rationality. Margaret's attempt to divorce art from the attribution of mimesis is, ironically, not unlike Leonard's idea that the Schlegels are 'pictures that must not walk out of their frames' (120). In both cases, there is a failure to recognise that art and culture are not hermetically sealed categories; that they are constituted by, and in turn underpin, social categories and divisions. Fry's distinction between 'actual life' and 'imaginative life' is undercut, for, in ways in which even Helen does not understand, her fantastical synaesthesia comments upon the incidents and symbolic undercurrents of the novel itself: it is she who sees, not only 'heroes and shipwrecks in the music's flood' (29), but also the profoundly unnerving goblins with their message of 'Panic and emptiness! Panic and emptiness!' (31).

Helen's response has its own hazards, however, for her desire to 'label' the music with meanings may lead to an interpretative fixedness which the music itself does not invite – suggested by her thoughts as she leaves the concert:

The music had summed up to her all that had happened or could happen in her career. She read it as a tangible statement, which could never be superseded. The notes meant this and that to her, and they could have no other meaning, and life could have no other meaning.   (32)

There is therefore a rigidity to her 'wool-gathering', for, whereas Tibby excludes referents completely, Helen fixes her referents too arbitrarily and uncompromisingly. The complacent assumption of meaning is shown to be as exclusive as a rigid formalism: both close off instead of opening out. Part of the problem is that Helen hears the romanticism in the music as well as that which is inimical to romanticism (namely the goblins), but she carries away with her only the romanticism. Another way of interpreting her response would be to say that she responds as a romantic to what, in its suggestiveness and interpretative fluidity, is an essentially *symbolist* experience. The implication seems to be that Beethoven, in 1910, must be heard with symbolist, not romantic, ears.

Britten, however, sees Forster's musical preferences as entirely romantic:

Forster prefers music based on striking themes, dramatic happenings, and strong immediate moods, rather than on classical control and balance, beautiful melodies and perfection of detail . . . he prefers the Romantic to the Classical. And why shouldn't he? – he was brought up musically at the end of the nineteenth century. (Britten 1969: 85)

Although he goes on to concede that this may be 'an overstatement' (85), his emphasis remains exclusively upon the romantic elements in Forster's responses to music. This has validity in relation to the use of music in the earlier, pre-modernist works; it is with regard to the later works that its limitations become apparent.

In the novels and short stories written before *Howards End*, music is frequently associated with latent or undiscerned romantic possibilities. This is evident in the description of the performance of *Lucia di Lammermoor* in *Where Angels Fear to Tread*, and of Lucy Honeychurch's piano playing in *A Room with a View*. Lucy, well on her way to making a catastrophically wrong choice, plays Schumann instead of Beethoven at

Mrs Vyse's London flat. Her choice and the quality of the music reflect on her rejection of George and her decision to marry Cecil:

> 'Now some Beethoven,' called Cecil, when the querulous beauty of the music had died. She shook her head and played Schumann again. The melody rose, unprofitably magical. It broke; it was resumed broken, not marching once from the cradle to the grave. The sadness of the incomplete – the sadness that is often Life, but should never be Art – throbbed in its disjected phrases, and made the nerves of the audience throb.   (*RV*: 121)

Here the emphasis is on the completion Art is believed to afford, and the 'Art'/'Life' dichotomy is boldly maintained. This is consistent with the movement towards completion and closure which the novel follows as a whole, and which, as the discussion in Chapter 2 has indicated, is expressed in particular in the formality of the comic mode. The sense of completion is not wholly undisturbed, for there are unexpected and unsettling reversals in the behaviour of both Mr Beebe and Miss Bartlett that hint at the incalculability of human motivation, and that undermine the moral presumptions which the ending of the novel may seem at first to support; nevertheless, the passage describing Lucy's playing affirms that art must function as an alleviation of the 'brokenness' of life. Beethoven, it is here implied, provides both the formal wholeness of art and the romantic possibilities that Lucy denies herself if she does not escape from Cecil and his world. But this is not what Forster has Beethoven offer in *Howards End*: there the suggestion is that art, however complete and whole, must also express something of the inevitable 'brokenness' of existence.

In the short story 'Co-ordination', Beethoven features once more in order to provide the suggestion that true 'co-ordination' lies in the unfettering of the spirit, and may be heard in the sounds of a shell wherein Miss Haddon hears the freedom of the sea and the rapport of the waves. 'Melody and Victory' (*CS*: 178) come together, just as Beethoven and Napoleon are associated with one another: they are both conquerors. But there is no victory suggested by the melody of Beethoven in *Howards End*, only the temporary vanquishing of the goblins, who threaten to return.

Another way of articulating this is to suggest that, in Forster's earlier works, it is the *characters* who are challenged by the music, which is in keeping with the humanistic values proposed in these works; thereafter, it is increasingly the *novels themselves* that are shaped and tested by music.

In contrast to Britten, Linda Hutcheon discerns in Forster's responses to music a manifestation of a wider dualism which she describes as 'a two-way pull between an interest in objective form and a concern for subjective responses [that] is reminiscent of the struggle between classicism and romanticism' (Hutcheon 1982: 96). This emerges clearly in what Forster calls 'rhythm', which, as a critical concept and a fictional method, works against 'formal relations' (89), even as it constructs and utilises them. 'Rhythm' is one way in which Forster introduces the idea that aesthetic form is a type of order, but that it is only *one* type of order; that it cannot be regarded as presupposing other kinds; and that, if others do exist, there is no necessary correlative relationship between them. This is essentially where the pejorative distinction Forster makes between 'pattern' and 'rhythm' lies, for 'pattern', as he conceives it, betokens an extreme formalism, one which does not make provision for or intimate the formlessness onto which it has been imposed. James's *The Ambassadors* – which Forster regards as 'pattern triumphant' (*AN*: 104) – is seen as suffering from this kind of attenuation, for '[a] pattern must emerge, and anything that emerged from the pattern must be pruned off as wanton distraction' (110). Significantly, 'pattern' is visual, not musical – Forster associates it with shapes that are fixed, and therefore seen as inflexible:

> It is this question of the rigid pattern: hour-glass or grand chain or converging lines of the cathedral or diverging lines of the catherine wheel, or bed of Procrustes – whatever image you like as long as it implies unity. Can it be combined with the immense richness of material which life provides? (112)

'Rhythm', on the other hand, is 'a technical resistance *against* too much ordering' (Bradbury 1970: 22); a way of seeking containment without 'castrating' (*AN*: 111) the characters in order to achieve 'a particular aesthetic effect which is certainly gained, but at this heavy price' (111). 'Rhythm' is offered by Forster in contrast to formal structures that are imposed from without: it 'lessens our need of an external form' (115). Proust's *À la Recherche du Temps Perdu* is presented as a work which makes substantial use of 'rhythmical' devices: it is 'chaotic, ill-constructed, it has and will have no shape; and yet it hangs together because it is stitched internally, because it contains rhythms' (113).

Forster distinguishes between two types of 'rhythm'. The 'easy' type, which is described as 'repetition plus variation' (115), depends for its effectiveness upon its irregularity and subtlety – in contrast to the extreme inflexibility implied by the Bed of Procrustes, this type of 'rhythm' is presented as flexible and formalistically discreet. Forster sees it as having been used with great success in *À la Recherche du Temps Perdu*, where the 'little phrase' in the music of Vinteuil 'crosses the book again and again, but as an echo, a memory; we like to encounter it, but it has no binding power' (114). The 'little phrase' develops 'a life of its own' (115), and, by 'stitching Proust's book together from the inside' (115), it contributes significantly towards our eventual sense that 'the book, which seemed as we read it so rambling, has an architectural unity and pre-ordained form' (*TC*: 216). Proust's use of the 'little phrase' thus illustrates 'the function of rhythm in fiction [which is] not to be there all the time like a pattern, but by its lovely waxing and waning to fill us with surprise and freshness and hope' (*AN*: 115).

The shifting and widening significations imbued by the 'rhythmical' recurrences distinguish this type of 'rhythm' from the *leitmotifs* in Forster's earlier fiction. 'Rhythm' is symbolist in its assumption that referentiality and meaning are elusive, but it most pointedly does not provide 'symbols' in the debased sense of a circumscribed range of correspondences – the distinction which E. K. Brown makes between the 'fixed symbol', which is 'almost entirely repetition' and the 'expanding symbol' which is 'repetition balanced by variation, and that variation . . . in progressively deepening disclosure' (Brown 1950: 56–7) captures something of the idea of ever-widening reference. The entire effect is lost if 'rhythm' becomes crudely representational: 'Done badly, rhythm is most boring, it hardens into a symbol, and instead of carrying us on it trips us up' (*AN*: 115).

'Rhythm' involves the contrived repetition of words and phrases – it is 'a sophisticated analogue of *déjà vu*' (Kermode 1966: 55). When words and phrases are used 'rhythmically', they accrue meaning through their changing contexts, but they also require of those contexts that they be considered in the light of previous circumstances and associations. They suggest the need for contingent rather than essential truths. Assumptions regarding the attribution of significance constantly require reworking as a result of these changing contexts, and the reader is forced to cede his or her prior expectations and engage with the text as an interlacing of its own referential systems. The implication is that the attribution of meaning is a process, one that gains fluidity and expansiveness because of the associations which the words bear with them. This sense of language as encoding memory and yet indicating that memory will not suffice – since new contexts bring new shades of meaning – is a crucial aspect of the modernist perception that meaning cannot simply be received, but must always be remade; that it must continually be wrested from sound and silence.

The purpose of Forster's use of 'rhythm' is to 'keep the contingent ... in a state of dissonance with the structured' (Graham 1988: 156). Its effect is thus double-edged:

> [Repetition can suggest] the presence of form in the universe; and can also satisfy the harmony-hunger, the form-seeking, of the reader. But ... repetition also undercuts by reminding that in a universe of echoes nothing is new, and therefore nothing is redeemed; and that the symmetries of art, equally, can be an imprisoning imposition and a delusion. (200)

This can be seen very clearly in *A Passage to India*, where each 'echo' not only draws attention to what it communicates itself, but also to the echoing principle at work in the novel as a whole. All echoes, too, refer forwards and backwards to the Caves, from which they cannot be dissociated. Hence, the Caves can never be obliterated or left behind: even when their immediate impact seems to have subsided, the echoing patterns built into the novel suggest that, like Helen's goblins, they could return. There is indeed the suggestion that 'nothing is redeemed'; nothing can be dispensed with or excluded from future consideration. This is not the case in the earlier, premodernist fiction: whenever the violets in *A Room with a View* or the smuts in Harriet's eye in *Where Angels Fear to Tread* reappear, they take us back to their initial romantic or unromantic significance; they do not signify something subtly different each time they recur, thereby implying that the past can neither be discarded nor recaptured intact.

The type of oscillation which 'rhythm' establishes subverts the apparent linearity of the narrative; at the same time, it accommodates 'eternal moments' and other intimations of a different level of experience, including 'prophecy'. 'Rhythm', used in this way, invigorates the narrative, making prose less prosaic and assisting the novelist in what Forster regards as his or her most important task – to 'reveal the hidden life at its source' (*AN*: 31).

The second type of 'rhythm' is the 'difficult' type, which Forster describes by means of a symphonic analogy:

> Is there any effect in novels comparable to the effect of the Fifth Symphony as a whole, where, when the orchestra stops, we hear something that has never actually been played? The opening movement, the andante, and the trio-scherzo-trio-finale-trio-finale that composes the third block, all enter the mind at once, and extend one another into a common entity. This common entity, this new thing, is the symphony as a whole, and it has been achieved mainly (though not entirely) by the relation between the three big blocks of sound which the orchestra has been playing. I am calling this relation 'rhythmic'.   (*AN*: 115–16)

This is the 'rhythm' of wholes, incorporating that of parts. The discussion, later in this chapter, of the sonata-like structure of *A Passage to India* will indicate how this type of 'rhythm' functions. It is process at its most extensive, yet it also moves *beyond* process, so that the work of art is made and being made at the same time. In the essay 'The Raison d'Être of Criticism in the Arts', Forster describes its effect:

> I can conceive myself hearing a piece [of music] as it goes by and also when it has finished. In the latter case I should hear it as an entity, as a piece of sound-architecture, not as a sound-sequence, not as something divisible into bars. Yet it would be organically connected with the concert-hall performance.
>
> (*TC*: 116)

The conflation of the spatial and the temporal in the notion of 'sound-architecture' constitutes an attempt to unite the aural and the visual, the moving and the static. The fact that it eludes most novelists is not surprising; Forster concedes that he cannot find 'any analogy to it in fiction' (*AN*: 116), although he wonders whether there may be 'something of it in *War and Peace?*' (116).

The symbolist quality of 'rhythm' as Forster perceives it emerges more strongly when one considers how much it has in common with the symbolists' views on the importance of rhythm in poetry, as expressed, for instance, in Mallarmé's 'Crisis in Verse':

> The structure of a book of verse must arise throughout from internal necessity . . . a subject will imply inevitably the harmony of the parts brought together and, since every sound has an echo, their corresponding locations in the volume.   (Mallarmé 1980: 8)

The fluidity of the rhythmic devices is also emphasised by Mallarmé:

> everything will be fluid, the arrangement of parts, their alternation and interruption by blank spaces, and will yield a total rhythmic movement, the silent poem itself, translated in its own way by each unit of the structure.   (8–9)

It is precisely for its capacity to include 'silence' and 'blank spaces' within a formal structure that 'rhythm' is commended by Forster. Its elusiveness reflects the mind's capacity to grasp only fleetingly the significance of that which confronts it. In Yeats's 'The Symbolism of Poetry', the effect described is very similar:

> The purpose of rhythm . . . is to prolong the moment of contemplation, the moment when we are both asleep and awake, which is the one moment of creation, by hushing us with an alluring monotony, while it holds us waking by variety, to keep us in that state of perhaps real trance, in which the mind liberated from the pressure of the will is unfolded in symbols.   (Yeats 1969: 159)

Through the liberation of the mind 'from the pressure of the will', the apprehension of the non-rational experience – of 'prophecy' – is made possible. As Kandinsky says, repetition 'will not only tend to intensify the inner harmony but also bring to light unsuspected spiritual properties of the word itself' (Lavin 1995: 143). From that perspective, 'prophecy' and the more 'difficult' type of 'rhythm' reach a point of convergence: rather than being examples of formalism and anti-formalism respectively, of 'the impressionistic and the structural' (Hutcheon 1982: 96) in Forster's critical thinking, the 'rhythm'/'prophecy' division is actually indicative of the *blurring* of formalist lines, for the broadest and most difficult type of 'rhythm' is a formal device transporting itself to an evocation of that which lies beyond form.

Although, as suggested, *Aspects of the Novel* is too idiosyncratic to serve as a comprehensive introduction to the novel in general, it is an extremely useful guide to one novel in particular: *A Passage to India*. Although Forster's own work is never mentioned in *Aspects of the Novel*, it may be argued that the only novel which it truly elucidates or justifies critically is *A Passage to India*. Most of the 'aspects' discussed appear in that novel; whether this leads to 'conciliat[ion]' (*AN*: 73) or not remains to be seen.

From the perspective of the writers and critics who favour 'selection' rather than 'saturation' – and Forster is, in a qualified way, one of them – the attempt to write a truly 'inclusive' novel is doomed to failure: a work that attempts to include everything in an undifferentiated way cannot be aesthetically impressive; one that is aesthetically immaculate must, of necessity, have excluded a great deal of material. *A Passage to India* deals in many ways with the implications of failure, including the failure of the British Raj, of friendship, of attempts to achieve 'connection' in general; and it is also an exploration of its own failure, of the impossibility, as it were, of escaping the curse of the eclectic. But, as Mrs Moore says, 'there are so many kinds of failure' (*PI*: 70).

What we find, consequently, is that where an 'aspect' of the novel is employed in *A Passage to India*, it tends to be pushed to the limit: the 'story', for instance, is engrossing, but there are lacunae in it which may disappoint or frustrate the reader; the 'people' are among the most vivid and memorable ever created by Forster, yet, as we have seen, the rationalistic ones end up feeling baffled and the non-rationalistic ones tend to be baffling. India becomes the site where the techniques of novel writing, as designated by Forster, are subjected to the same intense scrutiny as the other codes or traditions which are investigated. There is a sense in which India as subject matter proves too demanding for even the most ingenious of methods:

I have always felt that the most interesting thing about *A Passage to India* is Forster's using India to represent material that according to the canons of the novel form cannot in fact be represented – vastness, incomprehensible creeds, secret motions, histories, and social forms. (Said 1994: 241)

Characters such as Aziz, Adela and Mrs Moore are haunted by the episode at the Caves; beyond that, the entire novel is haunted by the constant presence of failure – its form by the prospect of formlessness and chaos, its very words by the possibility of their collapse into nothingness or the obverse of the meanings they customarily communicate.

Where 'rhythm' is concerned, it is clear that the novel is constructed by means of both the 'easy' and 'difficult' types. In the case of the former, the 'rhythmical' repetitions invite a reflection upon the capacities and limitations of language itself. Just as spirituality and benevolence are 'nothing' in the Caves, whereas they are ambiguously efficacious elsewhere, so, too, is language 'nothing' in the Caves, but tenuously meaningful outside of them. As we have seen, making language itself function as a 'rhythmic' device underscores the arbitrariness of presumptions of meaning, for, as words and phrases are 'rhythmically' repeated, signification becomes more diffuse. The tendency for words to break free of their original referents may be manipulated for political or chauvinistic purposes: for the Anglo-Indian community, for example, the National Anthem – the 'meagre tune, the curt series of demands on Jehovah' – is 'fused into a prayer unknown in England' (47), while the phrase 'women and children' becomes so dislocated from its referential context that it becomes a 'phrase that exempts the male from sanity when it has been repeated a few times' (190–1).

Mrs Moore's much-discussed wasp is an example of the use of the 'easy' kind. Its smallness and ostensibly negligible status are in contrast to its thematic and structural importance, which is another way of suggesting that inclusion is sometimes as simple as not *overlooking* what seems at first to be insignificant. The wasp is also used to pay tribute implicitly to an aspect of Hinduism that Forster admires, namely its respect for life in all its manifestations. The first appearance of the wasp suggests that Mrs Moore shares this pantheistic sense of the divinity of all life: ' "Pretty dear", said Mrs Moore to the wasp' (55).

The wasp itself demonstrates a complete disregard for the demarcations and categories to which most of the colonials are so attached:

> Perhaps he mistook the peg for a branch – no Indian animal has any sense of an interior. Bats, rats, birds, insects will as soon nest inside a house as out; it is to them a normal growth of the eternal jungle, which alternately produces houses trees, houses trees. (55)

When it reappears, it features in the novel's satirical treatment of the divisions and exclusions which Forster discerns in Christianity, a religion which (except for Mrs Moore's non-doctrinaire variety) is shown to reinforce the Anglo-Indians' attempts to circumscribe, label and exclude. Shortly after the wasp is first mentioned, old Mr Graysford and young Mr Sorley, the Chandrapore missionaries, discuss whether or not animals may be admitted to heaven:

> All invitations must proceed from heaven perhaps; perhaps it is futile for men to initiate their own unity, they do but widen the gulfs between them by the attempt. So at all events thought old Mr Graysford and young Mr Sorley, the devoted missionaries who lived out beyond the slaughter-houses, always travelled third on the railways, and never came up to the Club. In our Father's house are many mansions, they taught, and there alone will the incompatible multitudes of mankind be welcomed and soothed. Not one shall be turned away by the servants on that veranda, be he black or white, not one shall be kept standing who approaches with a loving heart. And why should the divine hospitality cease here? Consider, with all reverence, the monkeys. May there not be a mansion for the monkeys also? Old Mr Graysford said No, but young Mr Sorley, who was advanced, said Yes; he saw no reason why monkeys should not have their collateral share of bliss, and he had sympathetic discussions about them with his Hindu friends. And the jackals? Jackals were indeed less to Mr Sorley's mind, but he admitted that the mercy of God, being infinite, may well embrace all mammals. And the wasps? He became uneasy during the descent to wasps, and was apt to change the conversation. And oranges, cactuses, crystals and mud? And the bacteria inside Mr Sorley? No, no, this is going too far. We must exclude someone from our gathering, or we shall be left with nothing. (58)

Here the wasp is being used to satirise the notion that unity may be achieved through exclusion and the presumption of hierarchies of significance. The 'rhythmic' recurrence of the insect suggests, in itself, that the novel is not prepared to endorse the forms of exclusion satirised here. The wasp had been associated with jackals on its first appearance – 'There he clung, asleep, while jackals in the plain bayed their desires and mingled with the percussion of the drums' (55) – and the continued association here implies a refusal to partake of the exclusions practised by Mr Sorley, who will accept jackals into heaven, but deny wasps entry. What the 'rhythmic' recurrence of the wasp seems to promise is that the novel will itself make 'many mansions' available; that it will enact a near-cosmic capaciousness and inclusiveness, granting small creatures their importance, permitting 'men to initiate their own unity' (as suggested by the friendships across racial barriers that develop in the 'Mosque' section), distancing itself firmly from the gross discourtesy shown to Aziz, who is summoned by the Civil Surgeon, only to be 'turned away by the servants on [the] veranda'.

When the wasp appears once more, in the 'Temple' section, it is in the context of the collapse of that promise, and we see how the changing contexts which 'rhythm' relies upon compel the reader to recognise that the attribution of significance can only be provisional, subject to constant re-evaluation. Professor Godbole is caught up in the religious ecstasy of the Gokul Ashtami festival:

They loved all men, the whole universe, and scraps of their past, tiny splinters of detail, emerged for a moment to melt into the universal warmth. Thus Godbole, though she was not important to him, remembered an old woman he had met in Chandrapore days. Chance brought her into his mind while it was in this heated state, he did not select her, she happened to occur among the throng of soliciting images, a tiny splinter, and he impelled her by his spiritual force to that place where completeness can be found. Completeness, not reconstruction. His senses grew thinner, he remembered a wasp seen he forgot where, perhaps on a stone. He loved the wasp equally, he impelled it likewise, he was imitating God. And the stone where the wasp clung – could he . . . no, he could not, he had been wrong to attempt the stone, logic and conscious effort had seduced, he came back to the strip of red carpet and discovered that he was dancing upon it. (283–4)

Here we are made to revise whatever we have come to believe of the significance of the wasp, for, whereas it was associated with the demerits of exclusion upon its earlier appearances, here it is part of an inclusion that suffers limitations of its own. Godbole is able to love the wasp, but he is defeated by the stone. The wasp had seemed the most extreme representation of everything that is difficult to embrace in the world; but now we see that there are challenges that go beyond the wasp. Loving the wasp has seemed the ultimate test; now we find that it is not enough. Selection as a principle of exclusion – particularly relevant in terms of the debate about form – is ignored by Godbole: significantly, he does not 'select' the images of Mrs Moore and the wasp, they merely 'occur' to him; and yet the stone obtrudes amidst the 'universal warmth', and the implication is that there is something that refuses all human efforts to include, just as the final passage of the novel suggests that something larger than political differences opposes human efforts to unite. There is something intractable at the very heart of the 'universal warmth'. The promise of infinite accommodation, of 'many mansions', has been thwarted at the very moment when it seemed most likely to be fulfilled.

The stone which Godbole cannot love has its own 'rhythmic' associations, and takes us back to the Marabar Caves, which, if we had been reading the novel as a realist work, we would have expected to have left behind, since realist novels tend to construe and then resolve intrigue and dilemmas. Now we see that nothing is left behind: just as the Marabar came in the way of the commendable desire to deepen friendship, so the stone prevents Godbole from loving everything in creation. Significantly, Forster mentions stones in his discussion of Neo-Platonism and the philosophy of Plotinus:

> Not only do all things flow from God; they also strive to return to him; in other words, the whole Universe has an inclination towards good. We are all parts of God, even the stones, though we cannot realise it; and man's goal is to become actually, as he is potentially, divine.   (*A*: 59)

From this Idealist perspective, stones are included in the divinity of all creation. In *A Passage to India*, however, the stone is associated – before Godbole's attempt to love it – with the inevitable limitations of love and compassion:

How indeed is it possible for one human being to be sorry for all the sadness that meets him on the face of the earth, for the pain that is endured not only by men, but by animals and plants, *and perhaps by the stones*? The soul is tired in a moment, and in fear of losing the little she does understand she retreats to the permanent lines which habit or chance have dictated, and suffers there.

(*PI*: 247; my italics)

From deprecating hierarchies of sympathy and exclusions based on the notion that some creatures are more important than others, the narrative voice has moved to a position where it urges the necessity of such discriminations. Compassion is too scarce a commodity to be diffused; selection is not only a matter of aesthetic preference, but the corollary to every benevolent impulse.

References to snakes and worms also function 'rhythmically' in the novel. The initial mention of snakes seems to reinforce the Judeo-Christian connotations of evil as a postlapsarian inheritance: Mrs Moore is told by Aziz that she ought not to walk alone at night, for there 'are bad characters about and leopards may come across from the Marabar Hills. Snakes also' (43). Mrs Moore exclaims, for 'she had forgotten the snakes' (43). It is not surprising that she should do so, for her version of Christianity has no element in it of Original Sin or the innate depravity of humankind. Even at this early stage, an association is made between snakes and the Marabar Caves.

On the way to the Caves, Adela thinks she sees a black cobra; Aziz and the villagers agree, but, upon looking at it through Ronny's field-glasses, Adela decides that it is the stump of a toddy-palm. The others insist that it is a snake, however, and the narrative voice seems to side with Adela in her rational response:

The villagers contradicted her. She had put the word into their minds, and they refused to abandon it. Aziz admitted that it looked like a tree through the glasses, but insisted that it was a black cobra really, and improvised some rubbish about protective mimicry. (152–3)

However, the empiricist orientation implied in the desire to identify and label is precisely what is confounded at the Marabar Caves. There are snakes, of a kind, in the Caves, and the 'bad characters' Mrs Moore was warned to avoid, but they appear in so unexpected a guise, that

Judeo-Christian morality itself, with its reliance upon attributions of evil and good, of guilt and innocence, is called into question.

At the Caves, snakes and worms are associated with Mrs Moore's feelings of nullity and the assault upon her benevolent Christian impulses. In that nadir of pessimism, transcendentalism and spirituality, romantic or otherwise, are denied, and language is rendered meaningless. In contrast to the echoing principle in the novel as a whole, which elsewhere is associated with the proliferation of significance, the echo in the Caves insidiously denies all meaning:

> Even the striking of a match starts a little worm coiling, which is too small to complete a circle, but is eternally watchful. And if several people talk at once an overlapping howling noise begins, echoes generate echoes, and the cave is stuffed with a snake composed of small snakes, which writhe independently.   (159)

In *Aspects of the Novel*, 'story' is described as the 'chopped-off length of the tapeworm of time' (*AN*: 59), but here, in contrast, there is nothing finite about the worms and snakes; nor is the worm able to complete its circle and take its tail in its mouth in order to suggest completion and infinity. Notions of time-as-sequence and time-as-infinity are simultaneously denied, and 'echoes generate echoes' not in order to achieve a multivocal plenitude, which the method of the novel had seemed to be working towards, but merely to add nothingness to nothingness.

All teleological conceptions of the universe are confounded at the Marabar, which is why the expedition proves disastrous to Adela Quested, with her rationalist liberal-humanist inclinations, and to Mrs Moore, with her belief in the providential shape of the universe. The hopes that they cherish are disappointed, which is unsettling; but these same aspirations also turn on them and become the converse of what they had seemed to promise, which is devastating: Adela, who had been thinking of sexual love, accuses Aziz of an act that could not lie further from that ideal – attempted rape; and Mrs Moore, who had proclaimed the brotherhood and sisterhood of humankind, turns, after the expedition, to a sour misanthropy. In the 'Mosque' section, Mrs Moore had felt briefly a 'sudden sense of unity, of kinship with the heavenly bodies' (51), but in the echo in the Marabar she hears '[s]omething very old and very small. Before time, it was before space also. Something snub-nosed, incapable of generosity – the undying worm itself' (212), and in the hollowness of her 'vision' she sees that '[t]he abyss may also be petty, the serpent of eternity made of maggots' (213). The Judeo-Christian tradition promises the eternal life of the soul after the death of the body; but the message Mrs Moore receives is of the putrefaction of the spirit itself; a corruption at the very heart of metaphysics.

In the 'Temple' section, the snake becomes a 'cobra of papier-mâché' (285): during the Gokul Ashtami festival, the distinction between the natural and the artificial is elided, suggesting, once more, the presence of God in all things. Just as the 'red silk napkin' carried by Professor Godbole 'was God, not that it was. . . . It was just a napkin, folded into a shape which indicated a baby's' (285), so the snake is 'real' and 'artificial' at the same time. The narrative voice which had seemed to sympathise with Adela's insistence that a 'real' snake is not the same as one falsely identified as such, now seems prepared to accept a different kind of authenticity as almost everything is transformed and made part of the religious euphoria:

> All sorrow was annihilated, not only for Indians, but for foreigners, birds, caves, railways, and the stars; all became joy, all laughter; there had never been disease nor doubt, misunderstanding, cruelty, fear. (285)

Birds, caves, railways and stars all have 'rhythmic' associations of their own, which means that they are not to be discarded; even as the Gokul Ashtami festival purges them of their negative associations, the conclusion to the novel makes it clear that sorrow is never 'annihilated' – at best, it goes into abeyance.

Finally, after all the threats of snakes, wrongly identified snakes, and artificial snakes, a 'real' snake does appear. When the festival has ended, Aziz and Fielding go for their last ride together, and they see a cobra:

> Presently the ground opened into full sunlight and they saw a grassy slope bright with butterflies, also a cobra, which crawled across doing nothing in particular, and disappeared among some custard-apple trees. . . . They drew rein, to give the cobra elbow-room, and Aziz produced a letter that he wanted to send to Miss Quested. (311)

The 'real' reptile is in no way threatening; in fact, it is part of a pastoral setting that seems, ironically, to restore it to a prelapsarian innocence. Once more the cobra and Adela Quested appear in association, but now the emphasis is on the amelioration of the events in the Marabar through the forgiveness of Aziz. The association of the snake with forgiveness seems to take even the unpredictability of 'rhythm' to astonishing lengths; and yet it is not surprising that the 'real' snake should seem so innocuous, for, throughout the novel, the explicit, identified threat has been the least dangerous of all.

At times the narrative voice takes over a phrase initially used by one of the characters: an example of this is the recurrence of an observation made by Fielding in a comment offered by the narrator in a different context. After the trial, Fielding, in conversation with Adela, discusses the after-life with calm lucidity:

> it is difficult, as we get on in life, to resist the supernatural. I've felt it coming on me myself. I still jog on without it, but what a temptation, at forty-five, to pretend that the dead live again; one's own dead; no one else's matter.   (241)

Neither of them knows that Mrs Moore is dead; the reader does not know it either. Adela responds: 'Because the dead don't live again' (241).

Shortly afterwards, Fielding learns of Mrs Moore's death from Ronny Heaslop. The narrative voice describes the unimpassioned response of Fielding and Hamidullah to this news:

> They both regretted the death, but they were middle-aged men, who had invested their emotions elsewhere, and outbursts of grief could not be expected from them over a slight acquaintance. *It's only one's own dead who matter.*   (247; my italics)

Earlier, the remark was an example of the rationalism of Fielding, whose speech was described as being succeeded by 'a moment's silence, such as often follows the triumph of rationalism' (241). But when it recurs here, it does so as an ironic comment on the limitations of that creed. The observation that '[i]t's only one's own dead who matter' had seemed thoroughly sensible, suggesting that the individual's personal interactions must be more important to him or her than a generalised interest in humankind. But here the bathetic note and the comment that the men 'had invested their emotions elsewhere' imply that the 'personal relations' creed is, in its own way, exclusionary. Professor Godbole, to whom Mrs Moore is also 'a slight acquaintance' is, nonetheless, able to love her when she comes to mind during the Gokul Ashtami festival; Aziz continues to love her, although there is no rational basis for doing so; and her transformation into 'Esmiss Esmoor' during the trial makes her everyone's dead, as it were. She 'matters' greatly, but only when the cold logic and emotional conservatism of Fielding's stance are superseded.

This is borne out by the fact that Mrs Moore, like Ruth Wilcox before her, is able to 'survive' death, and to persist as a spiritual force. Even Fielding feels that 'people are not really dead until they are felt to be dead. As long as there is some misunderstanding about them, they possess a sort of immortality' (254). At the end of *The Hill of Devi*, Forster, with the death of the Maharajah of Dewas Senior in mind, makes an observation about the dead and their effect on the living which seems pertinent in this context too:

> One of the puzzling things about the dead is that it is impossible to think of them evenly. They all go out of sight and are forgotten, they all go into silence, yet we cannot help assigning them a tune. (*HD*: 113)

After her death, Mrs Moore becomes even more than a 'tune' – as 'Esmiss Esmoor', she becomes an incantation. What is more, she is transformed into a 'rhythmical' presence herself, appearing in the most unexpected contexts, such as in the mind of a devotee at a Hindu festival, far away from Chandrapore. Her 'immortality' cannot be explicated rationally; it is a 'misunderstanding' of the most profound kind.

The use of 'rhythm' ensures that the final sentence of *A Passage to India* is both climactic and anti-climactic. Whatever deflating communications it offers with regard to the friendship between Aziz and Fielding, it is also 'rhythmically' crescendo-like. Throughout the novel, the expectation of climax has been undercut: most notably the 'detective story' element of the plot has never been granted the steady movement towards identification and explication which the genre traditionally offers. India itself is presented as resistant to climax and closure, as suggested by the narrative voice in its description of the immersion in the waters of the Tank:

> That was the climax, as far as India admits of one. . . . Looking back at the great blur of the last twenty-four hours, no man could say where was the emotional centre of it, any more than he could locate the heart of a cloud.   (310)

The refusal of climax is true even of Forster's syntax. His description of the kind of sentence favoured, even in conversation, by the Alexandrian poet C. P. Cavafy bears upon the intricate structure of some of his own sentences:

> an immense complicated yet shapely sentence, full of parentheses that never get mixed and of reservations that really do reserve; a sentence that moves with logic to its foreseen end, yet to an end that is always more vivid and thrilling than one foresaw . . . it . . . stands at a slight angle to the universe: it is the sentence of a poet. (*PP*: 91–2)

This is praise indeed, for Forster, as he indicates in 'A Book that Influenced Me' – Samuel Butler's *Erewhon* – favours *indirection*:

> I have the sort of mind which likes to be taken unawares. The frontal full-dress presentation of an opinion often repels me, but if it be insidiously slipped in sidewise I may receive it, and Butler is a master of the oblique.   (*TC*: 214)

The final sentence of *A Passage to India* 'rhythmically' recalls the major sources of conflict and division in the novel:

> 'Why can't we be friends now?' said the other, holding him affectionately. 'It's what I want. It's what you want.'
> But the horses didn't want it – they swerved apart; the earth didn't want it, sending up rocks through which riders must pass single-file; the temples, the tank, the jail, the palace, the birds, the carrion, the Guest House, that came into view as they issued from the gap and saw Mau beneath: they didn't want it, they said in their hundred voices, 'No, not yet', and the sky said, 'No, not there'.   (316)

The rocks bring to mind the intransigent stones we have come across in the course of the narrative, as well as the Marabar Caves, suggesting once more that the Caves and all that they represent can never be 'left behind', and that one of the effects of the cyclical movements and echoes by means of which the novel is constructed is that they continually draw one back to the Marabar. The jail recalls Aziz's imprisonment (and thus the injustices perpetrated against him) even as he has finally found it in his heart to forgive Adela and recognise her courage. The reference to birds, ostensibly insignificant or connotatively neutral, draws the reader back to the bird Adela and Ronny could not name, and thus to all the unanswered questions which remain, even at the end of the novel. The very words of denial remind one of all the negations that have filled the novel from the first sentence. All that is fashioned by humankind and everything impervious to humankind seem to conspire here to make two friends who sought connection ride 'single-file'.

But, at the same time, there is a profound sense of linguistic 'connection' in this last sentence: whereas Aziz and Fielding have come together in order to be separated irrevocably, the words that describe their separation come together 'rhythmically' with great impact:

> Not a word has arrived in [the final sentence] untested. All have been explored throughout the fiction and have earned their place in this final, albeit paradoxical, description of landscape rendered audible.   (Herz 1985: 70)

Here, too, words have drifted from their initial contexts. A few pages earlier, Ralph Moore answers '[n]ot yet' when Aziz says '[b]ut you are Heaslop's brother also, and alas, the two nations cannot be friends' (306): the words as spoken by Ralph may suggest an optimistic belief that nations and the people who belong to them may become 'friends' when political injustices have been resolved. Now, by giving those very words to the 'hundred voices' that repudiate the friendship, that hope is denied: there are divisions that lie beyond the political.

While the phrases 'not yet' and 'not there' seem to anticipate a reconciliation in an undefined and possibly unknowable future, the 'rhythmical' associations point to the past, and seem themselves to deny the hope of escaping the cycle which they both represent and enact. Yet the symbolist quality of 'rhythm' makes the unattainable itself the 'here' and 'now' of the quest: like the 'emblems of passage' thrown into the water as part of the Gokul Ashtami celebration – 'a passage not easy, not now, not here, not to be apprehended except when it is unattainable' (309) – the final words that seem to unite in denial are themselves emblems of passage towards a silence that is never here and never now. Like Cavafy's sentence, Forster's too contains 'reservations that really do reserve'; it moves the ending of the novel away from closure and completion, shifting it into the realm of provisionality. It, too, stands 'at a slight angle to the universe'. Where most traditional narratives move towards the conclusion of a quest, this one implies that the journey is only beginning; where most convey either a sense of having come to terms with things as they are, or a suggestion that change is unavoidable, the last words of this novel communicate both the persistence of present circumstances, and an apocalyptic intimation of a fundamental change that cannot at this stage be grasped.

A Passage to India also makes use of the 'difficult' type of 'rhythm' described in *Aspects of the Novel*. In his discussion of Woolf's *To the Lighthouse*, Forster writes:

> *To the Lighthouse* is in three movements. It has been called a novel in sonata form, and certainly the slow central section, conveying the passage of time, does demand a musical analogy.   (*TC*: 243)

The same 'sonata form' which he discerns in Woolf's novel is clearly being utilised in *A Passage to India*. The structure of both novels is analogous to a three-movement sonata, involving an exposition, a development and a recapitulation:

> In the exposition section, the thematic material is exposed; in the development section, it is handled in new and unsuspected ways; in the recapitulation, it is heard again in its original setting.
>
> (Copland 1967: 115)

The physical setting of the 'Temple' section is, of course, not the same as the 'Mosque' section, but it does bring a series of 'returns', including the reunion of Aziz and Fielding, and, in the encounter between Aziz and

Ralph Moore, a near-repetition of the original 'eternal moment' constituted by the meeting between the former and Mrs Moore in the mosque.
The relative optimism of the 'Mosque' section corresponds to the traditional use of the sonata-allegro form, which has an 'affirmative quality'
(Copland 1967: 116). Although Forster sees the 'Time Passes' episode in
To the Lighthouse as 'slow', which is in keeping with the development section of the sonata, this cannot really be said of the middle section of his
own novel, except in the sense of the stultifying lethargy which the hot
weather brings; however, it certainly brings 'new and unsuspected' elements, and an emphatic retreat from the affirmativeness of the first section. In the third and final section we feel distinctly that sense of arrival
and return (but with variations) which characterises the recapitulation;
like the sonata, the progression of the narrative in *A Passage to India* is
cyclical as well as linear, so that the final impression is of circularity and
resumption, as well as of a movement forward.

   The sonata form is particularly well suited to the modernist crisis:

> The novelist's increasing awareness of polarity in the life of the indi-
> vidual and the social antagonism with which he is faced appeared
> most forcefully reflected in the sonata form with its play upon con-
> tradictory emotional pressures and tensions, its tendency towards
> introspective self-analysis and its striving for resolution. Both the
> twentieth-century novel and the sonata are founded on a dialect-
> ical structure: the greater the emphasis on individual alienation,
> the more evident will be the social antagonism out of which such
> inner division grows.   (Aronson 1980: 67)

Provided that one qualifies the phrase 'twentieth-century novel' as
referring more specifically to the modernist novel, this explication of
the dialectical structure of the novel/sonata is valuable, for it suggests
once more the modernist quest to negotiate continually with form
rather than to yield to it; to 'strive for resolution' and to withdraw
from it simultaneously. Using a structure of this sort constitutes an
attempt to find a fictional equivalent for 'the architecture of
Question and Answer' (87) – a form which will accommodate and further the idea of dialectic. Forster's predilection for musical structures
that communicate dialectical relationships is evident in his interpretation of the music of Hugo Wolf, which he discusses in the context of
what he regards as a lamentable dichotomy in contemporary life, a

'profound division between our private and our public outlook' (*PT*: 287):

> In many musicians (Schubert for instance) the piano accompanies the voice, in others it echoes the voice (e.g. Schumann's 'Nussbaum'), in others it alternates. Wolf alone seems able to create two independent and continuous streams of music, whose true relation is not revealed until the close.   (*PT*: 289–90)

From this perspective, Wolf's music resembles the more difficult type of 'rhythm': it too conveys the impression that there is no relationship between the component parts, the 'independent and continuous streams of music', only to reveal retrospectively a profound but oblique connection, a 'true relation'.

In *A Passage to India*, the 'three big blocks of sound' represent also the shape of the weather cycle in India: the 'Mosque' section corresponds to the cool or good weather; the 'Caves' section to the hot or bad weather; and the 'Temple' section to the monsoons, which break the terrible heat and renew the cycle. We are warned not to disregard the importance of the weather in India – ironically, the warning is given by Ronny Heaslop, who says '[t]here's nothing in India but the weather, my dear mother; it's the alpha and omega of the whole affair' (*PI*: 68). The idea of weather as destiny is implicitly confirmed by the fact that the novel's structure corresponds to that cycle, and to the movement in the three sections from affirmation to negation to a tentative and qualified reaffirmation. But the weather is a cycle without beginning and end – it is not an 'alpha and omega', and Ronny's phrase betrays once more the Western reliance upon linearity.

The Longest Journey also has a three-part structure, but what is lacking in that novel is precisely the dialectical structure that Aronson describes. The Cambridge – Sawston – Wiltshire progression does constitute a movement from what is positive to what is negative and then to a qualified return to the positive, but the dialectical implications are absent because there is nothing that is offered in opposition to that movement: there is no sense in which Sawston remains as a threat to the characters in the novel, for Rickie has been 'converted' before his death, and Stephen has always been beyond its influence. When Cambridge and the agrarian idyll come together in the rather curious alliance between Stephen and Ansell, this is a resolution which has triumphed over the Cambridge/Sawston antinomy. There is nothing resembling the extraordinary ambivalence of Aziz when he realises that the initial encounter with Mrs Moore is being replicated in his meeting with her son:

> 'Then you are an Oriental.' He unclasped as he spoke, with a little shudder. Those words – he had said them to Mrs Moore in the mosque at the beginning of the cycle, from which, after so much suffering, he had got free. Never be friends with the English! Mosque, caves, mosque, caves. And here he was starting again. (306)

Although the monsoons and the Gokul Ashtami festival both suggest the cyclical possibilities of rebirth and renewal, Aziz sees here that the cycles also constitute a form of imprisonment: 'rhythm' grants solace in that it may bring back what has been lost; but, as we have seen, it may also bring back what has been repressed or wished away. It is both a recovery and an imposition. Finding Mrs Moore again, as it were, brings back also the context of British rule in which the friendship developed. At the very beginning of the novel, Aziz and his friends debated 'whether or no it is possible to be friends with an Englishman' (33); now, by moving to the Hindu state of Mau, Aziz has asserted the impossibility of such a friendship – 'Never be friends with the English!' – only to find the resurgence, in one way or another, of his friendship with two English people, Mrs Moore and Fielding. 'Rhythm' and the cyclical movement of the novel have forced him to reopen what he had considered closed; they have compelled him to retain as a contingent possibility what he had rejected as an emphatic impossibility.

The tripartite structure of *A Passage to India* may also be seen as replicating the shape of a formal elegy. Peter Knox-Shaw has related the form of *To the Lighthouse* to the tripartite structure of the traditional pastoral elegy, and his observations may be applied with equal validity to *A Passage to India*:

> Basically, each of the three parts of *To the Lighthouse* corresponds to an essential feature of [elegy]. This becomes evident when we reflect that the elegist has, as a rule, three functions to perform: he

offers a life of the departed; he records the impact of death; he returns to the present, finally, with renewed affirmation.

(Knox-Shaw 1986: 33)

The elegy thus refuses, finally, the tragic note, for '[w]here tragedy presents, metaphorically speaking, the "darkening slope" towards death, the ascent from death is the concern of elegy . . . [it] ends by offering consolation' (32). Reading *A Passage to India* as an elegy enables one to see its structural intricacy in a different light: it becomes apparent that Forster's experiments with form express a sense of loss and dissolution, but also the impulse towards recovery and 'consolation'. Tragedy would bring too great a severance with what went before; so would a conventional ending which gave all the answers and resolved the intrigue. Elegy is the appropriate mode for 'a child of unbelief' (*AH*: 98), as Forster describes himself in an essay on Proust, to whom, significantly, he ascribes a similar avoidance of tragedy:

> He was too great an artist to indulge in the facile jiggle of a Dance of Death. . . . Avoiding tragic horror, which perhaps he mistrusted, and pity, which he could seldom supply, he has achieved a new view of the impermanence of the human race . . .   (*AH*: 96)

Between 'tragic horror' and 'pity', between despair and proscription, lies an awareness of 'impermanence' and conditionality; it is this awareness that the form of Forster's novel and its elegiac overtones communicate.

In contrast to the formal properties of the sonata, the novel offers also a type of music which seems to communicate (to the ear of someone who is not a Hindu) the kind of inscrutability which 'prophecy' conveys – Professor Godbole's song:

> At times there seemed rhythm, at times there was the illusion of a Western melody. But the ear, baffled repeatedly, soon lost any clue, and wandered in a maze of noises, none harsh or unpleasant, none intelligible. It was the song of an unknown bird. . . . The sounds continued and ceased after a few moments as casually as they had begun – apparently halfway through a bar, and upon the subdominant.   (*PI*: 95)

This song satisfies none of the Western expectations regarding aesthetic form: it is without a clearly delineated beginning and end, it attains no climaxes, and it seems to promise the consolations of rhythm and 'Western melody', only to disappoint the expectations that it invites. The difficulty experienced by someone unaccustomed to this kind of music is expressed by Forster in a letter to Florence Barger, in which he describes his ambivalent response to the singing parties at the Palace of the Maharajah of Dewas Senior:

> our singing parties at the Palace are only a debauch to the superficial observer. But there is much verbal and histrionic indecency which amused me at first, not now, because I see that it takes the place of so much that I value. I am afraid that Indian singing is doomed for this reason, because all the reformers and westernizers will have none of it. And it is, or has been, a great art.   (*HD*: 75)

The kind of music performed by Godbole has 'no definable beginning, middle, or end, [it is] ignorant of the relative validity of minor or major scales . . . – a music the best description of which would be one that claims the formlessness of infinity as its sole characteristic feature' (Aronson 1980: 145); it is 'essentially nondramatic since it expresses a sense of unity with a universal Being rather than the emotional conflicts of a composer or performer' (147). The music is, so to speak, its own hope and its own disappointment: that is why Krishna's refusal to come is not seen as a failure of vision or religious observance, but as another version of the interdependence of 'absence' and 'presence'.

Roland Barthes has described tonality as 'the fundamental code of the West' (Barthes 1977: 152), and it is the absence of tonality in Professor Godbole's song that estranges the Western listeners, for there is conventionally neither form nor romanticism in Western music without tonality. It is described as 'the song of an unknown bird', and it is not very long after this that Adela and Ronny come across the bird that they are unable to identify: the implication is that the song gives expression to those experiences and spiritual dimensions which elude the Western perspective. Significantly, Godbole's song is succeeded by a moment of untrammelled silence: 'Ronny's steps had died away, and there was a moment of absolute silence. No ripple disturbed the water, no leaf stirred' (96). The nature of this silence is, of necessity, difficult to determine: is it the silence which lies 'beyond the remotest echo', the apprehension of which was unsettling to Mrs Moore; or is it 'a revival of some primeval musical chaos' (Aronson 1980: 145), something not beyond form, but antecedent to it? All one can say for certain is that it is not the 'moment's silence, such as often follows the triumph of rationalism' (241) which succeeds Fielding's remark later in the novel. The bafflement of the English visitors points to the limitations of a response that cannot appreciate fully the sound of a bird that has not been identified. The strangeness of Godbole's song to Anglo-Indian and Muslim ears is related also to the fact that it is a musical enactment of the Hindu belief in polytheism, the 'polytheistic "maze" of Hindu worship, Hindu art, and Hindu mythology' (Aronson 1980: 147). Consequently, it finds its expression in the 'hundred mouths' (149) of India, whereas monotheistic beliefs and Western perspectives are confounded by so many voices, particularly when they seem to say different things.

The importance of 'prophecy' in the novel is also evident in the centrality of the novel's 'prophetic' characters, who play an even larger role than, for instance, Mrs Wilcox or Miss Avery do in *Howards End*. In keeping with Forster's notion that 'prophecy' lies 'outside words' (*AN*: 95), some of the 'prophetic' characters are noticeably non-verbal. Two of them – Stella and the punkah-wallah – never speak at all, while the others tend either to be laconic, or, as in the case of Godbole, cryptic and baffling in their utterances. Not surprisingly, they frequently succeed in intimating far more than they actually say: Adela, for instance, imagines that Mrs Moore had spoken the words 'Dr Aziz never did it', although she admits that it was the 'idea more than the words' (*PI*: 209). This comes when Mrs Moore is herself hostile to language, as a result of the harsh treatment of 'poor little talkative Christianity' (161) at the Marabar, and her recognition of the linguistic underpinnings of the beliefs that have now been soured:

> 'Say, say, say', said the old lady bitterly. 'As if anything can be said! I have spent my life in saying or in listening to sayings; I have listened too much. It is time I was left in peace.'   (205)

Her attitude here, after she has been established in the novel as a well-intentioned representative of a type of romantic Christianity, reflects critically upon the indispensability of the *logos* in Western thinking. Mrs Moore only 'speaks' to Adela by means of that which she does not actually 'say', just as it is only after she withdraws into misanthropy and then physically absents herself, that she is able to be transformed into 'Esmiss Esmoor'.

The 'prophetic' figure of the punkah-wallah subverts the trial and what it represents, extending the overt satire of Anglo-Indian justice to a satire of ratiocination itself. The legal procedures cannot unravel the incident at the Caves and prove patently inadequate; the 'prophetic', on the other hand, without resolving the inexplicable, succeeds somehow in communicating Aziz's innocence to Adela. In a mysterious – and certainly non-rational – way, the figure of the punkah-wallah and the transformation of Mrs Moore into 'Esmiss Esmoor' combine to transport Adela to a recognition that she herself does not begin to understand: her response becomes something distinct and separate from herself – '[s]moothly the voice in the distance proceeded, leading along the paths of truth, and the airs from the punkah behind her wafted her on . . . ' (230).

Amidst all the efforts to assign guilt and innocence – not only within the procedures of the court, but also within the novel's satirical treatment of British justice, which also amounts to a form of attributing guilt and innocence – the punkah-wallah sits, wholly detached and indifferent. He is an obvious contrast to Mr Das, the Assistant Magistrate, who is 'cultivated, self-conscious and conscientious' (221):

> [the punkah-wallah] scarcely knew that he existed and did not understand why the court was fuller than usual, indeed he did not know that it was fuller than usual, didn't even know he worked a fan, though he thought he pulled a rope. Something in his aloofness impressed the girl from middle-class England, and rebuked the narrowness of her sufferings. In virtue of what had she collected this roomful of people together? Her particular brand of opinions, and the suburban Jehovah who sanctified them – by what right did they claim so much importance in the world, and assume the title of civilization?   (221)

So unaware is he of even the most rudimentary kind of causality that he fails to see the connection between the pulling of the rope and the working of the punkah; his is that quality of seeing 'beyond cause and effect' (*AN*: 94) which is one of the characteristics of 'prophecy'. A part of humanity, he is yet apart from it; simultaneously an

'Untouchable' and a 'beautiful naked god' (*PI*: 233). (His status as an 'Untouchable' reflects upon the paradoxes within Hinduism, which sees all life as expressing the divine, finds unity in polytheistic multiplicity, and yet divides society rigidly into castes.) The punkah-wallah is imbued with symbolic significance to such an extent that the action of working the punkah – it cannot be coincidental that it must be worked *rhythmically* – becomes analogous to the irruption of 'prophecy' itself within the narrative:

> Pulling the rope towards him, relaxing it rhythmically, sending swirls of air over others, receiving none himself, he seemed apart from human destinies, a male Fate, a winnower of souls. (221)

As Adela sees the trip to the Marabar in a different light, she is herself granted, if only temporarily, the status of 'prophetic' aloofness, of being subject to time and yet free of it:

> She didn't think what had happened, or even remember in the ordinary way of memory, but she returned to the Marabar Hills, and spoke from them across a sort of darkness to Mr McBryde. The fatal day recurred, in every detail, but now she was of it and not of it at the same time, and this double relation gave it indescribable splendour. Why had she thought the expedition 'dull'? Now the sun rose again, the elephant waited, the pale masses of the rock flowed round her and presented the first cave; she entered, and a match was reflected in the polished walls – all beautiful and significant, though she had been blind to it at the time. (230)

She is remembering 'rhythmically', and thus not in the 'ordinary way of memory'. That the past itself has been changed in the process, and has been given a romantic hue that was wholly lacking before, emphasises the subjectivity of memory. Adela's romanticised perception of the expedition nevertheless leads to her recantation and the acquittal of Aziz: the implication is that the 'paths of truth' do not need to originate in an objective account or factual evidence. Instead, it is the attempt to impose a rational or empirical explanation of the events in the Caves that is presented as the distorting activity. The dissatisfaction with intentionality which one can trace back to Forster's earliest work culminates in the punkah-wallah: while others, in seeking to do good, have induced catastrophe, he is efficacious without the slightest desire to be so.

In withdrawing the charge, '[s]omething that she did not understand took hold of [Adela] and pulled her through. Though the vision was over, and she had returned to the insipidity of the world, she remembered what she had learned' (232). As we have seen, when the romantic was longed for and sought after – during the Marabar expedition – it conspicuously failed to appear. Now, when it is least expected, when Adela is expected to be most rational and intellectually lucid, she has a vision, a pragmatically *useful* one, which enables her to see the situation completely differently before she is returned to 'the insipidity of the world'. Whereas Mrs Moore is oppressed, even destroyed, by 'the twilight of the double vision' (212), the 'double relation' that Adela achieves somehow liberates her from the 'narrowness of her sufferings'. Here, too, one sees the characteristic modernist aversion to essentialist notions of truth: doubleness is not a good or bad thing in itself, but needs to be considered in the specific context in which it occurs.

The most extensive deliberation upon form in *A Passage to India* comes at the end of 'Caves' and the beginning of 'Temple', and includes once more the contrast between the East (specifically Hinduism) and the West as an aspect of that deliberation. It appears, significantly, between the two versions of 'chaos' depicted in the novel – the Marabar Caves and their denial of value, and the Gokul Ashtami festival, which Forster describes as 'represent[ing] the same thing as the scene in the cave, "turned inside out" ' (Wilde 1964: 151). The one is a chaos which reduces everything to nothing, the other a fructifying chaos that strives to attain the unity of everything. In the 'Mosque' section, exclusion was heavily satirised; in the 'Temple' section, by contrast, there is the suggestion that 'total inclusion is perhaps only another name for chaos' (Wilde 1964: 131). Both versions of formlessness are, as has been suggested, contained within an elaborate formal structure that is designed to express containment without denying the impact of the formlessness. It is a formidable task, and Chapters XXXII and XXXIII, straddling the second and third sections, comment upon the task, the level of success, and the implications thereof.

In *A Passage to India*, humankind seems 'to have reached not maturity but exhaustion' (Rosecrance 1982: 237), and it is with the relief born of his exhaustion, aesthetic and humanistic, that Fielding responds to the beauty of the Mediterranean as, on his return journey to England, he passes through Egypt and Crete and reaches Venice:

> As he landed on the Piazzetta a cup of beauty was lifted to his lips, and he drank with a sense of disloyalty. The buildings of Venice, like the mountains of Crete and the fields of Egypt, stood in the right place, whereas in poor India everything was placed wrong. He had forgotten the beauty of form among idol temples and lumpy hills; indeed, without form, how can there be beauty? Form stammered here and there in a mosque, became rigid through nervousness even, but oh, these Italian churches!. . . . In the old undergraduate days he had wrapped himself up in the many-coloured blanket of St Mark's, but something more precious than mosaics and marbles was offered to him now: the harmony between the works of man and the earth that upholds them, the civilization that has escaped muddle, the spirit in a reasonable form, with flesh and blood subsisting.   (*PI*: 277–8)

The phrase 'the spirit in a reasonable form' is crucial, for it combines the two aspects of the Western legacy of which Fielding is the best representative – the liberal-humanist quality of 'reasonableness', and the capacity for aesthetic appreciation, the ability to respond to 'form'. The Gokul Ashtami festival, on the other hand, is described almost immediately afterwards, in a particularly effective instance of 'repetition plus variation' (*AN*: 115), as a violation of both of these, 'a frustration of reason and form' (*PI*: 282). Whereas the Indian landscape is shown to be inimical to form and recalcitrant in the face of attempts to view it aesthetically, Fielding finds in Egypt and Crete and Venice a harmony so complete that, instead of the customary situation whereby form is imposed upon what is natural or inherently formless, in this case the formal impulse seems almost to have called the natural into being. There is what every romantic and every aesthete has sought: a 'harmony between the works of man and the earth that upholds them'. The 'works of man' occupy a place of importance that implies a heightened regard, Renaissance-like, for human accomplishment. It is no wonder that Fielding should find it so comforting, considering the difficulties encountered by his humanism in India.

Romanticism and form as significant human consolations had seemed to be lost after the expedition to the Marabar, but the message that Mrs Moore receives as she leaves India is of consequence to the reader too, reminding him or her that if one strives for the inclusiveness which comes from admitting many different voices, one must be prepared for the possibility that the voices may offer divergent, even irreconcilable perspectives:

> As she drove through the huge city which the West has built and abandoned with a gesture of despair, she longed to stop . . . and disentangle the hundred Indias that passed each other in its streets. The feet of the horses moved her on, and presently the boat sailed and thousands of cocoanut palms appeared all round the anchorage and climbed the hills to wave her farewell. 'So you thought an echo was India; you took the Marabar Caves as final?' they laughed. 'What have we in common with them, or they with Asirgarh? Goodbye!' (214)

The fact that there are a 'hundred Indias' with a 'hundred mouths' (149) had, prior to this, seemed entirely disconcerting in its implications – suggesting only irresolution, ambiguity and contradictory messages. But now the existence of the 'hundred mouths' assumes a different aspect, for the logic of such overwhelming multivocality must also mean that negativity and despair cannot have the last word; there should always be the possibility of a return to optimism and renewal, however guarded. There are no 'final' voices when language and meaning themselves have become provisional. Mrs Moore is rebuked for taking 'the Marabar Caves as final'; for allowing the negativity she experienced there to lead her into despair and misanthropy.

The reader who, like Mrs Moore, regarded the message of the Marabar as final, would be surprised to find the 'Caves' section being concluded thus:

> The Mediterranean is the human norm. When men leave that exquisite lake, whether through the Bosphorus or the Pillars of Hercules, they approach the monstrous and extraordinary; and the southern exit leads to the strangest experience of all. Turning his back on it yet again, [Fielding] took the train northward, and tender romantic

fancies that he thought were dead for ever flowered when he saw the buttercups and daisies of June.   (278)

The return in Fielding of 'tender romantic fancies that he thought were dead for ever' is the equivalent of Mrs Moore's belated understanding that the Marabar, however devastating, represents merely one of the 'hundred Indias'. After Grasmere and what it represents were so emphatically crushed at the Marabar, the resilience now of the delicate 'buttercups and daisies of June' of English romanticism makes one appreciate how the novel's determination not to permit anything to be discarded or left behind extends also to its most vulnerable occidental affiliations.

Fielding's response is less surprising than the apparently sympathetic wistfulness of the narrator. After the attempts on the part of the narrative voice to partake of other perspectives and thus to free itself of its limitations, the sentence '[t]he Mediterranean is the human norm' is startling, to say the least. For whom is it the 'human norm'? The claim smacks of cultural superiority, of the very tendency to universalise specific cultural experiences and expectations which was presented as reprehensible in, for instance, the behaviour of Adela. The narrative voice, in sharing Fielding's relief, seems to have become reactionary in its posture of cultural defensiveness, and in what it imputes to that which is culturally remote, suggesting that what is unfamiliar must be 'monstrous and extraordinary'. It has become the embodiment of the very attitudes which it satirised earlier in the novel; and, more than anything else, it is the solace and delights of form (and the threat of being deprived of them) which have provoked this surprisingly tenacious cultural loyalty.

It is not merely an instance of the narrative voice reneging upon its own implicit authority, of which the ultimate 'treachery' is the discovery that it too does not seem to know what truly occurred in the Caves. There is also the sense that the narrative voice is assessing with increasing self-consciousness its own success in the quest for inclusiveness and the reconciliation of East and West as a part of that. 'The Mediterranean is the human norm', while it testifies to certain types of cultural value, is also an admission of failure. It is a provocatively *excluding* observation; the voice that satirised exclusion must now find itself culpable of taking up the very same stance as the missionaries: 'We must exclude someone from our gathering, or we shall be left with nothing' (58).

Innocence and guilt are indeed difficult to determine in this novel, for who would have imagined that the narrative voice would become guilty of some of the attitudes from which it took such pains to distance itself? It has now lost almost every attribute which the omniscient narrator, used in so many realist novels, possesses securely: its omniscience, its consistency, and its immunity from the offences which it criticises or satirises in others.

It is also possible to consider the inclination of both Fielding and the narrative voice to take refuge at this point in the consolations of form as an act of political withdrawal. In the aftermath of Aziz's trial, the hope of a reformed or chastened Raj seems irrevocably to be lost, and what follows is a very powerful instance of a tendency identified by Edward W. Said – the increased reliance, in response to a perception of the 'vulnerability' of Europe, upon aesthetics as a form of control:

> [there is] the irony of a form that draws attention to itself as substituting art and its creations for the once-possible synthesis of the world empires. When you can no longer assume that Britannia will rule the waves forever, you have to reconceive reality as something that can be held together by you the artist. . . . Spatiality becomes, ironically, the characteristic of an aesthetic rather than of political domination.   (Said 1994: 229)

The success of an imperialist rule conducted along liberal-humanist lines would have constituted a form of 'synthesis'; in abandoning that ambition, the narrative voice offers, instead, an imperious assertion of the virtues of form and occidental aesthetics – something which is both sorrowful and culturally defensive.

This heightened self-consciousness in the narrative is taken further in the chapters that succeed the one describing Fielding's return to Europe – those in which the Gokul Ashtami festival is described. The extent to which the narrative voice in the 'Temple' section enters into the spirit of the Hindu festival has been much debated:

> [*A Passage to India*] represents [Hinduism's] ecstatic affirmation of the entire world, the ceremonial celebration of all matter and spirit as originating from and sharing in the Lord of the Universe. But if the text participates in the ambitions of Hinduism . . . to tie, weld, fuse and join all the disparate elements of being and existence in a

complete union, it withdraws from the incalculable and unassimilable enormity of the enterprise.   (Parry 1985: 28–9)

The validity of this may be seen in these chapters, where, for all its admiration, the narrative voice nonetheless marks its distance from what it describes. One of the indications of this lies in the extensive use of humour in this section: in part, the humorous tone proceeds from a desire to emulate the capacity of Hinduism to include merriment in religious ritual, combining it with profundity; but it is also edged with *satire*, and the satirical treatment of Hinduism and Hindu ritual, however gentle and sympathetic, is itself a mark of estrangement. The voice that approved of Hinduism's capacity for inclusiveness and satirised Western exclusions, cultural and religious, at the beginning of the novel, is now, in an unexpected inversion of its position, to be found satirising Hindu inclusiveness because it is unaesthetic.

Even the narrator's approval of the inclusion of merriment and practical jokes in the religious rites is a qualified one: 'By sacrificing good taste, this worship achieved what Christianity has shirked: the inclusion of merriment' (286). The narrative voice itself is clearly not willing to sacrifice 'good taste', even if the object is to be as inclusive as possible. According to Fielding, Stella and Ralph 'like Hinduism, though they take no interest in its forms' (313), but the narrator does not share their ability to warm to the doctrinal content and shrug off what they find aesthetically unpalatable.

In Forster's writings about religion in India, he tends to offer the Hindu temple as a synecdoche for Hinduism itself. Sometimes he suggests that it is precisely because it is so remote from what the West expects aesthetically or architecturally that it has so much to offer the Westerner:

> No one could love such a building. Yet no one can forget it. It remains in the mind when fairer types have faded, and sometimes seems to be the only type that has any significance. When we tire of being pleased and of being improved, and of the other gymnastics of the West, and care, or think we care, for Truth alone; then the Indian Temple exerts its power, and beckons down absurd or detestable vistas to an exit unknown to the Parthenon.   (*PT*: 228)

Elsewhere, however, he admits that what he dismissively calls the 'gymnastics of the West' is capable of resisting even the most fervent desire to embrace what the temple represents. While distancing himself from the extreme cultural chauvinism of Lord Macaulay, who declared in 1843 that '[t]hrough the whole Hindu Pantheon you will look in vain for anything resembling those beautiful and majestic forms which stood in the shrines of Ancient Greece. All is hideous and grotesque and ignoble' (*PT*: 256), Forster concedes that 'minds more sympathetic to India than [Macaulay's], minds less aggressively western, have also recoiled from the Hindu temple' (*PT*: 260). Goldsworthy Lowes Dickinson, for instance, 'used to cower away from those huge architectural masses, those polluting forms, as if a wind blew off them which might wither the soul' (260).

A less pronounced version of this is captured in the narrator's response in the 'Temple' section – evident, for instance, in the description of the singing of the devotees:

> They sang not even to the God who confronted them, but to a saint; they did not one thing which the non-Hindu would feel dramatically correct; this approaching triumph of India was a muddle (as we call it), a frustration of reason and form.   (282)

Although perhaps not 'aggressively western', the narrative voice is, nonetheless, insisting upon its own foreignness: it identifies itself implicitly with the 'non-Hindu' perspective; and, in the revealing parenthetical observation 'as we call it', it even aligns itself with those English characters (such as Mrs Moore) who had tried, unsuccessfully, to impose the terms 'mystery' and 'muddle', and the convenience of distinguishing between the two, upon the Indian situation. To partake fully of the experience, the narrative voice would have to cede its Western orientation, and it is not able or willing to do so. In fact, as has been suggested, the narrator's occidental sympathies become, perversely, even more pronounced at this point.

The failure of Hinduism to achieve full inclusiveness is stressed, not only, as we have seen, in relation to Godbole's discovery of the intractability of the stone, but also in comments such as the following:

> Hinduism, so solid from a distance, is riven into sects and clans, which radiate and join, and change their names according to the aspect from which they are approached. Study it for years with the

best teachers, and when you raise your head nothing they have told you quite fits.   (289)

The second sentence is the one which sets the greatest distance between the observer and what is being observed, for it denies the reader (whose foreignness and 'non-Hindu' identity are taken for granted) the opportunity of *ever* understanding Hinduism and its paradoxes; it entrenches the gap between East and West, between Hindu and non-Hindu, since even someone who takes the trouble to '[s]tudy it for years with the best teachers' will not be able to understand its complexities.

In 'The Mission of Hinduism' (1915), written before Forster's second trip to India, during which he was exposed much more extensively to Hinduism and Hindu society, he finds the paradoxes within Hinduism to be meaningful and appropriate:

> Stripped of its local trappings, of its hundred-handed gods and monkeys and bulls and snakes, and Twice-born, it preaches with intense conviction and passion the doctrine of unity. It believes in caste, it believes in Pantheism also, and these two contradictory beliefs do really correspond to two emotions that each of us can feel, namely, 'I am different from everybody else', and 'I am the same as everybody else'.   (In Das 1977: 5)

But the narrative voice in the 'Temple' section is not able to emulate this, to find a way of saying 'I am the same as everybody else'. It does not assert kinship and difference simultaneously, nor does it achieve the tolerance, the cultural largesse, which this would imply. Had it been able or willing to do so, this would have been the most profound 'connection' of all, making reparation for the political differences, the parting of friends, and the other divisions. It would have been a tribute to the compensatory capacities of narrative, to the power of art, both of which must now be seen as suffering a profound curtailment.

The absence of a transformation of that nature in the narrator marks an impasse which is equivalent, in narrative terms, to Aziz and Fielding's being compelled to ride 'single-file' (316). Despite all the attempts to attain a truly inclusive multivocality, the last chapters bring the admission that the narrative voice cannot have a 'hundred mouths' (149) that speak simultaneously and carry equal weight.

Instead it becomes culturally partisan: rather than striving for inclusiveness, it shows how ingrained are its own cultural predilections – including the admiration of aesthetic order, the tendency to make culturally specific value judgements, and to cling to a familiar secular scepticism – and how easy it is for these to become exclusionary.

The crucial point is that there are different kinds of exclusion and incompleteness, just as there are different kinds of failure. In locating itself between the rigid exclusions of the Club and the inclusiveness sought by the devotees at the Gokul Ashtami festival, the novel lies between two extremes, 'the one all inauthentic order, the other all transcendence and obliviousness of humanistic claims' (Price 1987: 151). It lies also between two versions of completion: the one is artistic in derivation, the result of a rigid formalism which Forster warns against when he says the novelist should strive for '[e]xpansion.... Not completion. Not rounding off but opening out' (*AN*: 116); the other is spiritual, and is associated with Godbole's creed: 'Completeness, not reconstruction' (283). The first refers to formal perfection, the second to the perfection of the soul in divine unity. Clive Bell states confidently that 'Art and Religion are . . . two roads by which men escape from circumstance to ecstasy' (Bell 1947: 92), but Forster, at the end of this, his most modernist novel, does not permit either to afford an easy escape. Lubbock, as an uncompromising formalist, commends Tolstoy, as we have seen, because he 'liberates and completes' (Lubbock 1947: 18); Forster, as a sceptical formalist, neither liberates nor completes. Artistic 'completion, in excising too much in the interest of 'completion', makes form too authoritarian; the spiritual variety, as sought by Godbole, in seeking to admit everything, gives up on form entirely. The first, applied to the novel, would close it in; the second would throw it open too widely.

The intermediate position makes possible the idea of form-despite-chaos and form-within-chaos; it expresses a recognition of something which is central to modernism:

the main figures of high modernism remained aware of inescapable duality, and uncollapsible distance between agent and world, between thinker and instinctual depths.... What was needed was a distinction between forms which gave us experience deadened and etiolated, and those which brought it back vivid and full.

(Taylor 1989: 472–3)

From this perspective, the complexities of the modernists' formal experiments point to a crucial paradox in the relationship between 'life' and 'art', experience and aesthetics: a perception that when the conjunction between the two is too neat or too 'complete', something is amiss; instead, there should always be the incompletion which communicates a sense of 'inescapable duality'. For many of the modernists, technique functions 'not as the provider of aesthetic absolutes, but as the focus for stylistic metamorphoses, which are mediated by a new idea, a shift in an artist's conceptual scheme' (Butler 1994: 15). Forster's technical experiments, as we have seen, have much to do with the avoidance of 'aesthetic absolutes', whether in the form of Lubbock's defence of James, or the ideas of the Bloomsbury art theorists. Change does indeed proceed from 'a shift in [his] conceptual scheme', but 'metamorphosis' would not serve as the appropriate term in this instance, for that implies a kind of completion. Instead *A Passage to India* moves into the interstitial space between the old and the new, where, as in Aziz and Fielding's friendship, the final severance of the old affiliations, although imminent, is endlessly deferred, while the introduction of an entirely new configuration has 'not yet' begun.

4
The Manuscripts of
A Passage to India

> The past once was alive and it now is dead, and if a writer
> succeeds in expressing these facts simultaneously . . . he has
> achieved a great literary effect. The expression must be simul-
> taneous, there must be a complete fusion of all tenses, or the
> spell fails.
>
> E. M. Forster, 'Literature and History' (*PT*: 37–8)

A Passage to India almost remained an uncompleted novel. Forster
abandoned the manuscript in June 1914, not long after visiting India
for the first time (1912–13), and resumed writing in earnest only in
1922, after his second visit (1921–2). A work in which gaps and fissures
are of such crucial importance had, thus, 'lacunae' (Beauman, 1993:
321) in its own creation, an interruption of approximately eight years.
The long abandonment means that it spans two very different experiences of India, one pre-War, the other post-War. Within the novel that
Forster was able to complete in January 1924 lies the shadow, the echo,
of the one that he could not complete in 1914.

What the manuscripts reveal is that, from the start, *A Passage to India*
was a work of nascent modernism, a continuation of the methods and
concerns of *Howards End*. When Forster took it up again, he intensified
and extended modernist elements that were already present in the first
drafts of the novel. The final version, far from simply replacing a 1914
perspective with that of 1922, retains many of the preoccupations of
the earlier period and charts their fate, as it were, so that a study of the
manuscripts shows how Forster's late-Edwardian perspective on India
(and what the British bring to it) was challenged and, in many
instances, chastened.

As the discussion of liberalism and humanism in Chapter 1 has indicated, Forster believed in 1914 that the Raj was capable of being rehabilitated politically; by 1922 he had moved to a position where he felt that the colonisers' refusal to take 'their stand upon a common humanity instead of the pedestal of race' (*PT*: 250), as well as the increasing militancy of the Indians – seen, for instance, in the widespread antipathy to the Prince of Wales's visit in 1922, described as an example of the imposition of 'Imperial pride and the will of a viceroy' (247) – had led to a situation where the hope of a 'democratic empire' (250), which he himself had cherished, must now be abandoned. The reforms which he noted in 1922 had come too late; when he resumed the writing of *A Passage to India*, he was presenting a situation which he now saw as irredeemable, beyond the reach of reform (and thus of satire); a political impasse:

> The mischief has been done, and though friendships between individuals will continue and courtesies between high officials increase, there is little hope now of spontaneous intercourse between the two races. The Indian has taken up a new attitude. Ten or fifteen years ago he would have welcomed attention, not only because the Englishmen in India had power, but because the etiquette and customs of the West, his inevitable destiny, were new to him and he needed a sympathetic introducer. He has never been introduced to the West in the social sense, as to a possible friend. We have thrown grammars and neckties at him, and smiled when he put them on wrongly – that is all. For a time he suffered, and it was with shame and resentment that he found himself excluded from our clubs. . . . Today he has ceased to suffer. He has learnt to put on neckties the right way, or his own way, or whatever one is supposed to do with a necktie. He has painfully woven, without our assistance, a new social fabric, and, as he proceeds with it, he has grown less curious about the texture of ours.   (*PT*: 243–4)

Forster presents the erosion of cultural supremacy as the precursor to the loss of political power. No longer can the 'etiquette and customs of the West' be regarded as the 'inevitable destiny' of Indians. In the establishment of 'a new social fabric' lies the increasingly politicised mood of the Indians in British India, including the impulse towards self-determination. This declaration of a political cul-de-sac describes in broad terms what *A Passage to India* represents specifically in the changing political attitudes of Aziz. He is excluded from the Club, scorned for putting on his collar-stud – the equivalent of the necktie – wrongly (or so Ronny thinks), and, in response to his treatment at the hands of the colonial officials, develops a nationalistic pride and a vehement distaste for all things English. From satirising the discourtesy of those who are rude, exclude people from clubs, and display so great a belief in the superiority of their own culture that they throw 'grammars and neckties' at people, Forster now satirises the political naïvety of those who believe that greater politeness and the suppression of the more blatant examples of British cultural chauvinism will address the demands arising from a developed and impatient political consciousness. In this excerpt (and in the completed novel), the attitude towards the Raj which Forster held in 1922 may be regarded as looking back and commenting upon what he wished for and believed to be possible in 1914.

This accounts, in part, for the strange time-scheme of the final version of the novel:

> if we begin to ask just when the events of the novel as a whole took place, it is not altogether easy to be sure. Some details of the novel, like the Lieutenant-Governor and the dog-carts, belong to an earlier period, while references to the Amritsar massacre place the timing of the novel as contemporary with its first publication.
>
> (J. Beer, 1982: 132)

Broadly speaking, the 'Mosque' section and parts of 'Caves' evoke a period coinciding with Forster's first visit to India, while the rest of 'Caves' and 'Temple' refer to a much later period, one that corresponds to his second visit. The blurring of historical specificity has the effect of emphasising in an unique way the hopes of personal and political 'connection' which Forster cherished in 1912–13, as well as his subsequent abandonment of these. The parts that belong to the first writing have not been recast in such a way as to make their political and historical perspective compatible with the later sections. In that sense, the notion of a chasm which cannot be bridged extends also to what one may call the political texture of the novel, in which no attempt is made to minimise the historical hiatus which lies at its heart.

Another consequence of this unusual situation is that it problematises greatly the representation of historical reference, especially in realist terms, replacing 'the close interface between the strands of historicity and fictiveness' (Furst, 1995: 92) evident in realist fiction, with a type of bifocality whereby the past is seen as coincidental with the present rather than culminating in the present. Any suggestion of history as a progression is thus repudiated, and the realist tendency to associate the movement from past to present with lessons learned and the authority of hindsight is supplanted by a vision of history as nonpurposive and contingent – a succession of hopes and disappointments.

The shadow of political developments that occurred between Forster's two visits to India falls over the parts of the novel that belong to the second writing: these include the Amritsar massacre and the attack upon Miss F. Marcella Sherwood during the disturbances at Amritsar, as well as the resultant response of the Anglo-Indian community. However, these events are not referred to directly, nor are they allowed to dispel the deliberate historical indeterminacy. The lack of specific reference to incidents such as the massacre and the attack on Miss Sherwood does not minimise their repercussions; instead, it extends the investigation to include a more general analysis of colonial anxiety itself, in which alarming occurrences (especially those associated with the possibility of vengeful uprising) are exploited to confirm deeply-entrenched fears. The years between Forster's two visits brought a renewed anxiety about insurrection: 'Those years had witnessed . . . local resistance in India to colonial and class exploitation and irregular but insistent insurrections across the subcontinent that recalled the still awfully remembered example of [the Great Mutiny] of 1857' (Harlow 1994: 82).

The earliest versions of the novel indicate that *A Passage to India* was conceived in 1914 as the transferral, broadly speaking, of the preoccupations and methods of *Howards End* to India and the question of British imperialism in India. *Howards End*, as the discussion in Chapter 1 has suggested, is, of course, also a novel about imperialism, where the territory to be 'colonised' is late-Edwardian England with, as Forster sees it, its acute sense of indirection and mythological impoverishment, and where the Schlegels, with the 'Imperialism of the air' (*HE*: 26) which is part of their German ancestry, vie for it with the Wilcoxes, whose imperialism derives from brute capitalism. Margaret sees at the offices of Henry Wilcox's Imperial and West African Rubber Company a map of Africa 'looking like a whale marked out for blubber' (193), and we are told that 'Imperialism always had been one of her difficulties' (193). Here in embryonic form is the conflict between English people of different political persuasions that was to feature so strongly in *A Passage to India*, and it is interesting to note that 'Miss Quested' (75) appears as one of the guests at the luncheon party that Margaret arranges for Mrs Wilcox.

As the earliest drafts of *A Passage to India* show, the novel was to test Bloomsbury values in India just as *Howards End* had tested them in England, undoubtedly with the same revelation of their magnanimous inefficacy and their moral complicity – in this case, in the misdemeanours of imperialism, with Aziz a victim of virtuous good intentions just as Leonard is in the earlier novel. There would have been a neat inversion in that *Howards End* is a condition-of-England novel which is also a condition-of-imperialism novel in that the erosion of old certainties and values has almost made England a foreign country, one that is being recolonised as the battle is fought as to who shall inherit it and what it is they are to inherit; *A Passage to India*, on the other hand, would have been a condition-of-imperialism novel that was also a condition-of-England novel, for the various Anglo-Indian characters embody several different strands of English moral and political life, all to be interrogated and found wanting in the inhospitable Indian landscape. In both cases a powerful sense of the strangeness of the familiar and the enforced questioning of prior assumptions would have been the prevailing note.

The focus in the completed novel is significantly different from this. In the same way as the novel moves from satirising the methods of the Raj, in the earlier sections, to a sense of the futility of satire in a political situation now wholly irredeemable, so, too, does it move from an exploration of the inadequacies and impoverishment of liberal-humanism, Western rationalism, romanticism and metaphysics, Christianity and Bloomsbury values, to a recognition that it is insufficient merely to indicate their limitations and their imposition as foreign codes and forces of alienation. In other words, the completed novel is a satire of satire, a consideration of the fact that the tools of criticism are constrained by the same exclusions and failures of vision as that which they criticise. What the manuscripts of *A Passage to India* show is that the novel progressed from one that set out to chart various failures and a few heavily qualified successes to a work that, as has been suggested in the previous chapter, includes within that task the failure and partial success of its own quest. In the movement from disappointment in what is to be commented upon, to disappointment also within the commentary itself, lies the evolution of the novel from a work of incipient modernism to one of full modernist self-consciousness.

This change is marked in the manuscripts by two important areas of revision: the one involves significant changes in the function and characterisation of Aziz, Adela, Fielding and Mrs Moore, while the other involves the intensification of the novel's 'prophetic' elements. Generally speaking, the changes in the manuscripts serve to deepen inscrutability and to replace explication with suggestiveness. An example of this is the incident, described in Chapter VIII of the novel, where the Nawab Bahadur's car collides with an unknown animal: this was based upon something which Forster experienced during his second visit to India, but it was later included in the 'Mosque' section, which, as has been indicated, conveys, for the most part, the experiences and mood of the first visit. In virtually each case, the revisions take the novel closer to the denial of a 'speakable truth' (Josipovici 1977: 138).

Of all the major characters, Aziz is the one who is changed least in the course of the manuscript revisions. Those changes which are discernible relate largely to Forster's sense of the changing political climate in India. In particular, he uses Aziz increasingly to show how, in his view, the politicisation of many Indians was provoked by the Raj itself, and that it was the abuses of the Raj which dissipated the existing goodwill and thus caused widespread anti-British sentiments. (The same point is made in the case of the Nawab Bahadur, who, like the renowned poet Rabindranath Tagore, gives up his imperial title; this is in response to the treatment of Aziz after the Marabar expedition.) The changes in the characterisation of the doctor are designed, therefore, to emphasise his goodwill before the Marabar trip, and his subsequent disillusionment and political awakening. Aziz embodies attitudes derived from both pre-Amritsar and post-Amritsar India, and encapsulates within one character the movement from 'the still largely acquiescent India of Forster's first visit' to 'the aroused India of a decade later' (Levine 1971: 23).

One of the ways in which this is done is to make the Aziz of the 'Mosque' section more of an initiate where relations with the English and friendship itself are concerned. Whereas in the final version of the novel it is Hamidullah only who has been to England and was hospitably received at Cambridge and by Reverend and Mrs Bannister, in the earliest drafts Aziz too has been to England, and speaks thus of Englishwomen: 'They are not all alike. . . . They have been my valued friends: ^I have known most accomplished and honourable ladies' (*MPI*: 9).* While the other men recall '^little kindnesses and courtesies', Aziz, 'with his experiences of England, could recall more important examples ^of angelic ministration' (9). This was transferred later to Hamidullah, no doubt in order to make Aziz a complete novice when it comes to having English friends, and thus wholly unaccustomed to 'angelic ministration', so that the kindness of Mrs Moore is all the more astonishing to him and all the more gratefully received. This early Aziz is also much more preoccupied with Western art and literature: one of his jobs is to teach drawing in the Government School, and he tells Hamidullah Begum that his students are copying 'the Venus of Milo' (10). He has also been to Germany, and recites some verses from Heinrich Heine:

> Vergiftet sind meine Lieder –
> Wie konnt' es anders sein?
> Du hast mir ja Gift gegossen
> Ins bluhende Leben hinein.

> Vergiftert [*sic*] sind meine Liede [*sic*]
> Wie konnt' es anders sein?
> Ich trage im Herzen viel Schlangen,
> Und dich, Geliebte mein.

(MPI: p.16)

> [Poisoned are my songs –
> How could it be otherwise?

---

* I have used Oliver Stallybrass's 1978 edition of the manuscripts of *A Passage to India*. However, I have taken advantage of computer technology to make the relevant extracts more iconic, and have replaced Stallybrass's system of brackets and oboli with the following:

- a line through a word or words indicates a *deletion*.
- characters in superscript indicate an *insertion*.
- Words that are underlined *and* have a line through them are *deletions within a larger, subsequent deletion*.

For you have poured poison
Into blossoming life.

Poisoned are my songs
How could it be otherwise?
I carry in my heart many serpents,
And you, my love.]*

One can see why Forster initially felt the verses to be appropriate, for the poisoning of life and love described here anticipates the fate of Aziz, as does the suggestion that it is *within* love itself that the poison lies. This would also have introduced a very appropriate instance of the 'rhythmical' proliferation of snakes in the novel, since it warns of the threat of serpents that are borne in the hearts of lovers, and thus of the corrosion of the affections where they should be most pure. It is also useful to consider in this context the sensibility which Forster attributes to Heine, whom he contrasts with Robert Burns:

> Burns sends his emotions outwards to mingle with human beings and become passions, Heine shuts his up in the circle of self-enclosure, where they fester. And Heine, not Burns, is the modern man. He is a typical product of repression . . .   (*PT*: 97)

The struggle to break out of 'the circle of self-enclosure', despite the sincere attempt on the part of several characters to direct their 'emotions outwards to mingle with human beings', is central to the novel; so too is the 'festering' of emotions which do not find a way of expressing themselves appropriately – a tendency which, significantly, Forster here associates with the Freudian concept of repression. Heine, as situated by Forster, would not have been out of place in *A Passage to India*; but the verses and their implications are inappropriate in the mouth of Aziz, who, in uttering them, seems too canny and too prescient.

More significant changes are evident in the evolving characterisation of Adela, Fielding and Mrs Moore. According to the final scheme of the novel, these three characters and Ronny Heaslop represent respectively four clearly defined strands of Western morality and sensibility – in Adela, a distinctly Bloomsbury-type liberal-humanism and

---

* Translated at my request by the late Mrs Hildegart Nicholas.

the creed of 'personal relations'; in Fielding, a more pragmatic, rationalist liberal-humanism with no links to Bloomsbury; in Mrs Moore, a Western mysticism that includes a type of romantic Christianity; and, in Ronny, a conformist conservatism. But this was not clearly laid out when Forster first began the novel, and one of the effects of the changes is that the Western inheritance, so to speak, of each of these characters becomes more precisely delineated. Only Ronny Heaslop remained largely unchanged. Adela, in the earlier drafts of the novel, is little more than the target of a satirical treatment of Bloomsbury abroad. Several subsequently deleted passages point to the rigidity of her ostensibly tolerant and broad-minded views – for example, there is a game of tennis after the Bridge Party:

> Miss Quested played, ~~but~~ in a very bad temper. She thought it [i.e. the Bridge Party] the most ~~ghastly~~ inhuman entertainment she had ever known, and it increased her wrath when she found that she was allowed to say so.   (*MPI*: 54–5)

The narrative voice directs a great deal of explicit antipathy towards this early Adela:

> She had little self control and had learnt at Cambridge that one ought to show when one's bored. She had not enjoyed her day, and ~~quite~~ forgot that busy men had planned it for her pleasure. Tired and cross, she swept off to bed before the last guest had left the verandah . . .   (*MPI*: 59)

It seems likely that the early Adela was to have been taught by the Marabar Caves that her confident Bloomsbury directness is hollow and self-deluding, which would, presumably, have turned her into a chastened Helen Schlegel.

Adela's Bloomsbury background is presented in the earlier versions of the novel even more emphatically than in the later drafts as an example of a foreign code being imposed upon India, one that is as excluding and rigid in its own way as are the conservatism and smugness of the 'Turtons and Burtons' (*PI*: 314). The early Adela is extremely irritable and aggressive – she attack[s]' (*MPI*: 180) rather than eats a guava – and, more significantly, she becomes racialistic very rapidly, feeling a momentary 'racial repulsion' (118) towards the 'Eurasian' driver of the Nawab Bahadur. The later Adela, however, is much more than a representative solely of Bloomsbury complacency and impetuousness and is presented in a far more sympathetic light. The gentler treatment of this character relates, in part, to the narrative voice's exploration of its own motivations and the Western cargo, so to speak, that it bears: once there is the recognition that it, too, cannot dissociate itself entirely from its cultural allegiances, there is less harshness directed towards her. When occidental prejudices of all kinds are being recognised with greater honesty, there is less inclination to use Adela to confirm the oriental prejudice, expressed by Hamidullah, that all English people turn out the same once they have been in India for a while, and that the women are particularly susceptible – 'I give any Englishman two years. . . . And I give any Englishwoman six months' (*PI*: 34). The novel, as initially conceived, would have implicated even a woman seemingly as enlightened as Adela in the reprehensible behaviour which Forster identifies in English women:

> If the Englishman might have helped the Indian socially, how much more might the Englishwoman have helped! But she has done nothing, or worse than nothing. She deserves, as a class, all that the satirists have said about her, for she instigated the follies of her male when she might have calmed them and set him on the sane course. There has been an English as well as an Indian *purdah*, and it has done greater harm because it was aggressive. Instead of retiring quietly behind the curtain it flaunted itself as a necessity, and proclaimed racial purity across a live wire.   (*PT*: 245)

Instead, in being placed both within and without modes of behaviour which are so readily satirised, she becomes a more complex and unpredictable character; what is more, this problematises the practice of satire itself, including the confidence of its judgements, and the ease with which its targets are held up for ridicule. Making her both rational and neurotic, sympathetic and unsympathetic, reprehensible and courageous, has the effect of exposing, confirming and repudiating the secret fears and vulnerabilities of the Empire. The Adela who becomes more difficult to insert into a pattern of behaviour and hold up for criticism is a manifestation of a waning confidence in the narrative voice in its own judgements in relation to what is estimable and what is not in the colonial situation, and a growing awareness of 'the contraries and contrariness that were central to colonial experience' (Boehmer 1998: xxxv). Instead of representing the inevitable decline of the English woman into prejudice and folly, Adela comes to embody these 'contraries and contrariness'.

Making Adela more 'rounded' is an ostensibly humanist gesture that, in fact, turns upon itself later, for the inability of the early Adela to understand her own experiences in the Marabar would have counted for little, in that she is presented as a person of limited insight and self-knowledge, perpetuating her own cultural and class predilections with no awareness of how discordant they seem in this new environment; but the bemusement of the later Adela, after she has been advanced so significantly in sympathy and intelligence, suggests that, however far she moves along that path, however much she changes, as it were, from Helen to Margaret, it is the inadequacy of the trajectory itself that will have to be confronted. Adela goes from caricature to character, but the Marabar Caves make character in realist and humanist terms as thin as any caricature; she becomes more 'rounded', but the Caves flatten everything.

Where Fielding and Mrs Moore are concerned, the subsequent revisions serve to make them more different from one another. Mrs Moore becomes less rationalistic and more mystical, while Fielding, in turn, becomes more analytical. It is clear that, as Mrs Moore's 'prophetic' status was enhanced, Fielding was increasingly presented as an embodiment of a wholly secular, wholly rationalist liberal-humanism. So different are the characters in the completed version of the novel that it is difficult to believe that they overlapped originally as much as they did, and that, in the earlier versions, Fielding was given thoughts and even actions that were later transferred to Mrs Moore. Their initial importance as foils to Adela decreases in the subsequent versions: whereas, at first, Fielding's pragmatism and sensibleness contrast strongly with Adela's lack of these qualities, and Mrs Moore's intuitive sympathies show up the younger woman's limitations, the movement of the rewriting is towards the challenging of the ostensibly superior qualities that Fielding and Mrs Moore embody, and towards a more widespread 'dwarfing' of what *all* of them have brought with them from the West.

The early Mrs Moore is a benevolent, intuitive character in the mould of Ruth Wilcox, but she is prone to intellectualising to a far greater extent than the later Mrs Moore, and her significance as a representative of Western mysticism and a type of romantic Christianity is not nearly as marked. In the course of the rewriting, she 'grows in two dimensions: besides her increased stature, her Christianity widens into mysticism' (J. Levine 1971: 106). Thus, in a deleted passage, Mrs Moore – who has said that the unknown animal that struck the Nawab Bahadur's car was a 'ghost' – retracts this, saying, 'What a foolish remark – I'd forgotten. No I don't believe in ghosts; I don't see how those of us who call ourselves Christians can' (*MPI*: 129–30); in the completed version of the novel, in contrast, Forster takes pains to indicate that her Christianity is not doctrinaire, which is why she is able to grasp intuitively certain tenets of Hinduism. The later Mrs Moore is quite capable of seeing ghosts, and even of becoming one. There is a consistent attempt in the revisions to suggest in Mrs Moore a capacity for moving beyond the range of her own experiences that sets her apart from the other Europeans, and that makes her collapse at the Marabar all the more disturbing in its implications. For instance, her response to the elephant that takes them to the Caves was deleted, presumably because it attributes to her the kind of mental rigidity of which she ought to be free:

> Mrs Moore had never liked elephants, feeling them excessive in proportion to the size of the globe. She preferred life in little pieces – wasps, lizards – not ~~these~~ in huge conglomerations. Had the soul once again strayed beyond its boundaries and been caught? Oh how life blundered . . . lumps clinging to the skin of a larger lump, and making noises at each other when it moved.   (201–2)

Mrs Moore is presented as one who gains the Hindu appreciation of life in all its forms, and should not therefore be perspicacious enough to appreciate wasps, yet resent elephants. She should also not be troubled by something which is not aesthetically pleasing – that is Fielding's role. The revisions further the idea that Mrs Moore is one who is willing, even eager, to shed her Western preconceptions, only to find herself defeated by the task.

Not surprisingly, the shifts in the characterisation of Fielding and Mrs Moore are impossible to consider without taking into account also the crucial changes in Forster's depiction of the Marabar Caves themselves, for, to a much greater extent than in the case of Adela, the changes made to these two characters are related to changes in the conception of the expedition to the Caves. It is *because* the challenges offered by the Caves are widened to include a challenge to Western mysticism and romanticism that Mrs Moore, prior to the expedition, needs to become more mystical and less rational. When one considers how devastating her experience there is, as described in the completed version of the novel, it is astonishing to discover that, at one stage, Forster intended to restrict her response to the Caves and their surroundings to this comment: 'Mrs Moore understood them, only too well, and was never again deceived by them' (276). Equally astonishing is the discovery that, in the earliest version of the expedition, Mrs Moore *does not enter a cave at all.* Instead, she tells Aziz that the Caves 'would be too much for her' (208), and asks him to let her rest. In the light of this, it is easy to see how Forster moved away from a conception of the Caves as embodying that which only Mrs Moore, of all the Europeans, could understand and counter with her inner resources, to that which crushes her so completely that her experience is, arguably, the most calamitous of all.

In the later versions of the novel, Mrs Moore's misanthropy – described as 'a hardness, a just irritation against the human race' (*PI:* 204) – is shown to be a direct result of her experience in the Caves. In the earlier drafts, however, she becomes irritable and is somewhat misanthropic even before the expedition. There are several passages, subsequently deleted, that show in Mrs Moore a disgruntlement that is not specifically linked to the Caves, so that once more we see how, initially, the Marabar was to be Adela and Fielding's testing-ground, and not hers. In an early version of the approach to the Marabar, Mrs Moore has the reaction which is later associated specifically with the effect of the Caves and the echo upon her:

> Mrs Moore awoke with a definite and alarming feeling all over her body. She had been ᵂᵃˢ ill. . . . Heart, nerves, or suppressed gout, the doctors had called the ˢᵘᶜʰ ᵃ symptom in England, but here she knew believed that it was spiritual, that the soul can stray out of its kingdom and be caught. . . . Mrs Moore recovered control, the sickishness and bad taste in her mouth were already ˢᵒᵐᵉ [*sic*] relics of something that she had forgotten, something ᵇᵘᵗ that had underlined the loneliness of human life. (*MPI*: 185)

Here Mrs Moore feels depressed on behalf of others, and senses the essential loneliness of people; in the reworked version of the expedition, she feels depressed more as the result of the collapse of her own beliefs. Her insights here, bleak as they are, are redeemed by the fact that she is perspicacious enough to gain them – she is a sibylline witness to the failure of 'personal relations'. That is presumably why it was not at first considered necessary that she should enter a cave, for she has seen already what the Caves will do to relationships between individuals, and even to Western romanticism. In reworking this episode, Forster shows that Mrs Moore's sibylline status is itself a product, at least in part, of that romantic tradition, and cannot thus remain unscathed. From being one who sagaciously identifies vulnerability in others and in the beliefs they adhere to, Mrs Moore has come to represent a vulnerability, even a paralysis, within the capacity for compassionate discernment itself.

In the 1913–14 writing, much more background material is supplied with regard to Fielding's life prior to the incidents described in the novel. There is an inconsistency to him that is not present in the later Fielding:

> he inspired confidence among his countrymen until he began to talk to them. A regrettable waywardness then appeared. He was always going off on a side issue and not even sticking to that: suddenly he would return, flourish an argument in their faces and be off again.   (*MPI*: 74)

A relatively long passage, completely deleted subsequently, describes an unsuccessful business venture, a clash with the wife of a business partner, a 'disreputable' period, and a subsequent 'repentance'. He labours among the poor for a brief period 'because he did not like them' (77) and wishes to mortify himself. His imperfections at this stage prepare the way for his later tolerance and equanimity:

> He regained equilibrium, and became ~~very~~ much . . . the decent fellow he had been ~~before~~ . . . though with increased sympathy and knowledge. He . . . lived to look back upon his period of 'repentance' as far more dangerous than the excesses that had induced it.   (77)

The quirkiness and impulsiveness of this early Fielding are minimised as more emphasis is placed upon his rationality (rather than his romantic tendencies), his level-headedness, and the fact that his experiences have taught him not to expect too much of life or of himself.

In the final version of the novel, his response to the Marabar Caves is confined to the following: 'Fielding ran up to see one cave. He wasn't impressed' (*PI*: 168). However, in the earliest drafts of the episode, his response is discussed at length, and much of what afterwards became Mrs Moore's experience is given to him. In the process of transferring the more significant response to the Caves from Fielding to Mrs Moore, the bleakness of the experience is accentuated, as well as the severity of the denial of consolation. Fielding experiences the Marabar Caves in the form of a 'colloquy' (*MPI*: 265). He is able to quarrel, as it were, with the Caves in a way that Mrs Moore is not. In the final version of the novel, one of the most unnerving aspects of the Caves is their *denial* of colloquy or dialogue in any form. On the way up to the Caves, Fielding 'converses' with the stones, a lone tree, and the Marabar Hills themselves. For instance, he is accosted by the tree:

> 'You want a mystery' it waved: 'human beings do, but ~~there is~~ [1]
> announce no mystery, only a muddle: the universe, incomprehensible
> to your reason, shall yet offer no repose to your soul.'   (265)

When these chapters were rewritten, much of what is said in these 'conversations' was given instead to the narrative voice, which suggests the extent to which the drama of dialectic and contestation is increasingly being represented within the narrative voice itself, and not merely in the responses of the characters. In the early version, the Marabar Hills themselves utter the refutation of romanticism later articulated by the narrative voice, and make a lengthy speech beginning, 'Devils are of the North. . . . Write poems about them on your romantic ~~English~~ moors.' (265). Fielding's response is admirably matter-of-fact under the circumstances: ' "... that's all very well, but one's got to carry on somehow" reflected Fielding' (265).

The clumsiness of this is an indication of the difficulties Forster experienced in writing about the expedition to the Marabar. (The extensive rewritings of the section as a whole show that this was the part of the novel which gave him the most difficulty.) The problem of how the Marabar was to deny the dialogic nature of language and communication, and yet respond with specific repudiations of the individual characters' beliefs and expectations, was a formidable one. The 'colloquy' described above clearly could not be satisfactory. Forster's solution involved giving the Marabar no 'voice' at all except the echo, which is the repudiation of all voices and all language, and giving the 'message' of the Caves in linguistic terms to the narrative voice.

Fielding's encounter with the echo is rendered in some detail in the earliest versions of the Marabar episode. In response to it, he recites poetry, including the opening lines of *Paradise Lost* and some of Meredith's 'The Woods of Westermain'. The significance of *Paradise Lost* in this context is not difficult to determine, for the inability of that monumental work of English literature and Christian morality to make any impression whatsoever upon the echo speaks for itself as a comment upon the impotence of Western traditions and values. The Caves antedate human existence and are impervious to the postlapsarian fate of humankind and the quest for a paradise regained: they are not to be construed in terms of human history, but of 'Geology', which, 'looking further than religion, knows of a time when neither the river nor the Himalayas that nourish it existed, and an ocean flowed over the holy places of Hindustan' (*PI*: 137). In harkening back to 'Geology', the Caves show the imperviousness of time to teleological constructs, and repudiate Milton's attempt, in *Paradise Lost*, to render the whole history of humankind, stretching from before the creation of the world until the cessation of time itself, for time is not purposive in the Marabar, and it has no concern with the fate of humankind. There is also an irony in referring in the Caves to 'man's first disobedience' and its consequences, for there is no *felix culpa* in the Marabar to assuage the misdemeanours of humankind, and, although serpents do indeed appear in the description of the echo, the Caves, as we have seen, abjure conventional notions of guilt and innocence.

The brief excerpt from Meredith's poem is also revealing. Whereas the lines from Milton have to do with that aspect of the Caves which opposes Christian paradigms, this extract emphasises also the Caves' disputation of English late romanticism. After a reference to 'Grasmere', which remained in the final version of the novel (although spoken of by Mrs Moore and Adela, not Fielding), we find a subsequently deleted reference to 'The Woods of Westermain' – from *Poems and Lyrics of the Joy of Earth* (1883): 'Enter these enchanted woods, / You who dare' (ll.1–2). Fielding admires this poem deeply:

[It was] a poem . . . that he had once admired even more than ~~Milton~~
Paradise Lost because it was adventurous and ~~brave~~ sane, and ~~spoke~~ sang of the ~~triumphs~~
triumph as well as the fall of man.   (*MPI*: 267)

Meredith's woods, if one considers the poem as a whole, are a place of
danger and enchantment, but both the perilous and the more affirmative aspects are imbued with a romantic significance, which is precisely what is lacking in the Caves. This makes the woods a place of
plenitude – 'Granaries you will have a store / Past the world of woe and
bliss' (ll. 64–5). In striking contrast to the Marabar Caves, the woods
offer also the bounty of the self, which makes possible a more satisfactory communion with others – 'You a larger self will find / Sweetest fellowship ensues / With the creatures of your kind' (ll.125–7) – and the
repleteness of individual identity is celebrated – 'Love, the sole permitted, sings / Sovereignly of ME and I' (ll.170–1).

When one considers the assault upon the sovereignty of the self in the
Marabar, not to mention what the Caves do to 'sweetest fellowship', the
ironies of the reference to 'The Woods of Westermain' are manifold.
More than anything, Meredith's woods are a place of constant change –
'Change, the strongest son of Life' (l. 259) – and change is what is absent
in the Marabar. It is impossible to romanticise that which never changes,
and yet has nothing to recommend it in its present form.

From the start, the Caves were envisaged as a place where hostility
between individuals would find expression:

Harmless in itself, it ~~put~~ ~~sucked~~ ~~human beings into a position where~~
pitted human beings against each other until they went mad.   (*MPI*: 234)

However, in the final version, the antagonism between people is over-
shadowed by the ways in which the Caves pit human beings against
themselves – a contest even more unnerving in its implications. There is
a partial recovery for those who, like Aziz, can blame others for their
misfortunes; however, for Mrs Moore, who has been the victim of an
attack from within, there is no recuperation.

The mystery of what actually occurred in the Marabar is so prominent an aspect of *A Passage to India* that it is astonishing to discover that,
in the very earliest account of the expedition, Adela is quite unambiguously attacked by someone, although the identity of her assailant is
not known:

At first she thought that ~~she was being robbed~~, he was ~~holding~~ taking her hand ~~as before~~ to help her ~~out~~, then she realised, and shrieked at the top of her voice. 'Boum' ~~went~~ shrieked[?] the echo. She struck out and he got hold of her other hand and forced her against the wall, he got both her hands in one of his, and then felt at her ~~dress~~ breasts. 'Mrs Moore' she yelled. 'Ronny – don't let him, save me.' The strap of her Field Glasses, tugged suddenly, was drawn across her throat. She understood – it was to be passed once round her neck, ~~it was to~~ she was to be throttled as far as necessary and then . . .

(242–3; Forster's suspension points)

She escapes by striking the assailant with her field glasses. The contrast between this version and the indeterminacy of the final account is a telling indication of the novel's movement towards 'unknowingness' and the widening of the implications of Adela's experiences. The removal of a definite assailant (another substitution of absence for presence), particularly after the attack upon Miss Sherwood at Amritsar, is also an effective way of commenting upon the irrational nature of Anglo-Indian paranoia, as well as the pervasive paternalism of various sectors of colonial society. As he rewrote this section, Forster increasingly used the expedition and its repercussions to show how deeply sexual and chivalric codes are implicated in the practice of colonialism. The manuscripts show the gradual introduction of the sexual element in the description of Adela's experience in the Marabar. In a passage subsequently deleted, we are told of her response to Aziz:

She had not, ~~she~~ and was not to have, ~~any~~ . . . sexual-feelings towards ~~him~~ the young man, but he ~~had touched~~ did touch her imagination and ~~impressed~~ impress her with his power.   (176)

This explicit denial was removed, presumably to accommodate the possibility of Adela's 'assault' being a reaction within herself to that which she desires but must deny; however, less is made of that suggestion than one might expect, even in the final version of the novel, and it seems that Forster wished to make the point about the politics of sexual relations in the Raj without offering the notion of sexual repression as too convenient an explanation. (David Lean's 1985 film version of *A Passage to India* does precisely the opposite, going to great lengths to emphasise the sexual frustration of Adela, and presenting her experience at the Caves as a hysterical sexual fantasy in such explicit terms as to leave very little mystery – or muddle – intact. In fact, Lean's film reverses the trajectory of the changes in the manuscript in that it emphasises Adela's experience at the expense of Mrs Moore's; not surprisingly, the greater part of the metaphysical menace of the Caves is lost.)

A crucial aspect of the deepening inscrutability that one finds in the manuscript revisions is the increasing propensity towards secretiveness on the part of the narrative voice. Although the general tendency in the revisions is to convert dialogue into narrative comment, this is, for the most part, not to clarify, but rather to subvert the 'knowingness' associated with authorial interpolation, and thus to make the reader more uncertain in his or her judgements, particularly where the urbanity and confidence of the voice are undermined. The apparently small matter of the news of Mrs Moore's death is an example of this: it is clear that Forster intended at first to share the news of Mrs Moore's death with the reader, while keeping the fact from the other characters in the novel, thus privileging the reader in a way that is common in many realist novels. Hence, the 'Esmiss Esmoor' chant is described in the manuscripts as giving her 'postumous [*sic*] fame' (394) and as an 'outburst of posthumous vitality' (395). However, Forster finally decided to withhold this information from the reader, and the result is that he or she is also made to think of Mrs Moore as a presence while she is, in fact, an absence, only to find that her absence through death has granted her a new kind of 'prophetic' presence.

This is not an especially unsettling version of what one may call narrative guile, for, although the narrative voice has chosen not to divulge an item of information, it has the power to exercise this kind of discretion and is therefore fully in control of the narration. But the question of what happened to Adela in the Caves involves something far more radical, for there the narrative voice cannot divulge for it does not know; it cannot protect us from the exposure of 'a sickening contingency in all human life' (Eagleton 1970: 40), and the void which opens up within its own endeavours.

As far as 'rhythm' and 'prophecy' are concerned, the manuscript revisions show both to have been present from the beginning, with, as has been suggested, a gradual extension of the 'prophetic' elements. The fact that instances of 'rhythm' are present even in the earliest versions of the novel is scarcely surprising, given the extensive deployment of this device in *Howards End*. Indeed, the revisions often show Forster deleting superfluous examples of 'rhythm', or replacing them with more effective ones. There are many more snakes, for instance, in the manuscripts than in the completed novel – Adela's decision not to marry Ronny is itself described as a snake:

> Instead of ~~renouncing~~ announcing her decision to him direct, as a civilised young woman should, she had revealed ^it^ incidentally ~~to Aziz, a stranger~~ while chatting to Aziz a stranger about mangoes: it had stolen up through a tangle of leaves and coiled round her hand. (*MPI*: 103)

The Caves themselves are at one point described as being snake-like – not merely the echo, as in the final version: Fielding, after his disturbing encounter with the echo, looks at the 'distended throats' which are the mouths of the Caves, and '[i]nto that which resembled a ~~serpent's~~ ^cobra's^ he chucked a stone' (268). The deletion of this reinforces the perception that the horror of the Caves lies in their non-purposiveness: they are too indifferent to be evil. In the face of their imperviousness, human action and speech become distorted and even malevolent, which is why, in the final version of the novel, the *echo* is described as being serpentine, but not the Caves themselves.

Even if one looks at the drafts of the 'Temple' section, which, as has been indicated, belongs wholly to the 1922–4 writing, one finds examples of Forster's considering the introduction of 'rhythmic' repetitions, only to discard them subsequently. For instance, the green bird that Adela and Ronny were unable to identify recurs during Aziz and Fielding's last ride together, as if to taunt the reader with its still-unidentified status; this was, presumably, considered redundant since the reader needs little reminding at this point of his or her inability to label and identify. It is also interesting to note that Forster considered letting Aziz and the English visitors to Mau hear, amidst the frenzied notes of the Gokul Ashtami festival at its height, the words 'Esmiss Esmoor' (563). Instead he settled for the repetition of the phrase 'Then you are an Oriental' (*PI*: 306), which, spoken this time to Ralph Moore, is a sufficiently cogent way of indicating the 'survival' of Mrs Moore, and the way in which 'rhythm' works to guarantee it.

It is not possible to know with any degree of certainty whether or not Forster already envisaged the sonata-like structure of *A Passage to India* in 1914. If he did have a tripartite structure in mind, the third section could have borne no resemblance at all to the 'Temple' section as it exists, for, as indicated earlier, the experiences described in that section are based, for the most part, upon his second visit to India. In itself, the move from Chandrapore to one of the Princely States in the last part of the novel is an abandonment of the hope that British India could reform itself and become viable politically. Along with Aziz, the novel has relocated itself physically as an act of political refusal. Any tentative reaffirmation invited by the sonata structure in the 'Temple' section cannot, therefore, include as an ingredient the reformation of the Raj, and that in itself must distinguish the structure of the completed novel from any large 'rhythmic' pattern which Forster may have had in mind in 1914, even if, as is likely, he already intended to use the Indian weather cycle as a way of shaping the novel.

Two earlier versions of a passage from Chapter XII indicate the nature and direction of the deepening of the 'prophetic' elements in the course of the revisions. Chapter XII is one of those chapters which, according to Forster's terminology, are pure 'plot' – 'plot' without 'story', or as close to it as is feasible. Human action and interlocution die down, as it were, in these chapters, and this allows the 'prophetic' note to be sounded more clearly than elsewhere. The chapter describes the geological antiquity of India, looking back to a time that antedates both the Ganges and the Himalayas. Something of the antiquity that is so vast that time itself seems to make virtually no imprint upon it, is preserved in the Marabar Caves, which are then described. The chapter ends with a suggestion that there may be caves which have no entrances, whose nothingness cannot be penetrated:

An entrance was necessary, so mankind made one. But elsewhere, deeper in the granite, are there certain chambers that have no entrances? Chambers never unsealed since the arrival of the gods? Local report declares that these exceed in number those that can be visited, as the dead exceed the living – four hundred of them, four thousand or million. Nothing is inside them, they were sealed up before the creation of pestilence or treasure; if mankind grew curious and excavated, nothing, nothing would be added to the sum of good or evil. One of them is rumoured within the boulder that swings on the summit of the highest of the hills; a bubble-shaped cave that has neither ceiling nor floor, and mirrors its own darkness in every direction infinitely. If the boulder falls and smashes, the cave will smash too – empty as an Easter egg. The boulder because of its hollowness sways in the wind, and even moves when a crow perches upon it; hence its name and the name of its stupendous pedestal: the Kawa Dol.   (*PI*: 139)

The manuscript versions of the chapter include two drafts of this passage: the differences, although subtle, are illuminating. This extract follows the sentence beginning 'Local report . . .':

Their guide, in his ignorance, said so, but he did not suggest that ~~these~~ such chambers contained ~~anything~~ . . . their ~~darkness~~ void was untroubled by echoes, that was all. The rock at the summit of the Kauwa [*sic*] Dol was itself ~~hollow~~ ~~a chamber~~ of this type, he declared, hollow and that was why it did not fall off its perch: it was a shell of stone enclosing a bubble-shaped cave . . . which had neither ceiling nor floor.   (*MPI*: 169)

Attributing 'ignorance' to the guide suggests the superior knowledge of the narrative voice, and thus degrees of competence in relation to the enigma of the Caves – a suggestion which the later version removes. The very fact that the guide and his explanations were abandoned is significant, for the 'inhuman' emptiness of the Caves is thus emphasised. The narrative voice in Chapter XII seeks as disembodied a condition as is possible, in order to convey something of the vacuity of the Caves. The impersonal, detached voice becomes the only permissible 'guide'. From a certain perspective, this may be a way of straining towards the extinction of personality that is required in the symbolist quest to achieve that elusive silence, the stillness that speaks more than words.

However, the narrative voice is also confronted with the silence that appals, that betokens only vacuity. The caves that have no entrance may or may not exist. On the one hand, there is an attempt to summon them into existence, as it were, through language and speculation, and thus to provide a way in of sorts; on the other hand, this only lays further 'nothingness' bare – 'nothing, nothing would be added to the sum of good or evil'. The word 'nothing' has been endowed with a 'rhythmical' quality from the first sentence of the novel; through 'rhythm', it has become a presence – *something*. But its meanings can only be provisional, never secure. 'Nothing' threatens always to slip back into nothingness, for there is a sense in which the word can accrue only nothing. In this excerpt we see language seeking to render what seems to be the very source of nothingness, the primordial emptiness which has the power to dismay and erode the narrative of human history itself, and make inconsequential its activities, good or bad. Symbolism is a 'revolt against exteriority . . . against a materialistic tradition' (Symons, 1899: 10); but here the symbolist language grapples with an *interiority* which is not the source of revelations or transcendental truths, but which makes all attempts to construe meaning fold in upon themselves, because nothing emanates from it. Instead of the 'chimerical search after the virginity of language (131) which Symons discerns in the work of Mallarmé, Forster gives us the ever-virginal nothingness which can never assume a substance or a story in the world, and in relation to which all language seems chimerical, stripped both of the referential potency which the realists relied upon, and of the 'idealist substratum' (Williams, 1989: 71) discernible in the work of the romantics and the symbolists.

The other telling revision in this chapter has to do with the way the Kawa Dol – which is suspended between the nothingness of its own perfect hollowness, and the nothingness which would ensue if it fell and smashed – is described. The Kawa Dol is the perfect symbolist metaphor, for its self-referentiality is complete in that it is 'a bubble-shaped cave that has neither ceiling nor floor, and mirrors its own darkness in every direction infinitely'; but its inaccessibility is the necessary condition of that perfection. In the second of the two drafts of this passage, we find a prognostication as to the eventual fate of this unusual rock:

> Some day the boulder will fall and smash like an egg. It has not fallen yet because of its lightness, which causes it to sway in the wind and even to swing when a bird perches upon it.   (*MPI*: 170)

The difference between this and what Forster finally settled upon – 'If the boulder falls and smashes, the cave will smash too – empty as an Easter egg' – is more than syntactical. The earlier version grants the narrative voice several kinds of prerogative, including the power of prediction, of unequivocal assertion, of finding finitude in the presence of infinity. The subjunctive mood of the later version suspends the already-suspended Kawa Dol in a limitless state, a condition of perpetual precariousness. This change, small as it is, is deeply suggestive for the novel as a whole. It communicates something of the waning authority of the narrative voice, as well as the increasing importance of projections which – like 'No, not yet' and 'No, not there' (*PI*: 316) – have always to remain provisional, speculative and infinitely deferred. It is another example of how the manuscript revisions in almost each case bring the novel closer towards those unsatiated truths of which modernism was made.

5
Looking Past Polemic: Forster and Modernism

'in eras of transition writers are all half-blind to one another.'
Edwin Muir, *Transition: Essays on Contemporary Literature* (1926: 203)
'Our quarrel . . . is not with the classics.'
Virginia Woolf, 'Modern Fiction' (1966, vol. II: 103)

What the modernists proclaim often differs markedly from what they actually do; it is therefore notoriously difficult to reconcile modernist polemic and modernist practice. The complexity that arises as a result of these inconsistencies points to a number of important considerations that ought not to be overlooked in any discussion of modernism. Not least of these is that, in looking back, we may be flattening differences which, to the practitioners themselves, were so great that they saw little common ground and were struck only by discrepant aspirations and strategies. In addition, there is the danger of overemphasising the vigorous polemic engaged in by many early twentieth-century writers in an attempt to define difference or settle upon convenient categories. The disputes engaged in by these writers 'appear now more like family or intergenerational quarrels in which the contending parties seem to be putting up a spirited defense against the lurking threat of co-dependency' (DiBattista 1996: 4). Polemic, in other words, should not too readily be read as dissent, nor should it be accepted too eagerly as an infallible indication of a literary agenda.

The perceived need for polemic does, however, convey something in and of itself, particularly where the modernists are concerned: it is, most obviously, an example of 'one of the tropes of modernism', namely 'its insistence on its own novelty' (G. Beer 1989: 139–40). At the same time, the very tendency to be strident may be read as an expression of defensiveness and vulnerability, rather than as a mark of confidence. In that case, the partiality for polemic may be something more than the understandable tendency for newness to be assertive and iconoclasm to be critical: it provides another demonstration of how the modernists' engagement with the historical circumstances in which they wrote was marked by acute uncertainty, both in terms of how contemporaneity should best be rendered and evaluated, and with respect to their own status within it.

One very obvious expression of this uncertainty is the curious lack of sympathy or insight discernible in many of the critical responses of the modernists to their fellow modernists. Muir's comment, quoted above, that 'in eras of transition writers are all half-blind to one another', assumes an added relevance in the modernist period, where the defensiveness of the modernists in relation to their own standing in historical and literary-historical terms affects greatly their responses to contemporary writers, often blinding them – so it may seem to us – to marked affinities.

A particularly revealing instance of this and of the ways in which the modernists read or misread modernism may be found in the critical relationship between E. M. Forster and Virginia Woolf. The relationship between the two has been described as 'an uneasy collision of two writers' (Herz 1988: 139); they 'spoke out of a shared set of assumptions, even if at certain times each could be oddly out of touch with the other's achievement' (142). Forster is the less vehement in the criticisms he expresses; Woolf's polemic is the more vigorous. Yet, as the ensuing discussion will suggest, it is Forster's more temperate and qualified response which is the more reliable indicator of the 'shared set of assumptions'.

'Again and again she eludes' (*AH*: 104) complains Forster, while Woolf writes that '[t]here is something baffling and evasive in the very nature of his gifts' (Woolf 1966, vol. I: 342). The complaints are odd, to say the least, coming as they do from two writers who have such an elaborate sense of the virtues of inscrutability. But this is only the beginning of a long list of critical curiosities: one would, presumably, have been able to predict that Woolf would have criticised Forster for relinquishing too few of the methods of the realists, and that Forster would have accused her, in turn, of not creating sufficiently 'convincing' characters; but could one have envisaged, for instance, that the creator of Mrs Ramsay would object to Mrs Moore, and on the grounds that 'we doubt both things – the real and the symbolical: Mrs Moore, the nice old lady, and Mrs Moore, the sibyl. The conjunction of these two different realities seems to cast doubt upon them both' (347), when Mrs Ramsay is herself a nice middle-aged lady and a sibylline figure, and her creator is herself enamoured of symbolical possibilities and of the 'conjunction of ... different realities'?

Woolf notes the extraordinarily dense and elaborate mixing of modes in Forster's fiction, but she responds to it pejoratively:

> Here, then, is a difficult family of gifts to persuade to live in harmony together: satire and sympathy; fantasy and fact; poetry and a prim moral sense. No wonder that we are often aware of contrary currents that run counter to each other and prevent the book from bearing down upon us and overwhelming us with the authority of a masterpiece.   (344–5)

The expectation that this 'family of gifts' should be 'persuade[d] to live in harmony together', when her own modernism relies to such a great extent upon mixing and juxtaposing different generic and stylistic traditions, upon 'contrary currents that run counter to each other', constitutes another critical oddity – evident also in her memorable description of Forster as the 'light sleeper' in the dormitory of fiction:

> [Mr Forster] is like a light sleeper who is always being woken by something in the room. The poet is twitched away by the satirist; the comedian is tapped on the shoulder by the moralist; he never loses himself or forgets himself for long in sheer delight in the beauty or the interest of things as they are. For this reason the lyrical passages in his books, often of great beauty in themselves, fail of their due effect in the context. Instead of flowering naturally – as in Proust, for instance – from an overflow of interest and beauty in the object itself, we feel that they have been called into existence by some irritation, are the effort of a mind outraged by ugliness to supplement it with a beauty which, because it originates in protest, has something a little febrile about it.   (349–50)

It is strange to find such antipathy to the mixing of genres in one of modernism's foremost publicists and practitioners. As we have seen,

Forster's writing does indeed straddle many conventional distinctions: his work could readily be included in most of the categories Woolf identifies in her essay 'Phases of Fiction' – he would not be out of place amongst the 'Truth-tellers', the 'Romantics', the 'Character-mongers and Comedians', the 'Psychologists', the 'Satirists and Fantasists', and the 'Poets' (Woolf, vol. II: 101ff.); yet, as the description of the 'light sleeper' suggests, this is something to be regretted, rather than an admirable versatility. What seems to underlie her designation of Forster as the 'light sleeper' is the complaint that he is not a sufficiently thorough or convincing *realist*: he 'never loses himself or forgets himself for long in sheer delight in the beauty or the interest of things as they are'; his lyricism does not emanate from 'an overflow of interest and beauty in the object itself'. The chief difficulty with this is that Woolf is urging Forster to commit himself to a mode of writing which, from her perspective, has ceased to be credible. The reference to 'things as they are' and 'the object itself' brings to mind her tribute to Defoe's achievement – as she sees it – in *Robinson Crusoe*:

> by reiterating that nothing but a plain earthenware pot stands in the foreground, [Defoe] persuades us to see remote islands and the solitudes of the human soul. By believing fixedly in the solidity of the pot and its earthiness, he has subdued every other element to his design; he has roped the whole universe into harmony. (Woolf, vol. I: 74–5)

Defoe is able to make his readers accept 'the solidity of the pot and its earthiness' because there is still available to them all a consensual belief in the status of objective reality; as a result of this, he is able to make the spiritual inhere in the physical, the exotic in the mundane, and thus to rope 'the whole universe into harmony'. In her fiction and criticism, Woolf communicates her perception that the modern age has eroded the 'solidity' of the pot, its objective status and the consensus assumed by Defoe; yet her description of Forster as the 'light sleeper' does not make allowance for the possibility that the fitful sleep she attributes to him is a symptom of his own awareness of the conditions of modernity. What this shows is that, even though Woolf is prepared to include Forster amongst the 'Georgians' – her term for what we now call the modernists – the premise underlying all her responses to his work is that he is at heart a realist. Flowing from this, there must be something anachronistic and self-defeating about his fictional endeavours, for Woolf in her polemic will not accept that contemporary realism has any validity at all; nor does she allow for the possibility that it may be combined, in an innovative way, with other modes: this is seen in her reaction to the 'romantic realism' of Forster's early work, where, instead of recognising that the two strands interact with and are dependent upon one another, she sees the realism as obfuscating the romanticism. She notes the extent of Forster's attention to two cornerstones of realism – the fact that he is 'extremely susceptible to the influence of time' (Woolf, vol. I: 342), and his concern with environmental influences:

> Mr Forster is a novelist . . . who sees his people in close contact with their surroundings. And therefore the colour and the constitution of the year 1905 affect him far more than any year in the calendar could affect the romantic Meredith or the poetic Hardy.
>
> (Woolf, vol. I: 342–3)

However, it seems that this is merely an ostensible or supplementary concern: 'observation is not an end in itself; it is rather the goad, the gadfly driving Mr Forster to provide a refuge from this misery, an escape from this meanness' (343). Within the hierarchy that she imputes to his early work, realism lies on the surface, while romanticism is the deeper truth:

> Beneath bicycles and dusters, Sawston and Italy, Philip, Harriet, and Miss Abbott, there always lies for him . . . a burning core. It is the soul; it is reality; it is truth; it is poetry; it is love; it decks itself in many shapes, dresses itself in many disguises.   (343)

Although Forster's 'eternal moments' have so much in common with Woolf's own 'Moments of Being', she fails to recognise that the 'irradiation' of the mundane is one of the main aims of 'romantic realism':

> It is the soul that matters; and the soul . . . is caged in a solid villa of red brick somewhere in the suburbs of London. It seems, then, that if his books are to succeed in their mission his reality must at certain points become irradiated; his brick must be lit up; we must see the whole building saturated with light. We have at once to believe in

the complete reality of the suburb and in the complete reality of the soul.   (346)

Because he retains aspects of the realist tradition in his work, Forster should, in other words, supply what Woolf attributes to Defoe and his eighteenth-century text: the ability to summon a 'complete reality'. The possibility that aspects of the realist tradition, particularly when deployed in conjunction with other modes, may themselves be used to reflect a loss of confidence in a positivistic view of life, is not broached. The polemical stance insists that the new must repudiate, not rewrite, the old, yet Woolf's own practice is not consistent with this: '[Woolf] did not simply reject the Victorians and their concerns, or renounce them. Instead she persistingly re-wrote them' (Gillian Beer 1989: 140). What appears in her own work as the subject of elegy or an opportunity for revision is regarded in his as an anachronism which is criticised both for its persistence and for its inefficacy.

Woolf's criticisms of Forster's work provide a very obvious example of the myopia evident in the critical responses of the modernists, and of modernism misreading itself, or failing to recognise a version of itself. In addition, it sets the tone for a great deal of subsequent criticism of Forster's work, in that it begrudges him his status as a modernist because he does not denounce the old in favour of the new, because the elegiac quality evident in so much of his writing is perceived as not sufficiently iconoclastic. Yet Forster is keenly aware of how easily what is new may itself become dated and fail to endure. This is made explicit in his review, published in 1920, of a book which he concedes is not palatable to 'the modern point of view' (*PT*: 51), Stopford A. Brooke's *Naturalism in English Poetry*:

It is . . . impossible to read the book without feeling a trifle superior. The banquet of literature, as the modern critic serves it, seems far more dainty and varied. Still, the good old School Feast had its points. It realized that literature, and poetry in particular, is of supreme importance, and that no man can flourish without partaking of it. By stressing the ethical importance it has passed out of date: but how soon, and for what reasons, will the criticisms of today suffer a like oblivion? Living as we do in the backrush and onrush of immeasurable tides, is it likely that any words we utter about the past will be durable?   (*PT*: 53)

This passage encapsulates many aspects of Forster's attitudes to change, to what has 'passed out of date' and to what is now seen as 'modern': a willingness to recognise the merit of the past (especially its 'ethical importance'), even as he concedes that the modern temper will not be satisfied with what it has to offer; a sceptical attitude towards modern taste, born of an awareness of the ephemerality of all traditions; and a recognition that there is always the co-existence of forward and backward movements – 'the backrush and onrush of immeasurable tides' – even in an age intent upon proclaiming itself as modern and jettisoning what it sees as obsolete.

In responding to Woolf's fictional experiments, Forster is, for the most part, far more receptive than Woolf is in her judgements of his work. In particular, he consistently grants Woolf her status as an innovator: the importance of her fictional experiments will be overlooked, he suggests, only by those 'who are blind to the newer developments of English prose' (*PT*: 27). He also recognises that what is keenly modern in Woolf's work is conveyed by every aspect of the writing – the subject matter, the form and even the syntax:

> Mrs Woolf's art is of a very unusual type, and one realizes that quite good critics, especially of the academic kind, may think it insignificant. It has no moral, no philosophy, nor has it what is usually understood by Form. It aims deliberately at aimlessness, at long loose sentences, that sway and meander: it is open to tensity and intensity, and willingly reveals the yawn and the gape.   (26)

Except for the prophetically inaccurate suggestion that Woolf's writing may not appeal to 'critics . . . of the academic kind', this is astonishingly insightful and sympathetic. It is all the more perspicacious if one considers that, in this assessment, published in 1919, Forster is responding to *The Mark on the Wall* and *Kew Gardens*, and that, when he wrote this, Woolf's most important modernist works had not yet been written. It shows that, for Forster, there is something in the modern spirit which can best be conveyed by writing that offers an unusual kind of obliquity – it 'aims deliberately at aimlessness' – and, at the same time, reveals 'the yawn and the gape'.

Yet, in other areas, Forster is less generous in his judgements of Woolf's work, and may himself be regarded as one of those who are 'blind to the newer developments of English prose'. This is most in evidence in one particular criticism, to which he returns again and again. It centres on her failure, as he sees it, to create sufficiently convincing characters, 'to allow her readers to inhabit each character with Victorian thoroughness' (*AH*: 111). Although his review of her first novel, *The Voyage Out* (1915), is favourable, this is the major flaw which he identifies:

> there is one serious defect in [Mrs Woolf's] equipment: her chief characters are not vivid. There is nothing false in them, but when she ceases to touch them they cease, they do not stroll out of their sentences, and even develop a tendency to merge shadow-like. (*PT*: 15–16)

The idea that characters should 'stroll out of their sentences' speaks of a naïve realism, a disingenuous belief in the possibility of an uncomplicated movement between the textual and extra-textual domains, an attitude which we do not find in Forster's own fictional practice or in his theoretical work. It is profoundly surprising that a writer so prepared, as we have seen, to accept that there are vast differences between 'Homo Sapiens' and 'Homo Fictus' (*AN*: 38–9) should neglect this distinction in considering whether Woolf's characters 'live':

> I feel that they do live, but not continuously, whereas the characters of Tolstoy (let us say) live continuously. With her, the reader is in a state of constant approval. 'Yes that is right', he says, each time she implies something more about Jacob or Peter: 'yes that would be so: yes.' (*AH*: 110–11)

Forster's own 'prophetic' characters, as we have seen, have precisely the effect of throwing into doubt the apparent self-sufficiency of characters constructed by means of more traditional methods, and the result is that the reader is constantly drawn into granting or withdrawing his or her 'approval'. Characters such as Mrs Wilcox, Miss Avery, Professor Godbole and Mrs Moore cannot be regarded as 'liv[ing] continuously' either, for it is in their elusiveness and inscrutability as characters and, literally, in their tendency to withdraw at crucial moments and to reappear when least expected, that their 'prophetic' significance is felt. Here Forster is demanding traditional psychological realism when he is prepared to move beyond it himself.

It is, however, significant that, although – as we have seen – Forster sides with Wells rather than James when he refers in *Aspects of the Novel* to their famous quarrel, in another context he nonetheless makes the same criticism of Wells's work as of Woolf's:

> Wells' lucidity, so satisfying when applied to peoples and periods, is somehow inadequate when individuals are thrown on to the screen. The outlines are as clear as ever, but they are not the outlines of living men. He seldom has created a character who lives . . . (*PT*: 58)

The fact that this criticism (published in 1920) is so similar to the charges levelled consistently against Woolf reveals more about Forster than it does about either Wells or Woolf. The realist and the anti-realist are being accused of precisely the same failing and the implication is clear: although Forster may not be prepared to embrace – or even to approve – all the techniques used by Woolf in seeking new methods of characterisation, he nevertheless finds little to admire in the methods of conventional writers, especially the Edwardian realists. For the most part – as the earlier discussion of *Aspects of the Novel* suggests – they are damned with faint praise.

Hence, in his criticism (albeit inconsistently), as in his fiction, Forster is to some extent moving beyond the reductive tendency – evident in many of the critical positions assumed by Woolf – of equating conventionality with etiolated practices and unconventionality with newness. Instead, he shows how the modern temper is often most effectively characterised by an uncomfortable confluence of the old and the new, and he accepts, even as he laments, the incontrovertibility of that awkward admixture. In that admission lies an intimation of the version of modernism which his work provides.

Implicit in much contemporary research on modernism is the attempt to broaden the definitions which are applied and to establish it as a more extensive terrain than earlier conceptions had granted – modernism has truly become 'a capacious country' (Brooker 1994: 1). To a significant extent, this has been the result of studies which have shown how tendentious earlier conceptions were, and how many modernist strands and voices were excluded from those definitions or canonical selections. Feminist literary scholarship has played a significant part in showing the extent to which modernism was 'unconsciously gendered masculine' (Scott 1990: 2). The effect of such attempts to expose 'all that Modernism has repressed, put aside, or attempted to deny' (Benstock 1987: ii) is far more than simply a matter of adding more writers to the modernist canon: it 'points towards – indeed, calls for – reevaluation and redefinition of Modernism itself' (Benstock 1987: 6). The tendency to refer to *modernisms* rather than *modernism* goes some way towards recognising this, and thus towards refuting a perception of modernism as a 'monolithic ideological formation' (Nicholls 1995: vii).

More inclusive definitions call into question the validity of former criteria for selection. They also bring a fuller awareness of the complexities of modernism, of its varieties, divergences, inconsistencies and the panoply of its socio-historical and aesthetic responses. From that perspective, 'the task of rendering a fuller account [of modernism] is justified . . . by the desire to provide richer, thicker narratives' (Levenson 1999: 1):

> we now have a dramatically enlarged perception of the range and reach of achievement. What once seemed the exclusive affair of 'modern masters,' the 'men of 1914' (as Wyndham Lewis called them), now stands revealed as a complex of inventive gestures, daring performances, enacted also by many who were left out of account in the early histories of the epoch, histories offered first by the actors themselves and later produced within an academic discourse, willingly guided by the precedents of the eminent artists.   (2–3)

To read modernist works only in terms of the most strident modernist polemic is to ignore many of the women modernists, as well as those male modernists who may have been marginalised by 'a more virile modernist ethos' (Scott 1995: 169) – Forster and Lytton Strachey being the two examples provided – or those, like Forster, who have 'seen deeply into the times without taking their typology of the artist or his work from the *avant-garde*' (Bradbury 1971: 27).

One of the aims of this study of Forster's modernism has been to delineate its characteristics, identify its component parts, and accommodate it within the 'dramatically enlarged perception of the range and reach of achievement' referred to by Levenson; to show that it has its place within a more flexible and inclusive conceptualisation:

a more subtle, adaptable, and traversable model of literary culture in which the richly textured life of the modern arts might be newly appraised in all its variegated, anomalous, disparate strands, some of which are elevated from, some lying closer to, the common weave.   (DiBattista 1996: 18)

These 'variegated, anomalous, disparate strands' in Forster's case would include his responses to the crisis of liberal-humanism, the unravelling of the 'romantic realism' of his earlier works and the complexities of what he requires of form. Those interrelated and often competing concerns, some socio-political, some generic, some aesthetic, come together to form what Levenson calls 'a complex of inventive gestures'. They reflect concerns which are by no means unique, and which find expression in the work of other modernist writers, even if Forster's responses are distinctly and unmistakably his own.

This will certainly encourage 'a new, cannier Forster to emerge behind the beloved traditional figure' (May 1997: xii). It is not just a matter, however, of finding a space for Forster's work within a sufficiently flexible account of modernism; it is also that, in doing so, our understanding of modernism itself is extended and enriched. Forster's modernism, for all its singularity, nonetheless lies close enough to what DiBattista calls 'the common weave' to direct us towards a number of important strands within modernism itself which may not have received sufficient emphasis. In particular, his modernism provides a compelling example of a tendency identified by Robert Wohl, whereby 'the modern does not replace the traditional; it joins with it to produce something new' (Wohl 1986: 67); seen in that light, modernism is 'the product of a many-layered culture in the process of disintegration and recomposition' (68). This describes precisely the kind of modernism Forster's work represents, with its interweaving of old and new, modern and traditional in a complex process of 'disintegration and recomposition'. Of necessity this cannot be a triumphant or euphoric modernism, for it is permeated with elegies for past traditions, even as it admits, with a mixture of reluctance and suspicion, the new. If '[t]he modern' is 'for most of us . . . that which we have always to catch up with' (Eagleton 1986: 139), then this is especially true of Forster, in whose later work the strain of trying to catch up with newness and modernity is always in evidence. Hence, although Richard Poirier has argued that what lies behind 'the modernist cult of difficulty' is the idea that innovation in the arts is a form of 'cultural heroism' (Poirier 1987: 112), Forster's modernism demonstrates instead that experimentalism is not always perceived chauvinistically by the modernists themselves, and does not invariably have to be seen in that light by those who read them. Rather than confirming Fredric Jameson's description of Forster as 'at best a closet modernist' (Jameson 1990: 54), it suggests rather that there is a significant strand within modernism itself which is distrustful of its own innovations and reminds us that to be experimental does not necessarily imply that newness is being embraced for its own sake, or that the past is being abjured simply because its traditions no longer have the same cogency:

> Not all [modernist] experiment took place for the sake of experiment, but out of a conviction that the old forms did not capture something important in life, a 'spirit', a force, a religious or spiritual dimension existing somewhere below or above consciousness but beyond the purviews of traditional fiction.
>
> (Phyllis Rose 1983: 142)

In other words, newness and experimentalism have no absolute significance, and can only be considered in the contexts in which they occur. Hence, instead of providing a sense of 'cultural heroism', Forster's modernism underscores the extent to which innovation may also be an admission of defeat and failure.

In relation to some of the major currents which have been identified in modernism, Forster's modernism may indeed occupy a marginal position; however, this ought not only to make us aware that accounts of modernism need to make a space for that kind of marginality, but also that the assumption of a position of liminality is itself an important characteristic of many modernist works. Forster's liminality proceeds from a sense of dual allegiances and the tentativeness that such a position engenders. It is also the result of lying somewhere between the two positions outlined below:

> The vaunted energy, formal experimentation, and psychic shock of modernist texts in the moment of their appearance . . . were hardly the sole property of culturally conservative writers, nor were their effects limited to the familiar circles associated with those figures.

In the vast array of contexts and places, writers during the era of high Modernism and beyond adapted its formalism and techniques, even its defining idioms, often so as to contest its political commitments. This was especially true for certain women, African-American, and socialist writers – what we can cautiously, with qualification, term writers on the left – attempting to open new public spaces or spheres for the expression of varied responses to modernity, and various political and social claims on its realities.

(Blair 1999: 162–3)

As far as this goes in refuting a monolithic perception of modernism, it still does not accommodate a position such as Forster's, whose politics and modernist practice are neither wholeheartedly conservative nor avidly iconoclastic. Indeed, as we have seen, what is most experimental technically in his work often emerges out of what is most conservative culturally or politically (as, for instance, in *Howards End*, where the movement into symbolism and nascent modernism is intertwined with a number of extremely reactionary responses to certain conditions of modernity); similarly, the most progressive socio-political attitudes may find no counterpoint in technical innovation (as in the writings which explicitly address homosexual themes, and which tend not to be experimental; or as in *A Passage to India*, where the critique of the abuses of the Raj is most overtly expressed by means of a quite traditional use of satire). The conservative and the contestatory (to use Blair's terms) are not as easy to identify in Forster's work as they may seem – either to those who, on the one hand, place stress only upon Forster's conservative responses to certain conditions of modernity and what he has in common with a number of reactionary male modernists; or, on the other, to those who wish to cherish the notion of him as an indefatigable liberal-humanist sage, bravely defending tolerance while so many others were flirting with variants of fascism or totalitarianism.

In his review, published in 1920, of H. G. Wells's *The Outline of History*, Forster argues that Wells as a historian is less successful in analysing modern history and contemporary developments than he is when he considers the more distant past. These shortcomings, it is suggested, are particularly evident in a chapter in Wells's study which is devoted to an analysis of events which took place as recently as 1914. Forster goes on to claim that the difficulties experienced by Wells are inevitable whenever people try to characterise situations which are still unfolding or trace historical trajectories which are inchoate:

> Our 'own' times, as they are ironically termed, are anything but ours; it is as though a dead object, huge and incomprehensible, had fallen across the page, which no historical arts can arrange, and which bewilders us as much by its shapelessness as by its size. (*PT*: 66)

The comment that '[o]ur "own" times . . . are anything but ours' is deeply revealing, particularly when one considers that it is specifically the modern age which Forster has in mind: it suggests a fundamental estrangement between the life of the individual and his or her status as an agent or subject of history. The alignment – which the realists make so much of – between private experience and the larger workings of history can, according to this, no longer be taken for granted. Between the two has fallen a 'dead object, huge and incomprehensible', shapeless and impervious, which causes profound bemusement. It is not surprising, therefore, that Forster objects to the note of optimism and the expectation of progress which he discerns in Wells's history:

> [Wells's] hand holds a lecturer's castanet, but his heart is Victorian, with a quite Tennysonian trust in the To-be. To him evolution is progress, and though a few events (e.g. the Punic wars) are condemned as purely toxic, he is on the whole inclined to give a good mark to everything that happens, on the ground that it makes the past a little more like the present. . . . it is only an optimist who could attempt a history of this planet. To the rest of us it is a planet full of scraps, many of which are noble and beautiful, but there seems not any proof that it progresses.   (*PT*: 61)

The capacity to 'trust in the To-be', despite the fact that it seems to be embracing the future, is, paradoxically, presented as anachronistic and 'Victorian'. It is telling that Forster sees this optimism as an attempt to reconcile past and present, to make 'the past a little more like the present', for his modernism proceeds, as we have seen, precisely from a belief that a fundamental disjuncture between past and present has taken place, and that no overarching scheme or ideological framework can be made to encompass them both. Wells offers the long view, but for Forster, who is so intensely aware of having inherited 'a planet full of scraps', modernity can bring only fragmentation and an inability to see through to the end of things. From this perspective, his modernism is an admission of myopia, an acceptance that there is no longer a vantage-point from which the shape of history may be viewed; an admission that history cannot be construed as linear, incremental or eschatological.

If the individual's relationship with history has changed, it must follow that '[l]iterature['s] . . . commerce with history' (*PT*: 38) has also to be understood differently. For the individual as for the writer, the difficulty lies in ascertaining how to proceed. Forster's intriguing comment, made in 1915, that 'our supreme choice lies not between body and soul, but between immobility and motion' (*PT*: 17), if seen in this context, seems particularly resonant. Frenetic and thoughtless motion, motion for its own sake, is strongly criticised in *Howards End*, as we have seen; at the same time, to submit to torpor is clearly another danger. The disenchantment which fuelled Forster's modernism could just as easily have become its own silence, its own nothingness, its own immobility; and perhaps, after *A Passage to India*, that is indeed what it became.

In *Pharos and Pharillon*, Forster describes the favourable circumstances prevailing in Alexandria during the second and third centuries, the time of Clement of Alexandria:

> in that curious city, which had never been young and hoped never to grow old, conciliation must have seemed more possible than elsewhere, and the graciousness of Greece not quite incompatible with the Grace of God.   (*PP*: 42)

This is a portrait of an idyllic city during an idyllic time. The ingredients of that idyll, as Forster conceives of them, are deeply suggestive: in particular, the notion that the passing of time does not threaten the city in any way, for it 'had never been young and hoped never to grow old'; and that the idyll is characterised by 'conciliation'. These are precisely the virtues which Forster does not find in the early twentieth century, and it is their loss which his modernism directly or indirectly addresses. Instead, the passing of time is seen as bringing the attrition and even the obsolescence of what had been valuable in the past, and it may be the resulting sense of unease, that uncomfortable habitation of contemporaneity evident in Forster's work which makes him seem 'both younger and older than his contemporaries' (Friedman 1995: 186). And it is the inability to *conciliate*, to appease contradiction and assuage incompatibility – to talk, as Forster puts it, 'this late nineteen century stuff with a twenty century voice' (*CB*: 118) – which characterises his modernism. As we have seen, this expresses itself in a variety of ways: a jostling of competing genres; a reluctant acceptance of duality and bifurcation, which may take the form of 'eclecticism' and 'inconsistency', described in *Aspects of the Novel* as lamentable necessities; and even the 'twilight of the double vision' (*PI*: 212) which so afflicts Mrs Moore.

The failure to 'conciliate' also implies a troubled awareness of the contingency of truth claims and the dilemmas which ensue when they prove to be incompatible:

> Especially in *A Passage to India*. . . . Forster experiments with narrative techniques to educate the reader about what has come to be seen in contemporary theory as a central dilemma of political life: How can one commit oneself to the realization of particular values and beliefs while maintaining an ironic awareness of their contingency and contestability, their incommensurability with other equally plausible ways of thinking? (Armstrong 1992: 365)

One of the ways in which one can chart how far Forster has travelled down this path is to compare *A Passage to India* with the poem which provides the title of the novel: Walt Whitman's 'Passage to India' (1871). Whitman's poem, commemorating the opening of the Suez Canal, celebrates connection and conciliation:

> Passage to India!
> Lo, soul, seest thou not God's purpose from the first?
> The earth to be spann'd, connected by network,
> The races, neighbors, to marry and be given in marriage,
> The oceans to be cross'd, the distant brought near,
> The lands to be welded together.

(ll.30–5)

Needless to say, Forster's novel stands in deeply ironic relationship to this, for *A Passage to India* charts instead the inability of people to 'connect' racially (and in other ways), and thus to achieve the cosmic 'neighbourliness' Whitman envisages. It also reveals the seemingly insurmountable chasms which confound the quest for the spiritual solace described later in the poem:

> Then not your deeds only O voyagers, O scientists and inventors,
>   shall be justified,
> All these hearts as of fretted children shall be sooth'd,
> All affection shall be fully responded to, the secret shall be told,
> All these separations and gaps shall be taken up and hook'd and
>   link'd together,
> The whole earth, this cold, impassive, voiceless earth, shall be
>   completely justified . . .

(ll.106–10)

The 'secret', as anyone who has read *A Passage to India* knows, is decidedly not 'told'; respond[ing] to 'affection' is shown to create problems of its own; the 'separations and gaps' proliferate; the earth, rather than being 'justified', produces the Marabar Caves, which are beyond justification, beyond language, and beyond conciliation. Between Whitman's poem and Forster's novel lies a shift in perception of gargantuan proportions. The use of the poem as a subtext may refer nostalgically to dreams of connection which can no longer prevail; the novel, the fullest expression of Forster's modernism, considers what has to be countenanced when nostalgia, however attractive, will not suffice.

References

Primary Sources

Forster, E. M., *Abinger Harvest* (London: Edward Arnold, 1936).
—— *Albergo Empedocle and Other Writings*, ed. George H. Thomson (New York: Liveright, 1971).
—— *Alexandria: A History and a Guide* (Garden City, New York: Anchor Books, 1961).
—— *Arctic Summer and Other Fiction*, ed. Elizabeth Heine and Oliver Stallybrass, Abinger Edition, vol. 9 (London: Edward Arnold, 1980).
—— *Aspects of the Novel*, ed. Oliver Stallybrass, Abinger Edition, vol. 12 (London: Edward Arnold, 1974).
—— *Collected Short Stories* (Harmondsworth: Penguin, 1954).
—— *Commonplace Book*, ed. Philip Gardner (Stanford, Cal.: Stanford University Press, 1985).
—— *Goldsworthy Lowes Dickinson* (London: Edward Arnold, 1934).
—— *The Hill of Devi and Other Indian Writings*, ed. Elizabeth Heine, Abinger Edition, vol. 14 (London: Edward Arnold, 1983).
—— *Howards End*, ed. Oliver Stallybrass, Abinger Edition, vol. 4 (London: Edward Arnold, 1973).
—— *The Life to Come and Other Stories*, ed. Oliver Stallybrass, Abinger Edition, vol. 8 (London: Edward Arnold, 1972).
—— *The Longest Journey*, ed. Elizabeth Heine, Abinger Edition, vol. 2 (London: Edward Arnold, 1984).
—— *The Manuscripts of 'A Passage to India'*, ed. Oliver Stallybrass, Abinger Edition, vol. 6(a) (London: Edward Arnold, 1978).
—— *Marianne Thornton: A Domestic Biography* (London: Edward Arnold, 1956).
—— *Maurice* (London: Edward Arnold, 1971).
—— *A Passage to India*, ed. Oliver Stallybrass (Harmondsworth: Penguin, 1985).
—— *Pharos and Pharillon* (London: Hogarth Press, 1961).
—— *The Prince's Tale and Other Uncollected Writings*, ed. P. N. Furbank (London: Penguin, 1999).

—— *A Room with a View*, ed. Oliver Stallybrass, Abinger Edition, vol. 3 (London: Edward Arnold, 1977).
—— *Two Cheers for Democracy*, ed. Oliver Stallybrass, Abinger Edition, vol. 11 (London: Edward Arnold, 1972).
—— *Where Angels Fear to Tread*, ed. Oliver Stallybrass, Abinger Edition, vol. 1 (London: Edward Arnold, 1975).
Lago, Mary and P. N. Furbank (eds) (1983) *Selected Letters of E. M. Forster*, vol. I (London, Melbourne: William Collins).
—— (1985) *Selected Letters of E. M. Forster*, vol. II (London, Melbourne: William Collins).

Secondary Sources

Advani, Rukun (1984) *E. M. Forster as Critic* (London, Sydney: Croom Helm).
Armstrong, Paul B. (1992) 'Reading India: E. M. Forster and the Politics of Interpretation', *Twentieth-Century Literature*, vol. 38, no. 4.
Arnold, Matthew (1965) *Culture and Anarchy*, ed. R. H. Super (Ann Arbor: University of Michigan Press).
Aronson, Alex (1980) *Music and the Novel: A Study in Twentieth-Century Fiction* (Totowa: Rowan and Littlefield).
Asquith, Herbert Henry (1902) 'Introduction', in Herbert Samuel, *Liberalism: An Attempt to State the Principles and Proposals of Contemporary Liberalism in England* (London: Grant Richards).
Barthes, Roland (1967) *Writing Degree Zero*, trans. Annette Lavers and Colin Smith (London: Jonathan Cape).
Barthes, Roland (1977) *Image, Music, Text*, ed. and trans. Stephen Heath (London: Fontana).
Beauman, Nicola (1993) *Morgan: A Biography of E. M. Forster* (London: Hodder and Stoughton).
Becker, George J. (1980) *Realism in Modern Literature* (New York: Frederick Ungar).
Beer, Gillian (1989) *Arguing with the Past: Essays in Narrative from Woolf to Sidney* (London, New York: Routledge).
Beer, John (1982) '*A Passage to India*, the French New Novel and English Romanticism', in *E. M. Forster: Centenary Revaluations*, ed. Judith Scherer Herz and R. K. Martin (London, Basingstoke: Macmillan – now Palgrave).
Beer, John (ed.) (1985) *A Passage to India: Essays in Interpretation* (Basingstoke: Macmillan – now Palgrave).
Bell, Clive (1922) *Since Cezanne* (London: Chatto and Windus).
Bell, Clive (1947) *Art* (London: Chatto and Windus; Toronto: Oxford University Press).
Bell, Michael (ed.) (1980) *The Context of English Literature: 1900–1930* (London: Methuen).
Benstock, Shari (1987) *Women of the Left Bank: Paris, 1900–1940* (London: Virago).

Bentley, Michael (1977) *The Liberal Mind: 1914–1929* (Cambridge: Cambridge University Press).

Bentley, Michael (1987) *The Climax of Liberal Politics: British Liberalism in Theory and Practice, 1868–1918* (London: Edward Arnold).

Bernstein, George L. (1986) *Liberalism and Liberal Politics in Edwardian England* (Boston: Allen and Unwin).

Bigelow, Gordon E. (1976) *The Poet's Third Eye: A Guide to the Symbolisms of Modern Literature* (New York: Philosophical Library).

Blackham, H. J. (1976) *Humanism* (Hassocks: Harvester Press).

Blair, Sara (1999) 'Modernism and the Politics of Culture', in *The Cambridge Companion to Modernism*, ed. Michael Levenson (Cambridge: Cambridge University Press).

Bloom, Harold (ed.) (1987) *E. M. Forster: Modern Critical Views* (New York, Philadelphia: Chelsea House).

Boehmer, Elleke (1995) *Colonial and Postcolonial Literature* (Oxford, New York: Oxford University Press).

Boehmer, Elleke (ed.) (1998) *Empire Writing: An Anthology of Colonial Literature, 1870–1918* (Oxford, New York: Oxford University Press).

Bradbury, Malcolm (1969) 'Two Passages to India: Forster as Victorian and Modern', in *Aspects of E. M. Forster*, ed. O. Stallybrass (London: Edward Arnold).

Bradbury, Malcolm (ed.) (1970) *E. M. Forster: A Passage to India* (Basingstoke: Macmillan – now Palgrave).

Bradbury, Malcolm (1971) *The Social Context of Modern English Literature* (Oxford: Basil Blackwell).

Bradbury, Malcolm and James McFarlane (eds) (1976) *Modernism: 1890–1930* (London, Harmondsworth: Penguin).

Britten, Benjamin (1969) 'Some Notes on Forster and Music', in *Aspects of E. M. Forster*, ed. O. Stallybrass (London: Edward Arnold).

Brooker, Jewel Spears (1994) *Mastery and Escape: T. S. Eliot and the Dialectic of Modernism* (Amherst: University of Massachusetts Press).

Brown, E. K. (1950) *Rhythm in the Novel* (Toronto: University of Toronto Press).

Bullock, Alan (1985) *The Humanist Tradition in the West* (New York, London: W. W. Norton).

Butler, Christopher (1994) *Early Modernism: Literature, Music and Painting in Europe, 1900–1916* (Oxford: Clarendon Press).

Carey, John (1992) *The Intellectuals and the Masses: Pride and Prejudice Among the Literary Intelligentsia, 1880–1939* (London, Boston: Faber and Faber).

Chefdor, Monique and Richard Quinones et al. (eds) (1986) *Modernism: Challenges and Perspectives* (Urbana, Chicago: University of Illinois Press).

Collini, Stefan (1979) *Liberalism and Sociology: L. T. Hobhouse and Political Argument in England, 1880–1914* (Cambridge, London: Cambridge University Press).

Colmer, John (1975) *E. M. Forster: The Personal Voice* (London, Boston: Routledge and Kegan Paul).

Cook, Chris (1976) *A Short History of the Liberal Party: 1900–1976* (Basingstoke: Macmillan – now Palgrave).

Copland, Aaron (1967) *What to Listen for in Music* (New York: Doubleday).

Das, G. K. (1977) *E. M. Forster's India* (Basingstoke: Macmillan – now Palgrave).

Das, G. K. and John Beer (eds) (1979) *E. M. Forster: A Human Exploration: Centenary Essays* (Basingstoke: Macmillan – now Palgrave).

Davies, Tony and Nigel Woods (eds) (1994) *A Passage to India* (Buckingham, Philadelphia: Open University Press).

DiBattista, Maria (1996) 'Introduction', in *High and Low Moderns: Literature and Culture, 1889–1939*, ed. Maria DiBattista and Lucy McDiarmid (New York: Oxford University Press).

DiBattista, Maria and Lucy McDiarmid (eds) (1996) *High and Low Moderns: Literature and Culture, 1889–1939* (New York: Oxford University Press).

Dickinson, Goldsworthy Lowes (1904) *The Greek View of Life* (London: Methuen).

Eagleton, Terry (1970) *Exiles and Emigrés: Studies in Modern Literature* (London: Chatto and Windus).

Eagleton, Terry (1986) *Against the Grain: Essays, 1975–1985* (London, New York: Verso).

Eagleton, Terry, Fredric Jameson and Edward W. Said (1990) *Nationalism, Colonialism and Literature* (Minneapolis: University of Minnesota Press).

Eccleshall, Robert (ed.) (1986) *British Liberalism: Liberal Thought from the 1640s to the 1980s* (London, New York: Longman).

Ellmann, Richard (ed.) (1960) *Edwardians and Late Victorians* (New York: Columbia University Press).

Emy, H. V. (1973) *Liberals, Radicals and Social Politics: 1892–1914* (London, New York: Cambridge University Press).

Eysteinsson, Astradur (1990) *The Concept of Modernism* (Ithaca, London: Cornell University Press).

Fletcher, John and Malcolm Bradbury (1976) 'The Introverted Novel', in *Modernism: 1890–1930*, ed. Malcolm Bradbury and James McFarlane (Harmondsworth: Penguin).

Freeden, Michael (1978) *The New Liberalism: An Ideology of Social Reform* (Oxford: Clarendon Press).

Friedman, Alan Warren (1995) *Fictional Death and the Modernist Enterprise* (Cambridge: Cambridge University Press).

Fry, Roger (1920) *Vision and Design* (London: Chatto and Windus).

Furst, Lilian R. (1995) *All is True: The Claims and Strategies of Realist Fiction* (Durham, NC, London: Duke University Press).

Furst, Lilian R. and Peter Skrine (1971) *Naturalism: The Critical Idiom* (London: Methuen).

Ganguly, Adwaita P. (1990) *India: Mystic, Complex and Real: An Interpretation of E. M. Forster's 'A Passage to India'* (Delhi: Motilal Banarsidass Publishers).

Gardner, Philip (ed.) (1973) *E. M. Forster: The Critical Heritage* (London, Boston: Routledge and Kegan Paul).

Graham, Kenneth (1988) *Indirections of the Novel: James, Conrad, and Forster* (Cambridge: Cambridge University Press).

Greenslade, William (1994) *Degeneration, Culture and the Novel, 1880–1940* (Cambridge: Cambridge University Press).

Halperin, John (ed.) (1974) *The Theory of the Novel: New Essays* (New York, London: Oxford University Press).

Harlow, Barbara (1994) 'Law and Order in *A Passage to India*', in *A Passage to India*, ed. Tony Davies and Nigel Wood (Buckingham, Philadelphia: Open University Press).

Harrison, Bernard (1991) *Inconvenient Fictions: Literature and the Limits of Theory* (New Haven, CT, London: Yale University Press).

Harrison, Charles (1994) *English Art and Modernism: 1900–1939* (New Haven, CT, London: Yale University Press).

Herz, Judith Scherer (1985) 'Listening to Language', in *A Passage to India: Essays in Interpretation*, ed. John Beer (Basingstoke: Macmillan – now Palgrave).

Herz, Judith Scherer (1988) *The Short Narratives of E. M. Forster* (Basingstoke: Macmillan – now Palgrave).

Herz, Judith Scherer and R. K. Martin (eds) (1982) *E. M. Forster: Centenary Revaluations* (Basingstoke: Macmillan – now Palgrave).

Hobhouse, L. T. (1934) *Liberalism* (London: Thornton Butterworth).

Hobson, J. A. (1902) *Imperialism: A Study* (London: James Nisbet).

Hobson, J. A. (1933) *Rationalism and Humanism* (London: Watts).

Hobson, J. A. (1986) 'The Crisis of Liberalism: New Issues of Democracy', in *British Liberalism: Liberal Thought from the 1640s to the 1980s*, ed. Robert Eccleshall (London, New York: Longman).

Hulme, T. E. (1924) *Speculations: Essays on Humanism and the Philosophy of Art* (London: Routledge and Kegan Paul).

Hunter, Jefferson (1982) *Edwardian Fiction* (Cambridge, MA, London: Harvard University Press).

Hutcheon, Linda (1982) ' "Sublime Noise" for Three Friends: Music in the Critical Writings of E. M. Forster, Roger Fry and Charles Mauron', in *E. M. Forster: Centenary Revaluations*, ed. Judith Scherer Herz and R. K. Martin (Basingstoke: Macmillan – now Palgrave).

Jackson, Tony E. (1994) *The Subject of Modernism: Narrative Alterations in the Fiction of Eliot, Conrad, Woolf, and Joyce* (Ann Arbor: University of Michigan Press).

James, Henry (1948) *The Art of Fiction and Other Essays* (New York: Oxford University Press).

Jameson, Fredric (1990) 'Modernism and Imperialism', in Terry Eagleton, Fredric Jameson and Edward W. Said, *Nationalism, Colonialism and Literature* (Minneapolis: University of Minnesota Press).

Johnstone, J. K. (1954) *The Bloomsbury Group: A Study of E. M. Forster, Lytton Strachey, Virginia Woolf, and Their Circle* (London: Secker and Warburg).

Jones, Vivien (1985) *James the Critic* (New York: St Martin's Press).

Josipovici, Gabriel (1971) *The World and the Book: A Study of Modern Fiction* (Basingstoke: Macmillan – now Palgrave).

Josipovici, Gabriel (1977) *The Lessons of Modernism* (Basingstoke: Macmillan – now Palgrave).

Keating, Peter (1989) *The Haunted Study: A Social History of the English Novel, 1875–1914* (London: Secker and Warburg).

Kermode, Frank (1966) *The Sense of an Ending: Studies in the Theory of Fiction* (London, Oxford: Oxford University Press).

Kiely, Robert and John Hildebidle (eds) (1983) *Modernism Reconsidered* (Cambridge, MA, London: Harvard University Press).

Knox-Shaw, Peter (1986) '*To the Lighthouse*: the Novel as Elegy', *English Studies in Africa*, vol. xxix, no. 1.

Landow, George P. (1993) 'Ruskin' in A. L. Le Quesne, George P. Landow, Stefan Collini and Peter Stansky (eds), *Victorian Thinkers* (Oxford, New York: Oxford University Press).

Lavin, Audrey A. P. (1995) *Aspects of the Novelist: E. M. Forster's Pattern and Rhythm* (New York, Washington: Peter Lang).

Le Quesne, A. L., George P. Landow, Stefan Collini and Peter Stansky (1993) *Victorian Thinkers* (Oxford, New York: Oxford University Press).

Levenson, Michael H. (1991) *Modernism and the Fate of Individuality: Character and Novelistic Form from Conrad to Woolf* (Cambridge, New York: Cambridge University Press).

Levenson, Michael H. (ed.) (1999) *The Cambridge Companion to Modernism* (Cambridge: Cambridge University Press).

Levine, George (1974) 'Realism Reconsidered', in *The Theory of the Novel: New Essays*, ed. John Halperin (New York, London: Oxford University Press).

Levine, June Perry (1971) *Creation and Criticism: 'A Passage to India'* (London: Chatto and Windus).

Lodge, David (1977) *The Modes of Modern Writing: Metaphor, Metonymy, and the Typology of Modern Literature* (London: Edward Arnold).

Lubbock, Percy (1947) *The Craft of Fiction* (New York: Peter Smith).

Lukács, Georg (1981) *Essays on Realism*, ed. R. Livingstone, trans. D. Fernbach (Cambridge, MA: MIT Press).

Mahood, M. M. (1977) *The Colonial Encounter: A Reading of Six Novels* (London: Rex Collings).

Mallarmé, Stéphane (1980) 'Crisis in Verse', in *Symbolism: An Anthology*, ed. T. G. West (London, New York: Methuen).

Masterman, C. F. G. (1911) *The Condition of England* (London: Methuen).

Masterman, C. F. G. (1980) *From the Abyss: Of Its Inhabitants by One of Them* (New York, London: Garland).

May, Brian (1997) *The Modernist as Pragmatist: E. M. Forster and the Fate of Liberalism* (Columbia, London: University of Missouri Press).

Meredith, George (1979) *The Egoist*, ed. Robert M. Adams (New York, London: W. W. Norton).

Miller, Jane Eldridge (1994) *Rebel Women: Feminism, Modernism and the Edwardian Novel* (London: Virago).

Minogue, Kenneth (1963) *The Liberal Mind* (London: Methuen).

Moore, G. E. (1903) *Principia Ethica* (Cambridge: Cambridge University Press).

Moore, R. J. (1966) *Liberalism and Indian Politics: 1872–1922* (London: Edward Arnold).

Muir, Edwin (1926) *Transition: Essays on Contemporary Literature* (London: Hogarth Press).

Muir, Edwin (1928) *The Structure of the Novel* (London: Hogarth Press).

Nicholls, Peter (1995) *Modernisms: A Literary Guide* (Basingstoke: Macmillan – now Palgrave).

O'Day, Alan, (ed.) (1979) *The Edwardian Age: Conflict and Stability, 1900–1914* (Basingstoke: Macmillan – now Palgrave).

Owen, John E. (1974) *L. T. Hobhouse, Sociologist* (Columbus: Ohio State University Press).

Parry, Benita (1979) '*A Passage to India*: Epitaph or Manifesto?', in *E. M. Forster: A Human Exploration: Centenary Essays*, ed. G. K. Das and John Beer (Basingstoke: Macmillan – now Palgrave).

Parry, Benita (1985) 'The Politics of Representation in *A Passage to India*', in *A Passage to India: Essays in Interpretation*, ed. John Beer (Basingstoke: Macmillan – now Palgrave).

Poirier, Richard (1987) *The Renewal of Literature: Emersonian Reflections* (New York: Random House).

Price, Martin (1987) 'Forster: Inclusion and Exclusion', in *E. M. Forster: Modern Critical Views*, ed. Harold Bloom (New York, Philadelphia: Chelsea House).

Quinones, Ricardo J. (1985) *Mapping Literary Modernism: Time and Development* (Princeton, NJ: Princeton University Press).

Robbe-Grillet, Alain (1965) *Snapshots* and *Towards a New Novel*, trans. Barbara Wright (London: Calder and Boyars).

Rose, Jonathan (1986) *The Edwardian Temperament, 1895–1919* (Athens, Ohio, London: Ohio University Press).

Rose, Phyllis (1983) 'Modernism: The Case of Willa Cather', in *Modernism Reconsidered*, ed. Robert Kiely and John Hildebidle (Cambridge, MA, London: Harvard University Press).

Rosecrance, Barbara (1982) *Forster's Narrative Vision* (Ithaca, London: Cornell University Press).

Rosenbaum, S. P. (1982) '*Aspects of the Novel* and Literary History', in *E. M. Forster: Centenary Revaluations*, ed. Judith Scherer Herz and R. K. Martin (Basingstoke: Macmillan – now Palgrave).

Rosenbaum, S. P. (1994) *Edwardian Bloomsbury: The Early Literary History of the Bloomsbury Group*, vol. 2 (Basingstoke: Macmillan – now Palgrave).

Sackville-West, Vita (1924) *Challenge* (London, Glasgow: William Collins).

Said, Edward W. (1978) *Orientalism* (London, Henley: Routledge & Kegan Paul).

Said, Edward W. (1994) *Culture and Imperialism* (London: Vintage).

Samuel, Herbert (1902) *Liberalism: An Attempt to State the Principles and Proposals of Contemporary Liberalism in England* (London: Grant Richards).

Scott, Bonnie Kime (ed.) (1990) *The Gender of Modernism: A Critical Anthology* (Bloomington, IN: Indiana University Press).

Scott, Bonnie Kime (1995) *Refiguring Modernism*, vol. 2: *The Women of 1928* (Bloomington, IN: Indiana University Press).

Scott-James, R. A. (1908) *Modernism and Romance* (London, New York: John Lane).

Searle, G. R. (1992) *The Liberal Party: Triumph and Disintegration, 1886–1929* (Basingstoke: Macmillan – now Palgrave).

Simons, J. B. (1936) *Arnold Bennett and His Novels: A Critical Study* (Oxford: Basil Blackwell).

Spender, Stephen (1937) *Forward from Liberalism* (London: Victor Gollancz).

Spender, Stephen (1963) *The Struggle of the Modern* (London: Hamish Hamilton).

Stallybrass, O. (ed.) (1969) *Aspects of E. M. Forster* (London: Edward Arnold).

Stern, J. P. (1973) *On Realism* (London, Boston: Routledge & Kegan Paul).

Stubbs, Patricia (1979) *Women and Fiction: Feminism and the Novel, 1880–1920* (Brighton: Harvester Press; New York: Barnes and Noble).

Symons, Arthur (1899) *The Symbolist Movement in Literature* (London: William Heinemann).

Taylor, Charles (1989) *Sources of the Self: The Making of the Modern Identity* (Cambridge, Melbourne: Cambridge University Press).

Trotter, David (1993) *The English Novel in History, 1885–1920* (London, New York: Routledge).

Waugh, Patricia (1992) *Practising Postmodernism, Reading Modernism* (London, New York: Edward Arnold).

Wells, H. G. (1953) *The History of Mr Polly* (London, Glasgow: Collins).

Wells, H. G. (1980) *H. G. Wells's Literary Criticism*, ed. Patrick Parrinder and Robert Philmus (Brighton: Harvester Press; Totowa: Barnes & Noble).

West, T. G. (ed.) (1980) *Symbolism: An Anthology* (London, New York: Methuen).

Widdowson, Peter (1977) *E. M. Forster's 'Howards End': Fiction as History* (London: Sussex University Press; Chatto and Windus).

Wilde, Alan (1964) *Art and Order: A Study of E. M. Forster* (London: Peter Owen).

Williams, Raymond (1989) *The Politics of Modernism: Against the New Conformists*, ed. Tony Pinkney (London, New York: Verso).

Wohl, Robert (1986) 'The Generation of 1914 and Modernism', in *Modernism: Challenges and Perspectives*, ed. Monique Chefdor and Richard Quinones et al. (Urbana, Chicago: University of Illinois Press).

Woolf, Virginia (1966) *Collected Essays*, vols 1–4 (London: Hogarth Press).

Yeats, W. B. (1969) *Essays and Introductions* (Basingstoke: Macmillan – now Palgrave).

Index